A Letter
An Ex
and Opal

TO MOM AND TERRY – WHO HAVE ALWAYS
BELIEVED IN ME.

.

PROLOGUE

Lucy was lounging on the couch, scrolling through Facebook on her phone, and wondering when Drew was going to get home when she heard a loud crash and what sounded like ripping metal.

Jumping off the couch and running down the hall, she threw open the front door, jaw dropping at what she saw.

Her car was smashed sideways against the garage, with a garbage can pinned between and the recycling bin sticking out from beneath the back bumper. The mailbox was lying in the middle of the yard, with the part of the wooden post that had held it up still attached. Tire tracks had ripped up the grass in a diagonal line leading up to the now totaled car.

Drew stood before her, cradling his right arm. "Hey," he said, pushing his way past her, into the house.

"What the heck happened?" Lucy called after him, shocked.

"Garbage cans are trashed and so is the mailbox. Oh, and your car. You're gonna wanna fix that," he responded as he grabbed an ice pack from the freezer and sat down on the couch. "Preferably tomorrow since I need the car for work."

Stunned, Lucy looked outside again, then back at Drew, closing the door quickly behind her. "Yeah, I can *see* that, but what *happened?*" she asked, walking into the kitchen to shut the freezer door that he had left open. Lately she felt more like his mother than his wife, and it was exasperating.

He sighed, long and loud, glancing over at her as she sat down beside him, and then offered, "You can't seriously tell me that you've never thought the gas was the break and the break was the gas, can you?"

"You've got to be kidding," Lucy asserted, "All of that happened—because you mixed up the break and gas pedals?"

"What?" Drew retorted, looking offended, "These things happen all the time, Lucy. It's really not a big deal. You need to loosen up, you're such a nag."

She was about to protest, to tell him she was just worried, when she smelt it, the distinctive tang of liquor. "Oh my gosh," she remarked, leaning back, away from him, "You've been drinking!"

"So," he said, "What are you going to do about it?" He smirked at her.

"Drew! You could have gotten into a wreck, something worse than what just happened out there. You could have killed someone, killed yourself!" she declared, raising her voice, upset.

"Seriously, Lucy. You act like it's against the law or something. What's your problem?"

"It *is* against the law, Drew. That's the problem!" Lucy cried.

"Oh, Lucy," he cooed, trying to sound endearing, "I sometimes forget how unlike me you are. How uncultured, how inexperienced. How little you actually know of the real world. I still can't get over what a shrew you are, though."

Fuming, Lucy got up and walked back into the kitchen. She sat down on a bar stool and bit her lip, willing herself not to cry.

She was beyond pissed at Drew—for drinking and driving, ruining her car, for being a jerk, for calling her a nag, a shrew. A nag? A shrew? How could she be a nag when the majority of her day was spent doing what Drew wanted her to do—picking up his dry cleaning, making the meals that he wanted, and even arranging manicure and pedicure appointments for *him*?

She normally would be happy to do these things for him, even if the weekly mani-pedi was a little embarrassing. She was the girl here, shouldn't she be the one getting pampered? It's just that he was never grateful for anything she did for him. He complained about everything. No matter how perfectly she had done something, it was never good enough. Never.

It wasn't just that either. He was hardly ever home, and when he was, he made her feel like she was the most pathetic person he had ever met. Making fun of how she looked—her hair, her clothes, even her body.

He had slowly started to change after they had gotten married, and the past few months had been worse than ever. Lucy knew how he treated her wasn't right. She knew she wasn't all the things he said she was when he was angry. Sometimes though, when they had had an incredibly bad fight, and he had said things she never thought he'd say... sometimes she believed it.

Lucy knew she shouldn't let him walk all over her. She should stand up for herself, tell him he can't talk to her like that, or maybe even leave him. She had thought about it, leaving him, many times. Each time though, she had talked herself out of it. She wanted to make it work or at least know that she had given it her all, before she gave up.

They did have fun together, or at least they used to. They used to have the best time going out to eat together, making up background stories for the people around them, putting on obviously fake British accents when they ordered their food. He had made her laugh, and she'd loved it. She wished for that back.

She also worried about what would happen to him if she did leave. Even though he was a major jerk, a lot of the time he did things that were incredibly stupid. She wasn't exactly worried about his dumb choices but worried more because so much of the time he didn't understand that he was being an idiot.

An honest to goodness, actual idiot. Like right now, for example. He honestly didn't think what he had done was a big deal. He had no regrets or guilt about it. Lucy could think of countless times when he had done or said something so dumb that people who had witnessed it had thought it was a joke. The sad thing was, it wasn't a joke. It was just Drew being Drew. That's what she worried about—about him being an idiot and not having anyone to look out for him.

Having heard him get up off the couch, she turned her head to watch him walk towards her, thinking maybe this once he'd apologize.

"Here," he said, dropping the ice pack on the floor by her feet, leaving a small dent in the floor.

She bent down to pick it up and heard him laughing at her.

"There's something I wanted to talk to you about," he began, hiccupping loudly.

"What's that?" she quietly inquired, shutting the freezer door, wishing for kindness.

"I want a divorce," he announced, then turned, and walked up the stairs to their bedroom. Once he got there, he tossed down a pillow and a blanket—his silent way of telling her, she's on the couch.

CHAPTER ONE

"Congratulations!" Mira declared as she grabbed her pen and shut the folder, "You are now officially divorced."

"Great," Lucy responded sarcastically, staring stoically at her best friend's mom, who was also her lawyer, "My life is turning out to be way more awesome than I could have ever imagined."

"Why don't you give Summer a call? She's always been good at cheering you up," Mira, Summer's mom, suggested as she got up from her desk and opened her office door.

Standing up and grabbing her purse, Lucy managed a very small smile and said, "Thanks for your help, Mira."

"Anytime, sweetie." Mira patted her back as Lucy walked out the door. "Good luck!" she called after Lucy before sitting back down at her desk to finish up for the day.

Grabbing her phone as she waited for the elevator, Lucy sent her best friend a quick text, then smiled despite herself at her best friend's quick response—*Meet me downstairs, I've been waiting down here FOREVER!*

Looking up when she heard the elevator ding, Lucy stepped in and wondered what Summer was up to.

"Lucy!" Summer screeched, as Lucy walked slowly out of the elevator, "Ready for some fun, girly?"

Looking around and feeling relief that there weren't many people there to witness Summer's loudness, Lucy weakly replied, "I don't know, Summer. I'm not feeling very festive today … given recent events. I'll probably go home, eat a tub of ice cream, and hang out with my cats."

Making an exaggeratedly confused face, Summer noted, "Uh, you don't even have cats."

"Yeah, but now is probably the perfect time to get a dozen," Lucy answered sarcastically.

"You never know, Luce, this could be the chance for you to do something amazing," Summer suggested, giving a big smile as she grabbed Lucy's hand, pulling her in the direction of the bar down the hall.

Lucy just glared as she pulled her hand back, not budging.

"Come on, let's go grab a drink. It's Friday, let's get crazy! I haven't gotten crazy for a long time, what do you say?" Summer asked insistently, shaking back her long blonde hair.

"Sure, why not. I haven't got anything better to do," Lucy grumbled, giving in. She knew Summer, so she knew she wasn't going to win this one tonight. Watching as Summer grabbed her compact, reapplied her lipstick, and added more mascara, Lucy added, "This better be worth it."

"Cheer up, Lucy, you're never gonna catch another man with an attitude like that!" Summer told her with a grin, as she stashed her compact back into her clutch.

"I have a feeling it's going to be a long night," responded Lucy, shooting a look at Summer and the mischievous look in her eyes.

"You got that right, girl!" Summer agreed, pulling Lucy down the hall, around the corner, and into the elevator that led to the secret "hot spot bar." Summer knew about all of those kind of places and was always dragging Lucy along with her. "And you, my friend, are going to have way too much fun! You never know, you just might get over-served."

"Don't remind me," Lucy uttered, thinking of the last time she'd gone out with Summer. They had ended up getting home just as the sun was rising, and Lucy definitely *had* been over-served. So much so that she spent the rest of the day praying to the porcelain gods. She really didn't want a repeat of that night, but as she watched Summer strut into "secret hot spot bar" in the office building basement and shimmy up to two men who were ogling her, Lucy wasn't sure she had a choice.

* * * * *

Lucy woke the next morning to snoring ... loud snoring, coming from her bed. She groaned and rolled her eyes. Summer was the last person you'd think would snore like a trucker with a cold.

"Summer," Lucy stated, poking her in the back, "wake up."

Summer didn't move. The only sign of life was that loud, insistent snoring. It was driving Lucy crazy, so she did the only thing she could do, aside from yelling (her head hurt just a little too much for that). She grabbed a pillow and hit Summer over the head. Once, twice, three times ...

"Ouch! Hey, what the heck? Luce!" Summer muttered, squinting at Lucy.

"Sorry, Sum, but that snoring has *got* to stop," Lucy maintained with a shake of the head. "I have no clue how you keep all those hot guys around with that *snoring*! No clue."

Wiggling her eyebrows, Sum responded, "Well, if you're asking ..."

"No! Nope. Don't want to hear it. I'm not that desperate. Not yet anyways." Lucy sighed, sitting up slowly.

"Oh, Luce, you'll be fine. I know things are hard now. I know this wasn't what you expected or planned or even wanted for your life. But

... you need to take it and run with it. This *is* your life now. Either you mope around, or you do something about it. Oh, and FYI, moping totally sucks and is extremely unattractive, so ..."

"I get it, I get it," Lucy affirmed, as Summer smiled at her, "No moping around. Do something amazing! Change my life for the better! It's just hard to be positive when I still feel totally blindsided by this whole divorce thing."

"Listen, if you ask me—"

"I'm not."

"Ha," Summer laughed, continuing, "If you ask me, Drew was a jerk from the beginning. He never treated you right. You deserve so much more. If he wants to jump ship and travel around the world *backpacking*, then good luck to him. But he'll never, never find someone as amazing as you! But you, Lucy, you're special. You always have been, and I know you are going to find someone who loves you so, so much."

"Hmm, I don't know. I'm not feeling too special right now, Sum," Lucy admitted, stretching.

"Lucy, you know me, and you know I'm always right! You're going to find someone who is going to make you feel like a million bucks! You're gonna find some hot-to-trot somebody, and he is gonna make you shine, baby!" Summer promised, eyes wide, as she popped up from her relaxed position on the bed.

Lucy laughed, "Shine, huh?"

"Bright like a diamond, baby!" Summer asserted, flashing her megawatt smile. "Now what time is it? I'm thinking I have a hot coffee date with one of those cute guys from last night in a few."

"Oh yeah, which one?" Lucy inquired, raising an eyebrow.

"That's the problem, Luce, I don't remember!" Summer admitted, making a face and jumping off the bed. "Better get to it! Oh, and you, girl, you need to find a job! Things don't come free around here, you know!"

"Yeah, yeah, thanks for the reminder," Lucy responded and sighed, watching Summer dance her way down the hall towards her own room.

It was kind of their thing, having sleepovers after their girls' nights, sharing their beds and daydreaming into the early hours of the night—or morning, depending on how you looked at it. Even though now they were both grown up, both twenty-four, it was still the same. Well, besides the fact that now Lucy actually lived with Summer.

If she could just be a little more like Summer, maybe things would be easier for her right now. It seemed as hard as she tried though, she could never really be as carefree as Summer was. She just wasn't like that.

Lucy was more cautious than Summer. She weighed each decision carefully, wanting to be sure things were just right before taking the plunge. Her mother had always told her she would make a good accountant. Lucy had asked her why, saying she was horrible at math and would find the job completely out of her league—not to mention a little boring! Her mom had just shrugged her shoulders, like she did when she didn't really want to answer a question, and explained to Lucy that her careful ways would make up for her lack of math skills.

Lucy wasn't sure she agreed. Actually, she really never seemed to agree with her mother, which was another problem altogether, best thought through when she had more energy and desire.

It seemed hard to be positive with all she was going through at present. When Drew had sat Lucy down after dinner that fateful night and told her he wanted a divorce, she had been completely caught off guard. He had told her he felt "bogged down" in their marriage, that he was sick of never getting what he wanted.

Lucy wasn't sure what he was talking about. When they had gotten married, Drew told her he wanted her to quit her job and stay home to "take care of the house." He would worry about the money, and she could worry about "all of their necessities." Reluctantly, Lucy quit the job she loved to please Drew. Giving up her salary had cut their income considerably, but Drew had a good job, made more than enough money, and was up for a promotion at the end of the year. It had been a difficult decision to make, and Lucy had been stressed about what they would do financially if Drew didn't get his promotion. Ultimately, she had decided, that being a good wife, and making a home for them, was more important than her career.

It had been fun at first, picking out decorations for their new house, planning out elaborate new meals for them to try, and even doing the errands Drew asked her to do.

The days wore on though, and those things didn't excite her anymore. Plus, they only took up a small part of her day. So Lucy started taking matters into her own hands, taking a few creative writing classes here and there to keep the creative juices flowing. She even made some friends with other women in her neighborhood who stayed home during the day as she did, some with kids, others without.

But even with the extra things that she took on for herself, Lucy never let the things Drew wanted her to do slip. She made every meal he asked for, picked up his dry cleaning when he needed it, and even arranged the endless pedicure appointments for him—seriously?! She had to laugh that between the two of them, he had the better-looking toenails.

So, yes, Drew told her he felt "bogged down." He wanted to "feel free." He just needed to be "released." He felt that he just needed to do something "different" to "regroup." He said that he and a couple of buddies were going to go backpacking around the world; he thought that might help him "free himself." He told Lucy that when he got back—he wasn't sure when that would be—that they could possibly try again. He wasn't sure though, he couldn't promise anything, but she should keep her options open.

When he finally shut up, Lucy laughed. She couldn't believe it, and she couldn't believe him! He sounded like such an idiot. Had she actually wanted to marry this man at some point in her life? She thought back to when they had been dating. Drew had seemed safe, always planning his next move, always two steps ahead. He had been big on putting money aside for an emergency and usually made good decisions. On paper, he had looked like the perfect guy, so Lucy had felt her choice to marry him was a good one. She was beginning to realize though, that looking good on paper didn't necessarily make you a good person.

At that point in the talk, Lucy had stood up, told him to go "blank" himself, and ran to the bedroom, slamming the door behind her.

Reality quickly set in, of , and she started sobbing. But not before Drew quietly suggested to her—through the closed bedroom door—that maybe she should find some way of "freeing herself," as well.

After what seemed like hours of crying, Lucy finally dried her eyes. "Ha!" she said to herself, "you think I need to find some way to *free myself,* do you? Well, lucky for you I have the perfect idea!"

She then walked over to his side of the dresser and proceeded to free his clothing out the bedroom window. When she was done, she felt amazing, very *free* indeed. But then she remembered she had been talking to herself and wasn't sure what to think. She decided to chalk it up to having to live with a moron like Drew for way too long.

Lucy shook her head, bringing herself back into the present, just in time to see Summer walking back into Lucy's room, looking way too cute for it being ten in the morning.

"Okay, babe, you get on that job thing, and I'll get on that hot guy thing!" Summer screeched as a pillow came flying at her.

"Get out!" Lucy teased.

"Hey, watch who you're talking to, girl, this is my place I'll do the—" Summer laughed and dodged another flying pillow.

"Bye, Sum, be good," Lucy called out with a grin. She then cringed and covered her ears as she heard the beginning of Summer's response before the door closed behind her.

Lucy lay back in bed and considered taking a quick catnap, but then thought better of it. Summer was right, moping around totally sucked. She needed to get up, take the bull by the horns, and do something. It was time for her, Lucy Caldwell, to do something amazing! It was definitely time for a change. So she jumped up and did her own dance to the shower, and to her surprise, it felt great.

* * * * *

Lucy was walking down the hallway toward the kitchen when she passed the small table where they tossed their mail and keys and other random things. She grimaced when she saw the large stack of mail and almost kept on walking, but instead, she grabbed the stack, praying it was either junk mail or, well, junk mail.

She flopped down at the kitchen table and flipped through the stack. Bills, bills, and oh, wait, could it be? Yes! More bills! She wasn't sure how she was going to pay all those bills without a job. Obviously, Drew wasn't financially responsible for her anymore because they were officially divorced. But to be honest, he had washed his hands of that "chore" the night he had told her he wanted out. She was sure she'd figure something out. Power of positivity, right?

Lucy sighed, setting the pile of joy down on the table. As she did, she glanced down and noticed another letter on the floor. This one was most definitely not a bill, though. This one was smaller and thicker than average, and the return address made Lucy's eyes bulge and her stomach twist.

Grandma Opal was definitely not someone Lucy wanted to think about, much less hear from at this point in her life. Lucy had met the lady only a handful of times, and each and every time had been extremely unpleasant and torturous. Lucy had no idea why Grandma Opal would be writing to her, but it probably had something to do with her recent divorce and Opal's opinion of Lucy's utter lack of whatever.

Nope, that letter was not to be opened now. Not yet anyways. Procrastination was the ticket for that one! Lucy was going to go for a walk, grab a coffee, and try to plan out the perfect job (bills, bills, bills!). Maybe when she had that figured out, she would be more inclined to open Grandma Opal's letter.

She set the letter down (actually, she buried it underneath the rest of the bills) and sighed. She knew that whatever Opal had to say would change her day, and she really wasn't ready for that right now. So she walked out the door in search of opportunity.

However, what Lucy didn't know was that she was right—Opal's letter would change her. But it wouldn't just change her day, it would change her life.

* * * * *

After a long day job-hunting, Lucy walked into the kitchen to find Summer sitting at the table, eyeing her letter, *the* letter. The letter she had been trying all day to forget about. That darn thing just wouldn't leave her alone.

She turned around and was about to walk back out the door when Summer stopped her. "What's this?" she inquired, holding it up towards Lucy.

"Huh, that? Oh, it looks like some kind of letter. Don't know, gotta go!" Lucy blurted out, trying to escape again.

"Whoa, hold it right there, girl." Summer ordered, eyeing first Lucy, then the letter. She held it up again, saying, "Here, it's for you. But I have a feeling this is something you already know."

Shaking her head, Lucy replied, "Nope, I don't know anything about that gem of a letter, nothing at all. So maybe you should just put it down."

Summer smirked, "This is getting interesting. Here, take it." She thrust the letter towards Lucy, waving it back and forth.

"No, thanks. Maybe next time!" Lucy asserted, backing away.

"Here!"

"No!"

"Take it!"

"No way."

"Lucy! Spill it," commanded Summer. She set the letter down on the table, and then spoke slowly while pointing to the chair next to hers, "Sit. Down."

Defeated, Lucy sat beside Summer at the table. "That letter is from my Grandma Opal."

"O-o-o-o-h-h-h-kay, and?"

"And what?"

"What's the big deal, Luce? Your Grandma Opal, huh? Well, I'm sure she's harmless, so just open the thing and see what she has to say." Summer pushed the envelope a few inches closer to Lucy.

"You don't understand, Summer. Opal is evil. And when I say evil, I mean *evil*. There is no way I am opening that letter! Who *knows* what could be in there!" Lucy disclosed, eyes large.

"Then I'll open it," Summer told her, grabbing the letter, ready to tear it open.

"No!" Lucy slammed her hand down on it.

"Why the heck not?" Summer demanded.

"I ... I need some time, is all," Lucy said quietly.

Summer squinted at her. "How much time do you need?"

Looking at Summer from the corner of her eye, Lucy replied, "How much do I get?"

Shaking her head, Summer announced, "You get three days' time, girl. If that darn letter isn't opened by Tuesday night, there'll be hell to pay."

Relaxing back into her chair, Lucy remarked, "Procrastination. Works every time."

When Summer just glared at her, Lucy quickly switched the subject, "So, how was your date?"

* * * * *

The next few days passed quickly, as they always seemed to do when Lucy had something to do in the near future that she wasn't looking forward to. She kept trying to forget about the letter, but it was always there, floating around in the back of her mind.

She spent her days looking online for jobs that piqued her interest, or in the local paper for help-wanted ads. There were a few that looked promising, maybe even some that looked fun, at least for the time being. She didn't think being a nanny to triplets could be *too* hard, could it? The kids probably just played or colored together all day anyway, and the family was offering a lot of cash for her time, so that could be an option.

There were also a bunch of dog-walking opportunities out there, and Lucy thought that might also be easy, and maybe even fun. That is, if she didn't have to pick up any dog poop and if the dogs were cute. Lucy doubted she could count on that, the latter maybe, but realistically not the former. Who was she kidding? They all sounded horrible so far.

Wherever she ended up working, it would have to be somewhere close—no car, thanks again, Drew—and it would have to be soon. She was very appreciative of Summer letting her stay temporarily rent-free in the apartment for now, but she would feel like a total loser if things didn't pan out for her in the next couple of weeks.

Summer insisted it wasn't a big deal. She said she understood what Lucy was going through with Drew, and she was in no rush for Lucy to move out. But Lucy still felt like a freeloader sometimes, and she really hated that feeling. Summer was the best thing going for her right now, and she didn't want to mess that up.

Lucy felt extremely lucky to have a friend like Summer. Summer was always understanding and never judged her, no matter what mistakes she made. She had always been like that though, even through their teen-age years when the push and pull of new friends and boys could cause anyone to make a mess of things.

Lucy grinned, remembering the day she had met Summer. They were in eighth grade English class, Lucy rushing in to get to her seat before the bell rang. She was always afraid of being late and being forced to sing in front of the entire class because of it.

Sliding into her seat just as the bell rang, she noticed the seat next to hers, which was usually empty, was now filled. She smiled a hello at the new girl, recalling the teacher mentioning something about a new student a few days previously.

Waiting for the teacher to start their lesson, she noticed the boy in front of her turning around in his seat to stare blatantly at Summer. When Summer noticed him staring at her, she promptly, not to mention loudly, asked, "What?" in a not-so-nice voice.

The boy, taken aback that Summer had actually uttered two words to him stuttered, "I, um … I like your socks!"

To which Summer directly responded, "Turn around and SHUT UP!"

Lucy couldn't help herself—she had to laugh and give Summer props for telling the boy exactly what she wanted him to do. Summer then looked over at Lucy, shrugged, and then laughed with her, and from that day on they were BFFs.

When Lucy had told Summer about Drew wanting a divorce, Summer had, of course, offered her mom's law expertise, free of charge. Lucy had suspected Summer had called her mom, immediately after hanging up with Lucy, to plead Lucy's case.

Lucy was proud of her friend. Summer had made something of herself, and she was happy doing it. Summer had accomplished something Lucy hadn't done for herself just yet—she'd found her passion.

Summer was an amazing stylist and had a weekly spot on the local news station featuring the up-and-coming fashions. She was also the girl the news station sent out to try new and crazy things. It was one of the most watched news spots, when Summer was on.

She also had one of the most popular boutiques around, which, in Lucy's opinion, was made even more popular by its irregular hours. Summer only had it open on the days she wasn't doing her styling or news spots. If she had gone out the night before and didn't want to get up early, then she wouldn't end up opening it until two or three o'clock in the afternoon. Even when she hadn't been up late, she would roll in at any old time. Lucy had no idea how people even knew when the store was actually open. Somehow someone must see the sign or see Summer pulling up in her parking spot behind the store because within twenty minutes of the store opening, there was always a line so far down the street that it sometimes wrapped around the block.

Lucy had gotten enough black eyes and twisted ankles trying to shove her way into the store to help Summer, that she had insisted Summer notify her ASAP when she was going to open the place. That way Lucy could get there before the madness happened.

When Lucy had quit her job at Drew's insistence, Summer had rolled her eyes and told Lucy she could always use the help at the boutique. At first Lucy would stop in after a writing class or on her way home from a coffee date, to chat with Summer and, of course, get first dibs on a cute pair of skinny jeans or a shirt she just couldn't pass up.

After a while, she was there most days the store was open, enjoying her time with Summer, grateful that she wasn't sitting home alone again and secretly wishing her life had turned out differently.

After Summer had offered Lucy her mother's services, she had also convinced her to come stay in her apartment for a while. Lucy was reluctant at first. She felt a little like she was taking advantage, but Summer kept badgering her about it until she finally gave in. Summer could be pretty convincing when she had her mind set on something.

Since she had moved in a few months ago, things had been going great. It was like being in high school again—discussing cute boys, complaining about the annoying ones, having sleepovers, and talking together other until all hours of the night.

It was just what Lucy needed to start the healing process. Plus, Summer was never afraid to say what she thought, and that was what got Lucy up and out of bed. This was good because otherwise she'd probably be crying into a pint of ice cream while watching a Lifetime movie marathon.

Even though she loved Summer to no end, Lucy knew what Summer was going to make her do tonight, and knowing that made her really not like Summer at that particular moment.

Hoping that maybe Summer was out on another hot date—seriously, the girl had guys kicking down her door—Lucy convinced herself she'd probably get an extra night to *not* think about the letter. She was really starting to believe it was going to happen since it was almost nine at night and there was no sign of Summer. Lucy was really starting to enjoy herself, snuggled in on the couch, watching *Revenge*, when the door swung open and in walked Summer.

"Hey, Luce!" Summer sang, making her hand into a gun shape and pointing it directly at Lucy. "I know what you were thinkin' and you're wrong, girl!"

"Oh, really? Just what was I thinking, Sum?" Lucy asked, raising an eyebrow, hoping Summer had forgotten.

"Ha! You were thinking I wasn't going to show for our little date tonight, weren't you? But, you were mistaken! Here I am, and you better be grateful too because I just walked away from a smokin' hot guy to come read a *letter* with you. This better be good, Luce." Summer sent her a look—half smirk, half glare.

"Oh, Summer, you know you didn't have to cut your date short on my account," Lucy responded, all innocence.

"Can it, babe. Let's do this thing." Summer strutted over to the table, picked up the letter, and tossed it at Lucy. "Open. Now."

"But …" Lucy started, pointing at the TV where Emily and Nolan were in what looked to be a serious conversation.

Picking up the remote, Summer switched off the TV, sat down on the couch next to Lucy, and declared, "*Revenge* can wait."

Lucy sighed. She knew when she was beat. To be honest, curiosity had been getting the better of her these past couple of hours. Weirdly, it had taken all her might not to run over and rip that letter open before Summer had arrived home. Lucy was happy Summer was with her because she knew she was going to need some moral support.

Ripping open the envelope, Lucy glanced over at Summer. "Here goes," she stated, as she pulled a thick sheet of stationary out of the envelope.

Dear Lucinda—

I have come to hear of your divorce from that Drew fellow. I'll let you in on a little secret—I was never quite fond of him. Even though, with divorce, it is most certainly a two-way street, and you may have had your many faults, nobody is perfect. I am most certain that moron Drew is the cause of this. Most men are idiots, Lucy, and they have no idea what they are doing and never will. If you find one who isn't an idiot, grab on to him and don't let go. The best thing for you to do now is to forget all about his existence and move on.

You are wondering why I am writing you, I am sure. It has nothing to do with the idiocy mentioned above. I am writing you to ask a favor. These types of things have always been hard for me to do. I'd rather be tough than let emotions shine through, I'm sure you know this.

I have recently been diagnosed with cancer. No one

besides my doctor, nurse, and house staff know about this. You are the first family member I have told. I am not sure how much time I have left on this earth, and in my reflections of this life I have some regrets.

One of them is not getting to know you better. I am hoping to change that—I am asking for a second chance with you, Lucy. So here is my proposition to you: come stay with me in the city. Come spend some time with your grandma. You may be surprised at all you might learn about me. And not all bad, I promise!

This is my wish—to spend my last days here getting to know you. You who reminds me so much of myself so long ago. I know this must be a huge shock, my asking you to come here. But if you can find it in your heart to forgive my ugliness of the past, I would so greatly appreciate it. I promise, Lucy, you won't regret it.

Love, your one and only Grandma Opal

Lucy took a deep breath and tried to steady herself. She definitely wasn't expecting this. She was shocked at Opal's proposition. And cancer? No matter how unpleasant someone was, no one deserved that, even if they had lived a long and full life. Come to think of it, had Opal lived a full life? Lucy wasn't sure. She knew next to nothing about her, other than the way she had treated Lucy and her mom all those years ago.

"You okay, Luce?" Summer asked, concerned.

Lucy, sighing, handed the letter over to Summer. "See for yourself."

Summer grabbed the letter and skimmed through it, exclaiming "Oh wow, Lucy! I don't know what to say … but … Holy heck, she wants you to move in with her!" Summer's eyes wide, she asked, "What are you going to do?"

"I think I'm in shock right now, Sum. I have no idea … I don't think I could just up and move in, I mean that would be weird, right?" Lucy stated, eyebrows scrunching together.

"I don't know, Luce. This is her dying wish. Can you deny her that? What if you said no, and then … after … you always regretted it? You never know, Lucy, it could totally suck or it could be amazing. Either way, it's going to be an experience you'll never forget. Honestly, what better time than now to do something totally crazy?" Summer suggested, grabbing Lucy's hands and squeezing.

"I don't know, Summer," Lucy stated reluctantly, eyeing her friend, who looked at her expectantly.

"Think about it, Lucy. You have no job, no commitments, nothing holding you back or tying you down. This is happening at the weirdest, yet most perfect time for you. I know it's a stretch, and I know your memories of your grandma aren't the best, but maybe this is exactly what you need. Plus, I don't know about you, but I have a feeling she has some pretty interesting stories."

With Lucy just staring at her, Summer continued, "You know I'm right. All those eccentric old bats do! I think you should go for it."

"You just want me out, so you can have your way with all those smoking hot guys you meet," Lucy declared, bumping her knee against Summer's.

"Ha! You're right. I do!" Summer laughed, smacking Lucy on the arm. "Now get packing, baby! You've got a wish to grant!"

* * * * *

Procrastination is a tricky thing. You don't want to suck at it because then you'd end up doing the things that you don't want to do, right away. You don't want to be too good at it either because then you wouldn't do anything. Ever. Lucy was good at it; in fact, it could be argued that it was one of her finer qualities. Normally she was okay with it, but today she just wished she could totally, totally suck.

She knew she should just bite the bullet and call her mom, tell her about the letter she had received from Grandma Opal and what she was thinking about doing. She knew her mom would flip a lid when she found out what Opal had asked, and she really didn't want to deal with that right now.

If her mom was good at one thing, it was drama, and Lucy had been having just a little bit too much of that lately. Plus, she was twenty-four years old! Why did she always feel the need to get her mother's approval all the time? Which, by the way, her success rate at that was very low since she and her mother had conflicting opinions on pretty much everything.

Lucy knew that the real reason she didn't want to call her mom right then, besides the awaiting drama fest, was that she wasn't sold on going to stay with Grandma Opal. If she was going to call her mom and share her plan, she had better darn well be sure it was what she wanted and have plenty of reasons to back it up. If there were any hint of wishy-washy in her tone, her mom would pick up on it right away and run with it.

Lucy had read and reread the letter from Opal. Sure, the beginning of the letter was the usual Opal, straight to the point, and a little hurtful, but Lucy was beginning to sense that it was just a front, Opal's way of protecting herself. Lucy wasn't sure why she felt this way, but something in the letter told her Opal wasn't really what she made herself out to be.

Even though Lucy didn't enjoy reading what Opal had written about Drew, she kind of agreed with it. Lucy was pretty sure the only reason reading it had hurt her was because she was still a little tender from the breakup.

Lucy remembered that when she was younger, going to visit Opal was always a nightmare. Opal was crabby, rude, and critical of her and her mother, and Lucy could never understand why. Lucy was Opal's only granddaughter. She was Opal's only anything, really.

Lucy's mother was an only child, and so was Lucy. They were the only relatives that Opal had. Lucy's mother felt bad for her mom, Opal, when Lucy's grandfather had passed away, so their trips to visit had become more frequent. Then, all of a sudden, the visits stopped. Lucy never knew why, and when she dared bring up the subject with her mother, she only got a shake of the head and a look, which she knew meant never to ask again.

Now, Lucy was curious. Opal's letter had dragged up old, forgotten memories, memories that had always been confusing to Lucy. Now Lucy had a chance to get some answers. Answers that her mother had never wanted to give her. Answers to questions Lucy had never before dared to ask.

If Lucy was one thing, it was curious. Her curiosity even overruled her cautiousness if that was possible. When Lucy thought about it that way, her opportunity to go and stay with Opal was a no-brainer. She was going, and that was that.

Of course, she wasn't ready just *yet* to call her mother and tell her of her plans, so she decided to check her email. Lucy had been bad about checking it lately, but now she wanted to see if there were any responses to the résumés she had sent out. Not that it would matter now, anyway, if she were moving. But just in case.

Sitting down at the desk she and Summer shared, tucked into the corner of the living room, Lucy booted up her laptop. Her eyes just about popped out of their sockets when she saw who sent the most recent email. She shook her head, rubbed her eyes, and looked again. Yup, there it was in black and white. She most definitely did have an email, and it was from Drew.

She stared skeptically at it for a few seconds, unsure if she wanted to see what he had to say. Then, taking a deep breath, she reluctantly clicked to open the email.

Slowly, she started to read. Then she started to laugh. What an idiot!

Dear Luce—

I just wanted to write hello and let you know that we are off! Our quest for freedom is moving along nicely. Our backpacking expedition is, if not exactly as expected, interesting at least ... You remember Corbin, my old college buddy? He has decided to join us on our quest! Corbin has been putting in extra effort, but things just aren't going his way. He booked us a room at the Four Seasons in Vail (that's in Colorado, if you didn't know), but when we got there, they said they had no record of a booking! Everything was packed because of some big goings on, so the only place we found to stay was at a friend of Corbin's. He has a wonderful townhouse, but all the rooms were already occupied when we arrived, so we had to sleep on the floor. That is not something I am comfortable with, Lucy. The next morning, I woke to a funny smell and a weird sound, When I opened my eyes, I saw a cat—A CAT—relieving itself on my backpack! Well, I couldn't get out of there fast enough, but Corbin wanted to catch up with his old friend, so we ended up staying a second night on the floor with those pesky cats!

You wouldn't believe the guys that live here, Lucy. One is a very successful entrepreneur. The other, his brother, is a young whippersnapper, who has a cast all the way up his arm from skateboarding. They are quite the pair, these two. Very interesting, and I must admit, intriguing. The businessman has a way about him. He could convince you the sky is green and the grass is blue, and then he'd sell you a piece of each without lifting a finger! The young one, well, he hasn't his

wits about him yet, so he is still learning, but he is always up for an adventure. I'm thinking of taking him up on a run on that skateboard thing of his, hahaha. My only hope is wherever we go next, we won't end up on the floor with cats! When backpacking around the world, Lucy, one should never set his sights too low.
Your best guy—
Drew

Shaking her head, Lucy said to herself, "Your best guy? You've got to be kidding me!" Then she typed a reply.

Drew—
It sounds like you are having more of an adventure than you bargained for! The funny thing is, when most people go backpacking, they stay in hostels or crappy hotels, not the Four Seasons ... so it sounds like sleeping on the floor and getting peed on by a cat is just the kind of experience you need. Your new friends sound nice, and I'm not sure why, but I think I'd really, really like their cat! Tell Corbin hello.
Lucy

Lucy couldn't help but laugh, Drew sounded so ... well, so Drew—the way he acts like he knows so much but is actually really ignorant in most situations. She wasn't sure what he expected when he decided to go "backpacking" around the country/world, but she was pretty sure slumming it in free, cheap, and dingy places wasn't what he'd had in mind.

The whole thing with Drew had her so stressed, and she was finally starting to feel a little bit better, like she could breathe a little now. She hadn't expected to hear from him, nor had she wanted to. But his email had made her feel really, really good. It wasn't that she wanted him to have a bad time, well, not really, but it was extremely entertaining to hear about the unpleasant things that were happening to him while he was "freeing himself." She secretly hoped that there would be another funny (for her, not for him) story coming soon because she could definitely do with another laugh like that.

Closing down her email, Lucy glanced at her phone. It was time to make the call. She wasn't happy about it, but she figured her enjoyment of Drew's misfortune could be a cushion for a little mama drama. So, reluctantly, she picked up her phone and dialed.

CHAPTER TWO

"Hello! Lucy, dear!" her mother answered, brightly.

"Hello, mother," Lucy said, taking deep breaths.

"Uh oh, whenever you start the conversation like that it's always some kind of bad news that you have to tell me. What is it, Lucy?" her mother asked, a hint of worry threading through her voice. She'd had her fair share of bad news over the past few months.

"I'll have to remember that next time, and then I'll have more of a head start to surprise you, ha-ha!" Lucy really didn't want to tell her where she was going in a couple of weeks.

"Lucy, quit stalling."

Whether Lucy wanted to admit it or not, her mother knew her too well.

"First off, you need to promise me you won't get mad. Because if you are going to get mad, then I'm not going to tell you and—"

"Yeah, yeah, I've heard that one before. Okay, Lucy, I promise I won't get mad," her mother offered with a sigh.

Lucy decided just to go for it. "Well, okay, so I got a letter from Grandma Opal. She wants me to come stay with her for a while, and after thinking it over, I've decided that I'm going to do it." Lucy spit it out, as fast as she could.

"WHAT? You got a LETTER from GRANDMA OPAL? What did it say? It couldn't have been very pleasant. Did she send over some kind of drugs for you to take too, so she could alter your mind and convince you to go stay with her?" She paused, and Lucy could hear her taking deep breaths. "I'm just so confused, Lucy. I just don't know what to think!" Lucy could hear her mom tapping her nails on the counter. This was what she did when she was upset, this was not a good thing.

Drama time, Lucy thought, but kept it to herself, and instead urged, "Calm down, Mom, it's okay! So yeah, the first part of the letter was how I remember Grandma Opal, but then … she told me something that changed the whole dynamic of the letter. I can't turn down her request, Mom. I just can't. I tried to reason myself out of it, but it's just not going to happen."

Lucy's mom, Stella, took a deep breath, "Okay, Lucy, I'm listening, and I'm trying not to be mad. Explain to me what the letter said, and I promise I won't say anything until you are done. I really need to understand what's going on here."

Lucy wasn't sure if she should tell her mom about Opal being diagnosed with cancer, but then decided she would. Opal hadn't said anything about not mentioning it to anyone, and Lucy knew it would help her mom understand why she was doing what she was about to do. Plus her mom, Stella, was Opal's daughter, and didn't she have a right to know?

"Okay, well, at first the letter was just what I had expected it to be. About Drew and me and how I make mistakes as does everyone, I should know that blah, blah, blah."

"What?" Stella interrupted.

"Mom, remember you said you'd listen and not say anything yet?" Lucy reminded her.

"Oh. Sorry, Luce. Okay, go on." More tapping.

"I mean, she didn't actually come right out and *say* I was an idiot for marrying Drew, but she said she was never fond of him. And you know what that means coming from Grandma Opal."

"Yes, that definitely wouldn't be a compliment. What else did she say?" Stella asked. Tap, tap, tap.

"Then she said something like she isn't good with emotions or feelings, but she had to share some news. Then she … well, she told me… " Lucy wasn't sure how to tell her mother that Opal had cancer. It was a big—no, huge—thing, and it felt weird to just blurt it out without at least warning her mom something like that was coming.

"What is it, Lucy?"

"I don't know, Mom, it's just, it's hard to say … "

"It's okay, Lucy. You can tell me, really."

Stella was beginning to worry. What was it that Lucy had to tell her? When it concerned Opal, you never knew what was going to happen.

"Mom … she has cancer," Lucy blurted out.

"What? Since when? And why don't I know this?" Stella asked, sounding stunned.

"Well, now you do. She said in her letter that she was just recently diagnosed and that no one knows, besides her doctor and the people that work for her."

"Why didn't she tell any of us? Isn't your family the first people you go to when something huge like this happens?"

Stella was obviously hurt. Of course, she wished Opal would have called or written her a letter. She knew things between them had been rough and weird for years, ever since Lucy was a little girl. But when things like this happen, weirdness flies out the window. Well it did for Stella, anyway. No matter what she and Opal had been through, Stella loved her mother and had always thought that when it came time, they'd all be together in the end. Opal was her *mother* for goodness sakes.

Neither Stella nor Lucy had been in touch with Opal since "the incident" from years ago. "The incident" is what Stella called it, to herself only, because no one else besides Opal, Stella's dad Henry, and Stella knew what had happened.

On that fateful day that Stella had hoped would be filled with surprise and acceptance, her parents had turned their backs on her when she had needed them the most.

She had been blindsided, and her pride had been crushed. They had told her to get out and not come back. Her father had yelled at her for the first time that afternoon, about how she had wasted their money. How her future was ruined now that she was knocked up, how the last four years of her life had been a waste. Not only to her, but to him as well.

She had tried to talk to him, to help him understand what she had been thinking. She wanted to sit down and explain how she had gone to the sperm bank and sat for what seemed like hours, picking out who she thought was the perfect "father" donor. Then, when it was all over and done with, how she could almost feel the baby forming inside of her, feel something magical taking place.

She had pleaded with him, begged him to understand. But he had just turned away from her and walked out the door, shouting "Get out!" as he left her crumpled on the floor, devastated and longing for her father's love and acceptance.

She then had sought her mother. She had always looked to Opal and was sure Opal would understand. Opal was a mother herself, so how could she not know what it felt like, to have something beautiful growing inside of her, her own little secret from the world? When her mom just shook her head and not meeting her eyes, commanded, "Leave. Go now, and pack your things," Stella felt like she had been slapped across the face.

She barely made it up the stairs and into her bedroom before she broke down, sobs racking through her body, over and over again.

When she finally stopped, having cried all her tears, she wiped her eyes, blew her nose, and resolved to be the best gosh-darn mother anyone had ever seen. She vowed then and there that she would give her child all that he or she would ever need or want. Vowed her child would never feel the pain of rejection of a parent turning her back when it mattered most.

Stella wasn't sure where she would go, but as she packed as much as she could into her old Volvo station wagon, she remember a friend from college talking about the town she had grown up in.

Alexandria was about two hours away from Minneapolis. Just far enough away to be out of sight, but not too far that her parents couldn't drive down for the day if they changed their minds about her situation. She had held out hope for a long, long time that the day would come when they would all be together again—but it never had.

Then she had gotten a phone call from her mom, telling her that her father had passed away. Though she was sad about her father passing away before they could mend their broken fences, Stella had been hopeful that she and Opal could make up.

She had taken Lucy a handful of times to visit Opal, and each time was more painful than the previous. Her mother was obviously still hurting from losing her husband, but Stella had hoped their visits would lessen the pain.

Nothing seemed to help, least of all their visits, which more and more often included Lucy crying for the entire trip, afraid of the "mean, crabby lady." She had been only four at the time and didn't understand what was happening, most of all why they were all of a sudden leaving their nice, peaceful town each weekend to go visit an irritable old woman.

It all came to a boiling point one weekend when Stella was trying to cheer Opal up, telling her a funny story about something Lucy had said. Before Stella could finish her story, Opal had started yelling at her, reminding her they had never wanted anything to do with her or her daughter. Opal had told Stella that her father had never forgiven her for what she had done to him and that he had gone to the grave with the pain still fresh in his mind.

"You're right," Stella had replied quickly, grabbing her purse, "I have absolutely no idea *what* we are doing here. Good-bye, mother." She then walked down the long hallway to the bedroom where Lucy was sleeping, picked up the toys there, and shoved them into her purse.

She had woken up Lucy, whisked her into her cozy car seat, tucked her favorite blanket around her, and drove away, never to return.

There had been times when Lucy was older that she had asked her mom about Opal, wondering what had happened. Still hurting from that afternoon years ago, Stella would just shake her head, and Lucy would try to forget about it.

Stella would sometimes think back to the vow that she had made in her bedroom so long ago and wonder if she was living up to it. She loved Lucy with all her heart, but sometimes it was hard to let her go and let her do her own thing, let her be hurt. She wanted Lucy to learn from her mistakes, to skip the dumb choices by listening to her advice and do the right thing from the start.

This had caused a space to form between her and Lucy, beginning when Lucy entered her teen-age years, and the space was still sometimes apparent now. With all that Lucy had gone through lately, Stella had learned to step back and let Lucy make her own choices. Lucy was her own person with her own dreams and desires, and there was nothing Stella wanted less than to stand in the way of her daughter's future.

Stella knew she would at some point have to tell Lucy what had happened with Opal, but she didn't want to hurt her. She didn't want Lucy to think that it was her fault. She didn't want Lucy to feel like she had ever been unwanted or a burden to anyone. If anything, Lucy had given Stella the courage to make her dreams a reality. That was what she wanted Lucy to learn from her story, that Lucy had given her the chance to be everything she wanted to be.

Even after everything that had happened with her parents, all that had been said, Stella was surprised that her own mother wouldn't think about telling her or possibly not want to tell her that she was dying. Would Opal go to her grave with the pain she felt Stella had caused, fresh in her heart too? Stella hoped not, but wasn't sure what she could do. She'd learned that sometimes people hold on to their pain, and there wasn't anything anyone else could do about it.

"I'm not sure, Mom. Maybe she feels like she *did* go to her family first," Lucy suggested, regretting it instantly. She knew her mom was going to take it the wrong way.

"What is *that* supposed to mean? That I'm not family to her? That *you* are? Need I remind you, Lucy, that I am her daughter?" Stella demanded, tapping louder.

"No, Mom, that's not what I meant at all. What I meant was that the people who work for her have been with her for years. They probably know her better than anyone else and are like family to her. I'm guessing they know a side of Opal that we've never seen. They live right there with her, they see her every day. If something is going on with her, they are going to see it and wonder what's up. So, in my opinion, she kind of had to tell them."

Stella was silent for a long time, and Lucy wasn't sure what her mom was thinking. Either she was really, really mad at Lucy, or … she was just really mad at Lucy.

After what felt like forever, Stella stated, "You know, Lucy, you're right."

Lucy wasn't sure she had heard what her mother had said correctly. She must be dreaming. "Mom, did you just say what I think you did?"

"Ha-ha. Yes, I did! You are right, I don't know why I've never thought of it before, but I bet they are like family to her. Of course, she would tell them. I just wish she would have said something to me. I know we've been through a lot, but …" Stella trailed off, losing herself in memories of the past.

Lucy knew it was as good a time as any to bring up what had happened, to ask her mom and see if she would let her in on her memories. But Lucy wasn't sure she wanted to open that can of worms right now. Strangely, she felt that if her mom wanted to tell her what had happened, she would, and she felt that until that moment came when her mom wanted to be open, she really didn't even want to know.

"Wow, okay, so how did she get to the part where she asked you to come and stay with her?" Stella asked from her end of the phone, raising her eyebrow in such a way that she looked similar to Lucy.

"Right, well, she said she had been diagnosed with cancer … and then she said she had regrets. She said that I was one of her regrets. That she wishes she had gotten to know me better. That I remind her of herself at times. She said that she really hopes for me to give her a chance so that I can also get to know the real her."

"Well, I can understand that. When you are faced with only so much time, your life kind of comes into perspective and you are faced with what you have or haven't done. I can see why she'd want to change that part of her life. Other than her staff, we really are all that she has. Are you sure you want to do this? Do you think you'll be okay there? I mean, I know you'll be safe but … I just hope she is good to you, that's all," Stella said, adding, "You don't need anyone else who is going to treat you like, well, you know."

Lucy smiled. She felt like she was having a moment with her mom, which was very weird because she couldn't remember the last time they'd had a moment. "I thought of that too, Mom. I mean she was really horrible back in the day. I don't know, I think, I *hope* she has changed. I just get a feeling that she really does want us to get to know each other, the whole thing where she said she isn't good with emotions. Well, it kind of makes sense that she would be crabby all the time. Plus, here's the kicker, she told me it was her wish that I would come and stay with her. How can I deny a dying person her last wish? I can't, I just can't, Mom," Lucy confided, shaking her head and forcing her tears back. Why was she suddenly so emotional?

"That is a kicker, Luce, but you know what? Even if it wasn't her last wish, I think you still would have given her a chance. That's just who you are," Stella said softly, between what Lucy could only decipher as sniffles, sans tapping.

"So, what do you think, Mom? Do you think it's a horribly bad idea?" Lucy asked, biting her lip as she waited for her mother's response.

"I think you should go with what you feel and with what you want,"

Stella recommended, her voice warm.

"What? Mom! What's the deal? You've never said that to me before! You love telling me what to do or not do! I thought you would totally flip when I told you about this and say that I shouldn't go or make me give you a million reasons why I should ... but you're ... you're not, and I'm not sure what to think." Lucy was bewildered.

"Oh, Lucy, I think you *should* go. I think going will be something great for you and for Opal. You two are both so much alike it would be a shame for you not to get to know each other before it's too late. Honestly, I've been trying not to influence your decisions lately," Stella revealed with a chuckle, knowing that if she could see Lucy right then, she would be raising her eyebrows. "I said *trying*. It's not as easy as it looks, either! But ever since your divorce, I've really wanted to take a step back and be here more for you. Just to listen and let you find out who you are, what you want. Maybe I didn't do so well at that when you were younger, and I'm sorry for it, but I can make up for it now, and I will. I love you, Lucy, and I think that if you don't go on this adventure, you may wish you had later on in life."

Lucy couldn't stop the tears now, and she didn't want to. It took a while to find her voice, but when she did, she said, "I love you too, Mom ... and I can't believe it, but I think we just had a moment."

Stella laughed, responding, "I wish you were here now, so I could give you a huge mama bear hug! It sounds like you need it right now."

"You know what, Mom, I can't believe I am going to say this but— you're the best. You really are a great mom, and I am so lucky to have you." It felt weird to be having a heart to heart with her mom again, but Lucy liked the way she felt. She could definitely get used to it. She had missed the way things had been when she was younger and they had been close.

"Look at us all emotional, and it only took ten years and a major event to bring us together!" Stella noted, grinning. She felt amazing—it was like they were finally breaking down all those walls they had built up around them. Why they were there, all those walls, she didn't care right now, it just felt good to be demolishing them.

"Ha-ha, well, okay, Mom, I better get going. I think I'm going to let Opal know I've decided to grant her wish." Lucy laughed—her "granting a wish" sounded absurd.

"Okay, Lucy, good luck. Call me later and let me know all the details."

"I will, Mom, bye," Lucy said, hanging up.

That had gone okay. No, it had gone amazing! With her mom being so surprisingly supportive, Lucy was actually a little bit excited for her trip to Opal's. The past few months had been horrible, but it seemed like things were turning themselves around, at least with her mom.

Who knew, maybe Opal was different, like she claimed in her letter? Maybe she had a little magic in her, something that could change the bad into good. Lucy hoped so because she really needed something different in her life, and for once procrastination wasn't the ticket; moving forward was.

*   *   *   *   *

Later that night, feeling much more relaxed than she had in a long time, Lucy was lounging around watching TV and waiting for Summer to get back from most likely some hot date. She couldn't wait to tell Summer about her conversation with her mom. She knew Summer would be floored that they'd actually had a civilized conversation.

She also couldn't wait to tell Summer about what Opal had said. Lucy had called her grandmother after talking to her mom, channeling the positivity from her most recent conversation. Opal had been more than friendly towards Lucy, even before Lucy told her she was accepting the offer to stay. Opal hadn't even asked or brought the subject up at all, but she was obviously very excited and happy when Lucy told her she had decided to stay and would like to get to know her better.

Then the conversation shifted to when Lucy should come and other details. Opal said Lucy was welcome to arrive anytime she wanted, but that she would like to get a room ready for her stay. She thought that a week's time would be about right for that to get done.

Opal then surprised Lucy with her next question. She asked her to describe her dream bedroom. Lucy wasn't sure how to respond. Of course, she had visions of the best bedroom a girl could imagine, but she wasn't about to spill it to Opal—only to arrive and have it laid out before her when she got there. Lucy would love to have all she desired in her dream room, but she didn't feel right assuming Opal would possibly indulge her like that.

Lucy had almost said as much to Opal, and Opal, surprising Lucy again, had insisted that she spill the beans. Opal honestly wanted to do something nice for Lucy, to make her happy, and she knew a beautiful bedroom could be something that would help Lucy feel welcome and comforted while surrounded by unfamiliarity.

So Lucy had reluctantly given in and divulged what she thought would be the perfect, most beautiful bedroom. And Opal in turn became more and more excited while the vision built in her own mind. Of course, Opal's excitement was contagious, and Lucy felt herself becoming even more excited, and before they knew it, they were laughing and gushing as if they were old friends.

At the end of their conversation, Opal had tried to finagle Lucy's dress size from her, but Lucy had adamantly refused. Opal just retorted with a half laugh, half snort, "Ha! You just watch. I'll have that info before you can bat those pretty little eyes of yours!"

Honestly, Lucy didn't doubt it. It was becoming more and more obvious that Opal had ways of getting what she wanted, and right now, that was just fine by Lucy.

After they hung up, Lucy had felt happier than she had in a long time. It wasn't just because she knew when she arrived at Opal's, she'd have something beautiful waiting for her, though that didn't hurt the situation. It was because she had thoroughly enjoyed conversing with Opal.

Despite the age difference, they seemed to get along great. There had been no awkward pauses in the conversation or times when Lucy wasn't sure what to say.

Just thinking about it made Lucy smile bigger than she had in forever, thinking about the fun times she hoped were ahead of her.

That's when Summer walked in, abruptly stopped, and stared at Lucy. "Uh-oh, don't tell me … you only get that in-the-clouds, dreamy look on your face for two reasons—one, when something amazingly great happens—and two, when you're in love … don't tell me you met someone!" Summer screeched, running over to give Lucy a huge hug. "So tell me, who is he? Where did you meet him?"

Lucy glared at Summer, remarking, "In the clouds? Thanks, Sum, that does wonders for my confidence right now."

"Oh, come on, babe, you know what I mean! It's like that 'o-h-h-h-h, I'm in heaven, life is so perfect, nothing can stop me now!' look. S-o-o-o-o-o tell, tell!" Summer's eyes were as wide as saucers, perfect, beautifully blue saucers.

"I haven't met anyone, Sum. Where would I meet anyone? All I've been doing is sitting around here or wandering around looking for random jobs. I'm sure all the normal guys see me and run." Lucy sighed. She hoped that one day she'd meet someone new, but it was a little too soon to be thinking about that right now.

"Oh come on, Lucy! You've got to be kidding, right? Have you really never noticed how men look at you? Their jaws drop, babe!"

"Summer, we're not talking about you here, we're talking about me. Jaw dropping is not my style …" Lucy's voice trailed off. She always felt that she paled in comparison when she was next to Summer.

Summer with the lush blonde hair, blue eyes, and curvy body. Guys were always drawn to her, and it was obvious why. Summer was the life of the party, laughing and dancing and singing in an altogether unselfconscious way, a way Lucy wished she could be.

Lucy, on the other hand, felt her long, wavy brown hair and big hazel eyes were boring, plain. She was always just a little self-conscious and sometimes a little awkward. But when Lucy pointed those things out to Summer, Summer just shook her head, saying, "Luce, do you really not see how gorgeous you are? You're like this cute, quirky little thing, with amazing eyes and a perfect smile. Then get talking to you and you have this innocence and genuine quality that people love, and you're also a little quiet, which translates to mysterious, which translates to intriguing ... I just described you perfectly! I'll need to remember that if you ask me to set you up some kind of Internet profile one day!"

Forehead crinkled, Lucy looked at Summer, delivering, "Well, that was a very complimentary description, Sum. Thanks ... but, if all that's true, then why don't I have men lined up around the corner—like you?"

Summer smiled, baffled. Lucy really was what Summer had just described, and the fact that she didn't actually know it made her seem that much cuter. "Lucy, you are all those things, and more! Honestly, I remember being at a party one time, and there was this group of guys talking about you. I, of course, stopped to listen in to what they were saying for two reasons, one—you're my best friend, and two—because one of the guys I thought was hot and, well, you know ..." Summer winked at Lucy, then continued, "They were saying how amazing they thought you were, how hot you were, how they wanted to ... well, I'll skip over that part. But when it came down to them actually approaching you, they couldn't, Luce, because they thought you'd shoot them down! They were totally intimidated by *you*!"

"Intimidated by me? That has *got* to be a joke!" Lucy asserted, rolling her eyes.

"Lucy, have some confidence in yourself! They were intimidated by you. You have this way about you that—I don't know any other way to describe it. That's probably why you don't have all the guys lined up around the block! They are terrified of you, in a good way! I'm not like that. I mean, I know I'm cute, but it's different, it's easier to approach a silly, giggly girl than it is to approach someone you can't read, who is mysterious."

Summer looked at Lucy raising her eyebrows and decided to elaborate, "See, it's like this. Me, I'm easy to read, right? I'm crazy and goofy, and people can see that in me right away. But with you, you're harder to read. You're mysterious, alluring. That's intimidating because you never know, you know?"

Deciding to take Summer's word for it, Lucy agreed, "I guess I can see that. I mean about you being easy to read and me not so much. But, like I was going to say, I didn't meet anyone. That's not what's put this dopey look on my face."

"It isn't? Then what? Don't tell me you and Drew ..." Summer looked horrified.

"No! No more Drew, *ever!*" Lucy screeched, waving her hands in the air. "It's Opal. I talked to her today, and it was really amazing, to put it mildly. I'm actually looking forward to this visit. I think I'm going to enjoy this time with her. Wow, I'm a little surprised I just said that."

"Luce! That's great! I thought old Opal had something up her sleeve, that old battleax!" Summer laughed, then her smiled dropped from her face and her eyes became like saucers again, "Uh-oh, so if you've talked with Opal, then that must mean you've also talked with your mom."

Summer knew her too well.

"You are never going to believe this, but my mom and I actually had a heart to heart. Our first since I was a little girl, I think."

Lucy didn't think Summer's eyes could have gotten any bigger, but they did when she heard what Lucy just said. "What? Are you kidding me? How the ... ? What ... ? I'm confused here."

"Oh yeah, I felt the same way when we were talking. I was worried I had somehow ended up in another dimension or some kind of alternate universe," Lucy affirmed, giving Summer a you-get-my-drift look. "But it really, truly happened. She said she's working on letting me make my own decisions and being more open, being a better mom than she has been ... it was all very unreal."

"Wow, okay ... I don't know what Opal has up her sleeve, but can she send some of that my way? Man, I want a dose of whatever is going around!" Summer exclaimed.

"Come on, Sum, you know you've never needed any extra luck. But sure, if I figure out what the deal is, I'll let you in on it," promised Lucy with a smile. She felt extremely lucky right now—good friends, family that was starting to maybe work itself out, and embarrassing emails from the ex ... "Oh, I almost forgot, I got an email from Drew, and you won't believe what he wrote!"

Lucy pulled Summer over to the computer to show her Drew's email, making Summer laugh like she hadn't in a long time. Throwing an arm around Lucy, Summer proposed, "Oh, Luce, let's go get some takeout and find something girly to watch on Netflix. We need to spend all the time we can together before you head out." Summer shook her head and laughed some more, adding, "Wow, that email just made my day. You ready to do this, baby?"

Taking her cue from Summer, Lucy responded, "O-o-o-o-o-h-h-h ye-e-e-a-a-a-h-h, let's do this, *baby!*"

Laughing together, as always, they headed for the door, ready to take the world by storm, or by chick flicks and takeout anyways. They spent the rest of the night watching horribly clichéd, but good nonetheless, girly movies, eating Chinese, and sharing a tub of Ben and Jerry's for dessert.

Knowing it was one of the last nights they'd spend together as roommates made the night bittersweet, but both girls went to bed with a feeling of happiness in their hearts, thankful that they had someone who understood them inside and out and who would love them no matter what.

CHAPTER THREE

The next week passed more quickly than Lucy could have imagined. Even though she hadn't found a job yet and at this point wasn't even looking—that could wait until she was settled in with Opal—she was busier than she thought she would be.

She and Summer spent almost every night together, watching bad TV, going to dinner, going out to celebrate Lucy's next phase in life, as Summer liked to call it. During the day, when Summer was at work, Lucy would hang out with her mom. It was a little awkward at first because they hadn't spent much time together since Lucy's wedding to Drew, but they soon fell back into how things were before they had grown apart.

Lucy's mom was a writer. Well, *she* liked to call herself a writer, but Lucy wasn't quite sure she would agree. Stella wrote an advice column for the local paper. Lucy was always embarrassed when people would ask about her mom and what she wrote because then Lucy would have to actually admit that her mother, well, she wrote about sex.

Lucy always blushed when she reluctantly gave out that information to people who were able to pry it out of her. Summer thought it was awesome. She often told Lucy if she had any questions or concerns she could just go ask her own mother, but Lucy didn't think it was that great. Her mom had been writing the advice column for what seemed like forever. She wrote and answered questions about anything from how-tos, to what happens when, to help! my blank, blank!

Lucy was mortified with the whole thing. She always had been and probably always would be. She purposely skipped over that section in the paper. Well, that was when she actually happened to be reading the paper. The worst part was when her friends would ask her mom advice in front of Lucy or when Summer would start talking to Lucy's mom about something that had happened to her during one of her escapades. Stella would usually get this look on her face, and Lucy knew that meant she had just found some new material to use in next week's paper.

Being the writer of an advice column, Stella could work from home. So Lucy spent most of her remaining daytime hours hanging out in her childhood home, sitting on a bar stool in the kitchen with her mother while she typed away, both of them sipping coffee in companionable silence. Even though they didn't always say much, with Stella writing and Lucy reading or checking email—she'd gotten a few more emails from Drew, nothing as good as the first one though—it was like they were silently getting to know each other again, or at least starting to understand each other.

Then, one day it just hit Lucy. She looked over at her mother, who was chewing on her lip as she debated what she should write next, and Lucy realized that she was going to miss these relaxing moments with her mom. Lucy cleared her throat and took a sip of her coffee. She wasn't used to this, feeling emotional about her mother.

Stella looked up at Lucy with a smile to inquire, "What's going on in that mind of yours, sweetie?"

Trying to hold it together, Lucy replied, "I'm just really going to miss you, Mom." Before she could get another word out, Lucy broke down, tears streaming down her face.

Stella came over to Lucy, giving her a hug. "Oh, Lucy, I'm going to miss you, too. Are you sure you still want to go? You don't have to, you know. There is still time to change your mind."

"No, I still want to go. It's not that. It's just, I don't know. Things have been so weird lately, weird but in a good way. You know, with you and me. I don't understand why I am getting so emotional lately. I've been so happy for the past few days, but then there are times where I just feel so overwhelmed," Lucy tried to explain, drying her eyes.

"I know exactly how you feel, Lucy. This," Stella pointed to herself and then to Lucy, "is still new to me, too. I wish things could have stayed this way between us during those years when you were struggling to grow up and I was afraid to let you go. We were so close when you were younger, and then things changed, but I'm so grateful for this time, right now. It feels like we might be coming back together. I've been happier than ever these past days, too, and it hurts to think you'll be leaving soon. It's like I'm losing you right when I found you," she shared, leaning her elbow on the table, her chin in her hand.

Sniffing loudly, Lucy declared, "Oh, Mom, you're not losing me. You'll never lose me."

"I know," Stella agreed, smiling her knowing smiling. "And you'll never lose me. It just feels like it right now. Change does that. It makes you feel amazing and excited and inspired, but it also scares the daylights out of you. But—sometimes we need to be scared, I think."

Lucy studied her mom, smiling.

Stella narrowed her eyes and then asked, "What? Do I even *want* to know what you're thinking?"

"You know, I'd never thought I'd ever say this but, you've actually had some pretty good advice lately. Weird ... maybe I should start reading your column, get some pointers for my new life!" Lucy revealed thoughtfully, waiting to see how her mom would respond.

Stella was speechless. For a second. Then a small smiled appeared, and she stated, "You know, that's actually a great idea, Lucy. I can set you up with a subscription to the paper when you're in the city with Opal, and I'm pretty sure you can log in online to see all the back issues as well. Plus, you can always call your dear old mom if you can't find the answer you're looking for there."

Choking on her coffee, Lucy replied, "Just forget I asked."

* * * * *

Lucy woke with a start. She had a weird feeling that someone was staring at her, but she had no idea who it could be or why she would feel that way. She flipped over onto her back to try to get back to sleep. And then she screamed.

"Hi, babe!" Summer was standing over her bed with a wicked grin on her face.

"Summer! Sheesh, I was trying to sleep here, what the heck are you doing?"

"It's today, baby!"

"What's today?" Lucy asked, eyeing Summer, "Are you drunk?"

"Of course I'm not drunk! Not yet anyways. Get up, baby," Summer ordered, as she yanked back Lucy's covers.

"Would you just please tell me what's going on here?" Lucy demanded, holding onto her covers for dear life.

"It's your last day today, you leave this afternoon, remember?"

"Uh-huh, okay. So ... why are you waking me up? By staring at me? And acting like a crazy person?" Lucy questioned with her head cocked, giving Summer a half glare, half smirk.

"Crazy? Me? That's not possible," Summer maintained, giving Lucy her crazy look, the one she had perfected in the mirror so long ago. Lucy always cracked up when she saw that look, only because the reason Summer had perfected it was for when she felt bad breaking up with a guy and wanted him to break up with her first. "If he thinks I'm just freaking psycho, then I won't have to do the dumping, girl!" Summer had explained.

Lucy covered her eyes and lay back down, pretending to be asleep.

"Okay, I get it. You want to know what's going on. Fine, I'll tell you. We're going hunting," Summer disclosed, hands on hips, head held high.

Lucy sat straight up, blowing some stray hairs out of her eyes, "What?"

"You heard what I said. Hunting. Man hunting, that is!" Summer clapped her hands together and sang, "Get u-u-u-u-p-p-p!"

Throwing a pillow at Summer, Lucy growled, "You woke me up at six in the morning for that? So I could go hunt men with you? You don't need any help with that. Good night." Lucy fell back against her haphazard pillows.

"Hello! It's not for me, silly. It's for you," Summer declared, pursing her lips and leaning in towards Lucy.

Lucy sat straight up again, asking "What?"

Pointing at the bathroom, Summer commanded, "Get in the shower. We'll talk when you're actually presentable."

She then strutted out of the bedroom, and Lucy knew she had no choice in the matter. They were going hunting, man hunting, that was. As she walked slowly into the bathroom she wondered just exactly what that would entail. She probably didn't want to know.

* * * * *

"I'm going to do *what*?" Lucy responded with a cringe. She hoped she hadn't heard Summer correctly.

"Oh, you heard me! You are going to walk up to that guy, say hell0, and give him your number," Summer repeated, pointing to a very attractive guy, standing in line to get a coffee.

They were sitting at a table outside one of their favorite coffee shops. It was a beautiful day, and besides Summer's mission for her, Lucy was enjoying the sunshine.

"So why do I need to do this again?"

Summer heaved a breath in and then out, and reiterated, "You need to acquire a quick batch of confidence, my dear, and this is just the way to do it."

"By being rejected?" Lucy asked.

"You'll see. You definitely won't be rejected," asserted Summer, wiggling her eyebrows.

"I'm still confused as to why, on our last day together, we can't just do something more low key," Lucy muttered, slouching down in her slightly uncomfortable, wobbly chair.

"Here's the deal, Luce. The other day when we were talking, I realized that you really don't see yourself the way you are—"

Lucy cut in, questioning skeptically, "And that is?"

"Beautiful! This is my gift to you, Lucy. Before you leave, I want you to feel sure of yourself. So no matter what or who you have to take on, you know you can do it!" Summer explained, smiling her megawatt smile.

"So you think that by me talking to that super hot model-esque guy, that I'll feel better about myself?" Lucy knew it was a waste of time, but she decided to play along with Summer. It *was* her last day with her bestie, after all.

"Just you wait, you'll see what I mean after we're done here," Summer maintained. Then she pointed at the guy, commanding, "Now go! You're gonna shine, baby!"

Lucy pushed herself up, took a deep breath, and channeled Summer. She walked over to the hottest guy she had ever spoken to and said, "Hi, I'm Lucy."

"Hello," he replied, giving her a quick once over, "I'm Drew."

DREW??!! Lucy almost ran away, but she kept her cool and, handing him her number that Summer had scrawled on a slip of paper, told him, "You should give me a call sometime." Before she had time to see his reaction, she turned and did her best Summer strut away.

When she got back to the table, Summer had a gigantic grin on her face, "So? That wasn't so bad was it? I bet you twenty bucks he texts you later today!"

"Well, it ain't gonna happen, no matter how hot he is," Lucy responded, stone-faced, flopping down onto her chair.

"Wha— ... huh?" Summer was confused.

"His name is Drew," Lucy disclosed, shaking her head and taking a giant sip of her mocha.

Summer busted out laughing, "Wow, out of all the guys in all the coffee shops in the entire town, we pick the one with the wrong name! But seriously, you should have seen his face when you were walking away! He looked like he had just won the lottery!" Summer held her hand up for a high five.

Lucy lightly slapped Summer's palm. "Ha-ha, I'm sure. Okay, are we done here? If not, can we go someplace else? Please!" Lucy begged. She just wanted to get the heck away from anyone with her ex's name.

Summer rolled her eyes and stood up, pulling Lucy toward a local park. "Alright, girly, a few more times, and then we'll call it good. Then we can go home and get you ready to jet."

Over the next two hours Summer forced Lucy to approach about ten more guys, all extremely good-looking, of course. Lucy thought it was overkill, but she wanted to appease Summer. She knew Summer was trying to help her out, even if it was in a cheesy way.

Surprisingly, by the end of their "man hunting," Lucy actually felt pretty good about herself. She had become a little more confident with each person she approached, and by the last guy, she was neither nervous, nor did she need to channel Summer. She was just being herself.

Walking home, Summer turned to Lucy and asked "So, how do you feel?"

"Astonishingly, pretty good." Lucy looked over and smiled at her best friend. She was going to miss Summer most of all.

"See, I knew it would work! The reason I had you do it wasn't because I think talking to hot guys is that important, but because I know that hot guys are basically the hardest people for you to talk to, to actually approach. I figured if you could get comfortable doing that, well, then there's nothing you can't do!"

Tearing up yet again, Lucy stopped and hugged Summer, saying, "Thank you, Summer. I'm going to miss you so much."

Lucy knew Summer had done her a huge favor. She had, in her own way, given Lucy a great gift. Lucy had always had trouble with confidence, and seeing that, Summer had pushed her to believe in herself.

"Luce! I'm going to miss you, too! Now let's get back home, so you can open your going-away gift before you have to leave."

They walked back to their apartment, laughing and enjoying their last few moments together before Lucy set off.

* * * * *

Stuffing into her bag the going-away gift Summer had given her, a framed photograph of the two of them together, Lucy looked around the room again, making sure she hadn't forgotten anything. She couldn't believe the time was finally here. Opal had sent a car to drive her the two hours it took to reach the city, and it would be arriving any second.

She had said her final good-byes to her mom the previous night, and she would be calling her when she arrived at Opal's, as promised. Even though she was only going to be a little over two hours away, it still felt as if she were leaving everything she knew. It wasn't so long of a drive that she couldn't come and visit them if she felt like it for a long weekend, but she obviously wasn't going to be seeing as much of them as she had been, and that was hard for her. Especially since the only person she knew in the city was Opal, and she barely even knew *her.*

Summer rushed into the room as Lucy was giving it the final once-over, "The car's here, Luce! I can't believe you have a *car* driving you to the freakin' city! Let's go, baby, it's your time!" She grabbed Lucy's arm and pulled her out of the bedroom, bouncing and dancing the entire time.

"Gee, you sure are excited to see me leave, Sum," Lucy remarked, acting glum. She knew Summer was excited for her, plus having a plush car pick her up was pretty cool.

"Oh, Lucy, you know I'm going to miss you like crazy! I just can't wait to hear all of your stories; I know you're going to have a bunch! Going to live with an old, mysterious grandma, in a huge two-story apartment in the city, with your dream bedroom just waiting for you! Come on, girl, who *wouldn't* be excited?" Summer exclaimed, pulling Lucy into a tight hug when the big black SUV pulled up.

"I know, Summer. Thanks for everything, honestly—putting me up, putting up with me, forgoing steamy make-out sessions while I was living with you, making me talk to Greek gods to make myself feel better! I'm going to miss you." Lucy hugged Summer back tightly.

"You're welcome, Lucy. It was my pleasure, and if you need a place when you're done with this adventure, my door is always open, you know that. Now, go have the time of your life! Don't hold back! Be crazy and adventurous! Just let go. This is an amazing time for you, girl. It's your time to shine! So shine bright, baby!"

"I'll try, Sum," Lucy told her, making a silly face before she handed off her bags and climbed into the waiting SUV.

"I'm serious, Luce. Like a diamond, baby! Love you!" Summer shouted and waved.

"Love you!" Lucy called as the door closed—and then she was off. Taking a deep breath, she watched Summer disappear as the SUV drove off down the road. She couldn't believe she was actually moving in with Opal. Well, she could believe it, but in the scheme of things it had all happened so fast. She hoped Summer was right, that it was an amazing time in her life. She supposed it could be, if that was what she wanted to make of it. The thought made her smile.

She could be whoever she wanted to be in this new adventure. No one knew her, well, except for Opal, but even she didn't *really* know her. If Lucy wanted to do something with her life, to make a change and really do something that would make her happy, satisfied, now was the time. She just had to figure out what that was, and a two-hour car ride was the perfect opportunity to do just that.

Besides the driver asking her if she needed anything or to let him know if she needed or wanted to stop at any time, her ride was filled with silence. Thankfully, it was the relaxing kind of silence, not the awkward I'm-not-sure-what-to-say kind. The driver must, well, drive often because he obviously didn't mind not keeping up a conversation, and that was just fine with Lucy. It was nice to just sit back and enjoy the ride, watching farms and smaller towns flash by.

The smaller towns eventually turned into bigger ones, and before she knew it, they were in the city. Lucy had a vague memory of being in the city before, but the memory was mostly of things that had scared her when she was a young girl—homeless people picking through the garbage, buildings with broken out windows, and kids playing in small grass yards with chain link fences surrounding them. It was fun to see the city now that she was older and able to enjoy it—all the shops and restaurants she could walk to, museums to visit, a huge baseball stadium. She loved baseball.

She felt like she had barely seen all that she wanted to see when the driver pulled up to an enormous building and announced, "We're here, Lucy. I'll get your bags, and you can follow me up."

Lucy took a deep breath; now that she was actually here she was nervous. She watched the driver open the tailgate and grab her bags. Then he opened her door and extended his hand to her.

Swallowing, she grabbed his hand and stepped out into the city, into Opal's world. The driver could obviously see that she was a little worried because he smiled encouragingly at her, offering, "You're going to do just fine, Lucy. Don't worry about a thing. If there is anything you need, you just come to me."

Feeling a little better, almost like she had someone on her side, she smiled and replied, "Thank you, sir."

He laughed quietly, then caught himself, explaining, "That's not necessary. You can call me Bowden."

Lucy looked up at the older gentleman, smiling. She liked him already and hoped he was one of the people who worked for Opal on a regular basis. "Okay then," she said, "Thank you, Bowden. I'm feeling a lot better already."

"Great, let's go. Opal has been anxious for you to arrive ever since you agreed to come and stay. To be honest, we all have been awaiting your arrival. It will be refreshing to have someone new around the place," he confided with a smile in his voice.

As they walked into the building, a doorman opened the door for them and another person behind a desk just inside the doors greeted Bowden with a nod. Bowden guided Lucy to the elevators, and when inside, he pushed the P button, which Lucy knew stood for "penthouse."

Just thinking that she was actually going to be living in the penthouse of one of the biggest and most expensive apartment buildings in the city made Lucy's heart beat a little faster. She hoped she didn't mess anything up because she had never lived anywhere *this* nice before. What if she … ? trailing off she shook her head. This wasn't the time for freaking herself out, this was her time to be whoever she wanted to be, and she was going to be fine.

Echoing her thoughts, Bowden smiled at her as the elevator chimed, signaling that they were at penthouse level, offering again, "You're going to be fine, Lucy. Just fine. I promise."

As the doors opened, Bowden made an after-you gesture with his hand.

Looking up, Lucy then saw Opal, waiting in the entry hall for her, all smiles.

"Lucy, dear! Get over here and give your grandma a hug!" Opal called out.

At hearing Opal's welcoming greeting and seeing her reassuring smile, all of Lucy's nervousness fell away. And much to her surprise, she ran to hug her old grandma. Breathing in the scent of Chanel No. 5 and soap, Lucy smiled and stepped away from Opal, saying, "Thank you so much for asking me here, Opal."

Opal waved her hand in the air and replied, "Oh, don't be silly, dear. It's you whom I should be thanking. Saving me from the boredom that is my life nowadays."

Smirking at Opal, Lucy insisted, "I highly doubt that. I have a feeling, Opal, that your life is far from boring." Looking over at Bowden, she caught him trying to hide a smile and laugh.

Opal, catching the exchange, sent Bowden a look that had him straightening himself up, though Lucy had a feeling it was more for show than anything else. "I'll take your bags to your room, Lucy," he stated as he grabbed Lucy's bags and turned down the hall.

"Ah, yes, your room," Opal remarked, smiling at Lucy, "I hope you'll approve. I had some very good suggestions from a few reliable sources, besides yourself, of course, and I'm excited to see what you think of the place. Now, being the hostess that I am, it would be rude not to ask you if you would like to have something to eat before you get a tour of the place, so?"

Lucy laughed at Opal's raised eyebrow, proposing, "Actually, Opal, I hope I'm not rude in saying this, but I'd really love to see my room first."

"Good answer! I knew you were a lot like me. Fun first and nourishment later. Ha! Let's go!" Opal bellowed, and off she went, surprising Lucy with all of her energy.

When Lucy walked into her new bedroom, she couldn't believe her eyes. She actually had to close and rub her eyes a few times to make sure that what she was seeing was real. Even her wildest dreams of what the most beautiful, relaxing, perfect bedroom would have looked like didn't come close to what Lucy was looking at right now.

Whatever Opal had done in the past, Lucy was sure she had

outdone herself when she had done this room. It was painted a soft grey, except for the wall that the bed was against. That wall was painted a darker, but still warm grey. Her bed was more than she could have ever even imagined. It was a huge four-poster canopy bed, with romantic, gauzy material, flowing down each side. It was piled high with far too many white pillows to count and was covered with the fluffiest, most comfortable-looking white bedspread she had ever seen.

There were nightstands with mirrors above them on each side of the bed, their style adding to the romance of the room. At the foot of the bed was a lounge chair covered in pillows that matched the bed perfectly. There was a huge flat screen TV mounted across the wall from her bed, which supposedly could somehow retract back into the wall when she didn't want to watch it.

On the far side of the room—"far" being the optimum word here—was a couch and two chairs, again piled high with pillows, and a built-in bookcase that took up the entire wall, filled with books. Lucy couldn't believe this was her *room*, and she didn't think she could get any luckier or happier; that is, until Opal pointed toward a door Lucy hadn't noticed yet.

Wondering what was on the other side, Lucy walked through and stopped dead in her tracks, "Oh, wow!" was all she could say as she looked around at what Opal was telling her was a bathroom.

Painted in an even lighter grey than her bedroom, it was massive! It had his-and-her sinks, which made Lucy laugh, wondering if she'd ever have a "his" in this place of hers to use it. There was a gigantic whirlpool tub that could easily fit more than a few people comfortably in it. A bigger shower than she had ever seen before, walled in glass, with showerheads jutting out from every direction, a steam shower, and a separate room for the actual toilet.

There were so many flat screen TVs in the bathroom—above the tub, in the toilet room, even in both of the showers—Lucy wondered if she'd ever need to watch that much TV.

Shaking her head, Lucy turned to Opal, "This is amazing, beautiful! It's more than the perfect bedroom. I can't even believe I get to live here! You're going to have a problem getting me out of here, I can tell you that much right now."

"I'm glad you like it, but you haven't seen it all just yet," shared Opal, grinning and motioning Lucy to follow.

Floored, Lucy turned to gape at Opal, inquiring, "What more could I need?"

Pulling Lucy over to another door beside the bathroom, Opal responded, "I'll give you a hint. What is one thing a girl absolutely needs when moving to a new place to start over?"

Shrugging her shoulders, Lucy just smiled, saying, "I have no idea just now, Opal, I'm still in shock from all the other amazingness I've seen."

Grinning like the Cheshire cat, Opal opened the last door and pushed Lucy inside. Again, Lucy was stunned. She stood inside a massive walk-in closet, which was filled to the brim with clothes and shoes and bags and anything she could think of that she might ever dream of having.

Taking a big breath, Lucy started wandering around, taking in Opal's generosity. She honestly couldn't believe Opal had done this for her. The closet was L-shaped, and when she was at one end of it, it seemed she could barely see the other. Walking back around to the end where she'd entered, she was just about to thank Opal profusely when she noticed another thing she had missed.

It was a smaller section of the closet that had what looked like a vanity you'd see in the movies, filled again with makeup and essentials that Lucy had only dreamed of using before because of the hefty price tag they were attached to.

Her whole room, bathroom, and closet, for that matter, were brightly lit with a natural light that made the place seem cheerful and romantic at the same time.

Turning to Opal, Lucy expressed, "Opal, I ... don't know what to say. Thank you so much. 'Thank you' seems like not enough to say right now. This is amazing, so much more than I would have ever expected, I just can't believe it."

Opal grabbed Lucy's hands and looked her straight in the eyes, asserting, "Lucy, you are more than welcome. I want you to know that I wanted to do this for you, I want you to feel comfortable here, even spoiled." Laughing softly, Opal sighed and then admitted, "I've felt guilty for a long time for how I treated your mother and you all these years. But I also want you to know that this isn't my way of saying sorry or trying to make up for those times. I am sorry, but buying you things isn't the way I want to show you that. Honestly, I like doing this kind of thing, and I can afford it, so why not? To see you so excited about something like this makes me happy, and happy is what I need right now."

Normally Lucy would have been a little more reluctant to share her feelings with someone she had just met. But there was something about Opal, and this place, that put her at ease. "Thank you so much, Opal, for doing this," Lucy repeated, pointing around her room, "but also for realizing that things weren't right between us all before and wanting to make them better. It means a lot to me, and to my mom."

"I know it's taken me a long time, but better late than never, I always say!" Looking at Lucy with a grin in her eye, Opal held out her hand and suggested, "Now, how about some food?"

"That sounds great, but there's just one thing I have to do first," Lucy explained, as she walked out of her closet and took a running leap towards her bed and jumped, surprising herself. She usually reserved jumping on big fluffy beds for when no one was watching. "Yep," she said after a few bounces, "I've always liked doing that, and it is just as amazing as I thought it would be!"

Laughing, Opal crooked her finger at Lucy and remarked, "Oh, I have a feeling that fun times are a comin'! You have no idea what I have planned for us. Now, let's eat."

Looking out of the corner of her eye at Opal, Lucy questioned, "Why do I have a feeling that I'm not going to like all of these plans? Should I be scared?"

Opal, shaking her fingers at Lucy, just told her, "Well, you're just going to have to wait and find out, now aren't you?"

Smiling, Lucy followed Opal out of her bedroom and down the hall towards the kitchen, thinking all the way how in a kind of cool way, Opal reminded her a little bit of Summer.

CHAPTER FOUR

Shutting the door to her very own amazing, new room, Lucy smiled. She'd had one of the best days of her life. Not just because she had just been given the best room *ever*, but because the little time she had spent with Opal, dinner and then catching up a little more afterwards, had been more fun than she could have imagined.

Lucy was on cloud nine, but she knew that could change at a moment's notice. Opal wasn't in perfect health, obviously, and Lucy knew she needed to make use of her time here, be thankful for every bit she had with Opal.

Plopping down on her superbly comfy bed, Lucy sighed. She was beyond exhausted, and she still had a lot to do before she could go to sleep. Well, it felt like a lot, anyway. She needed to call her mom and Summer, to let them know how things had gone, and she hadn't unpacked her stuff yet either. If she waited until tomorrow it would be all wrinkled.

Making a face, she got up and grabbed her bag to unpack before she made her phone calls. Pulling out a few items, she glanced at her closet and got an idea. Walking to the closet and opening the door made her smile again. She could stand there all day and look at all that Opal had given her.

Lucy was betting that somewhere in there were some perfectly unwrinkled, fresh pajamas. She wandered around until she spotted a long dresser tucked up against a sidewall. "Bingo!" she thought, opening the drawers. The first few contained all lacy underwear and bras. Lucy wasn't quite sure how she felt about Opal buying her *that* kind of stuff. She pulled open the two bottom drawers and saw rows of comfy, cute, and sexy-looking pajamas. Going for comfy tonight, Lucy pulled out a neon pink pair of pants and a matching grey tank that had neon pink stripes, and smiled to herself.

She really could stay in this closet forever, but she was exhausted and had phone calls to make still, so she tiredly walked into the bathroom. The problem with the bathroom was that she could stay in there forever too, sheesh! Was she ever going to get back to her bed? Thinking about her bed, she smiled and pulled her PJs on. The trouble with her bed was that she most definitely wouldn't ever want to be leaving that thing, so rushing out of the beautiful bathroom wasn't that difficult.

Falling into the comfort of the pillows and soft sheets, Lucy almost groaned with pleasure. This place *was the best*! Yeah, she was totally spoiled right now, and she really, really liked it.

Grabbing her phone, she dialed her mom. Lucy knew Summer would make her explain in detail everything about her room, so this conversation with her mom would be relatively painless compared to that. She really didn't mind explaining in detail to Summer, it just was that she was totally spent. She opened her eyes as she heard her mom's voice on the other end of the phone.

"Luce! Hi baby!"

Yawning, Lucy replied, "Hi Mom."

"You good, Lucy? You sound tired." Lucy wasn't sure, but she thought she might have heard a concerned tone in her mom's voice.

"Oh, Mom, I'm more than good, I'm great! But I am completely exhausted right now. Let me say, though, Opal really outdid herself. My room is amazing! I'm going to have to take pictures tomorrow and send them to you, so you can see this place!"

"Oh, Lucy, I'm so glad! I was wondering how that project was going to turn out. I thought it would be nice, lucky girl. So, Opal is … good?"

"She's been nothing but welcoming to me, Mom. Things are going well so far. We've actually had a lot to talk about, too. Surprisingly, it's been easy, not awkward."

Hearing Lucy's smile through the phone made Stella's day. "Good. Now get some sleep. When you're rested up, I want some pictures, and call again in a few days or whenever you want. I want to hear all about it!" Stella told her.

"I will, Mom, talk soon," Lucy promised, sleepily.

"Love you, sweetie, bye."

"You too, Mom. Bye." Lucy hung up.

Then she smiled, texting Summer. Summer was going to be pissed, but Lucy knew she wouldn't be able to do this place justice if she tried explaining it to Summer tonight. She'd just have to wait until tomorrow. Plus, what if she did call Summer and fell asleep while on the phone with her? Summer would never let her hear the end of it.

Leaning back and closing her eyes, Lucy fell asleep before she could read Summer's spicy reply.

* * * * *

Opening her eyes, Lucy smiled, again. Nope, there was no confusing herself on where she was today. She had remembered even before she opened them.

Taking a minute to relax and admire the view, she looked around, taking it in again. She also noticed a few things she hadn't the night before—all of her windows were floor-to-ceiling, and there was a sliding glass door that let out to a pretty good-sized balcony.

Lucy had forgotten to shut her gauzy curtains and the heavier ones that covered them in her sleepiness last night, so the sun shone through, making everything look even more exquisite. Sunshine always did that to Lucy, though. It always made things just a little bit brighter. Even when she was having a hard day, it brightened things a bit when she saw the sun.

Curious, Lucy stepped out of bed, opened the sliding glass door, and stepped outside into the sunshine and noise. The city was busy—people walking here and there, some in a hurry, others taking their time, taxis and buses and bikes zooming this way and that.

She spotted a coffee shop just down the street and was itching to go grab a latte and a muffin, just because she could. Well, and because she'd do about anything to be sitting on this balcony with a cup of coffee right about now. Deciding that was just what she needed, she spun around, leaving the door open a bit, and walked back inside the apartment and down the hall.

She found Opal in the kitchen, relaxing with the newspaper and a steaming mug of something in front of her. Looking up as Lucy approached, she said, "Oh, hello Lucy. Sleep well?"

"Oh yeah," Lucy replied with a big smile, "Did you even have to ask? That bed is a dream, I didn't want to move from it, that is until I noticed I had a balcony and, well, of course, that had to be explored. I saw a coffee shop just down the street, and I think I'm going to run and get something. Do you want anything?" Lucy asked, bouncing up and down a little, in excitement for the small adventure.

Grinning at Lucy, Opal inquired, "Excited for coffee?" Eyes lighting up as she noticed Lucy's giddiness, Opal went on to share, "Bowden actually made me my tea already this morning, but I'd love to go with you tomorrow morning. You go. Then we can talk about the day's plan when you get back."

Itching to make her coffee trek, Lucy responded, "Sounds good. So how do I get back up here? I'm a little worried they might not let me back in."

"Ha! That'd be something! They know you now, Lucy. They were informed of your arrival yesterday, but if they give you any trouble, just have them call me or Bowden. We'll set them straight." Smiling, Opal went back to her paper as Lucy rushed out the door.

It was clear that Opal was enjoying her granddaughter already. It was nice to see Lucy excited about all the little things that she herself had come to take for granted. Opal had high hopes she would get to see a lot more of that sparkle in Lucy before her time came. Opal didn't want to think about that now though; she'd focus on the positive, as her doctor had told her, so that was exactly what she was going to do. Cancer be damned.

As Lucy tried not to skip down the street, she wondered if she should have dressed in a special way for her first outing, then decided it didn't matter. She was surprised at her nonchalant attitude; normally she wouldn't set foot outside of her bedroom until she was at least dressed. She was only going about a block though, and she didn't know anyone around here anyway. It was a free pass to be lazy for a while before anyone actually knew who she was, and she was totally going to take it.

Lucy laughed as she looked up before entering the coffee shop and saw what it was called—GRINDER—spelled out in big black letters. Lucy thought impulsively of taking a picture and texting it to Summer but then decided against it since it might call attention to her out on the street in her pajama-ed state.

Opening the door, she also noticed a "Help Wanted" sign taped to it. Wondering if she should try her hand at working at a coffee shop, Lucy sidled up to the counter to order her drink.

"Hey, what can I do for you today?" a skinny, twenty-something guy asked.

"Hmm," Lucy stalled, looking up at the names of all the drinks. They were definitely interestingly titled, almost embarrassingly so. "Wow, okay. What's the Whipped B-witch like?"

Smirking at Lucy, the guy explained, "Basically a caramel latte with extra foam and an extra espresso shot to go with that."

Not wanting to ask about any other of the drinks because, well, she didn't want to name them, she quickly decided, "Sure, sounds good."

The guy just stared at her. Lucy, in response, was getting more uncomfortable by the second, especially because she was still in her pajamas. Then he finally spoke again, slowly, "What size?"

"Oh, sorry. Large, please." Looking around while the guy made the drink, Lucy thought the place was pretty cool. Well, besides the freaky drink names. It seemed pretty laid back, and Lucy was thinking it might be kind of fun to work there, that is, if they would hire a normal girl like her.

"WHIPPED B!" the guy shouted a little too loudly. He slid her drink toward her on the counter, startling Lucy.

Quickly grabbing the cup that was careening toward her, before it hit the ground, Lucy smiled and muttered a thank you as she bobbled the drink, almost spilling it. She looked up to see the guy chuckling at her.

Thinking she should probably just leave while she was ahead, Lucy got a good grip on her cup and turned to leave. She took a few steps toward the door, but changed her mind at the last second and turned back around. Normally Lucy was more reluctant to push herself out of her comfort zone, but she suddenly felt that she had nothing to lose.

Back up at the counter, the guy was cleaning the espresso machine while checking his phone. He looked up at Lucy when she approached, "Ye-s-s-s-s-s?" he inquired, looking somewhat annoyed.

"Hi. I, um, was wondering about the job—have you hired anyone yet?" Lucy asked, trying to sound sure of herself. For some dumb reason the guy made her nervous.

Looking at her for a few seconds, he replied, "Well, the sign is still up, so obviously we haven't hired anyone yet. You need a gig?"

"Yeah, I actually just moved here, so, yeah, I'm looking for something. I live right up the street, so … I can see this place from my balcony and …" Lucy had no idea what her deal was, this guy wasn't her type at all, but his total monotone personality was freaking her out. Which was making her talk. A lot.

"Have you worked at a coffee shop before? What's your experience?" he inquired.

Lucy shook her head, "No, none really," she smiled weakly at him.

He blinked at her, then asked, "Do you have any references I can contact?"

Lucy could feel the blush creeping up her face. This was turning out to be a lot worse than expected. She was usually so much more prepared. "No," she admitted glumly, but quickly changed her mind, "No, wait! I mean yes! I do have a reference! My best friend owns a boutique and I sometimes I would— "

He cut her off before she could finish, "Usually I wouldn't hire someone without experience, or valid references, but I'm desperate to get somebody on the afternoon shift. A few of my employees left a couple weeks ago to go on some backpacking adventure, and things have been a little hectic since."

Lucy almost choked on her coffee. Backpacking adventure? He couldn't be serious. She would have laughed if she hadn't almost choked.

"You okay?" he asked, looking at her like she had three heads, smirking.

"Yes," she replied, clearing her throat and putting what she hoped to be a normal expression on her face, "Afternoons work great for me!"

"Great," he replied, eyeing her strangely, then added, "Oh, and we're normally pretty laid back here, but—no pajamas at work. Think you can handle that?" he informed her, keeping up his smirk the whole time.

What was with this guy and his smirking? She didn't like the smirks and didn't like his attitude problem. But she needed a job, so, throwing her usual caution to the wind, Lucy agreed, "Yes. See you tomorrow."

Trying not to run out the door, she heard him say, "Uh-huh."

As the door closed behind her, she was pretty sure that if she looked back into the coffee shop, he would still be standing there, smirk on face and phone in hand.

Tightly holding her coffee and keeping her eyes down, she wasn't looking where she was going, just watching the pavement, trying to convince herself that she hadn't made as big a fool of herself as she thought she might have. When, all of a sudden, she bumped into somebody, hard. "Oh! I'm so sorry," she called out, glancing up to see whom she had just about spilled her coffee on. She was pretty sure her chin just about hit the ground.

The most gorgeous-looking guy stared down at her, dark brown hair falling into his dark brown eyes. He looked her up and down and asked, "You okay? Gotta watch where you're going around here. Don't want to run into the wrong guy, you know?"

"Yeah, I'm so sorry … that guy back there, in that coffee shop, just totally freaked me out, and then for some idiotic reason I asked him if I could have a job, and he said yes." Lucy looked up at him through her eyelashes, shaking her head to get the hair out of her eyes and added with some embarrassment, "I wouldn't go in there if I were you." She definitely had a problem with talking a little too much when she was nervous.

"Huh, I'll keep that in mind," he told her, as he reached up and tucked her misbehaving hair behind her ear. "See you around then?" he asked with a smile.

His grin momentarily made her speechless, and then Lucy blinked at him a few times and answered, "I guess?" It came out more like a question, which seemed to amuse him.

"Well, you did just tell me you applied for the job, and the scary guy in there said yes, so … I'll see you around, in there?" He pointed to GRINDER, lifting an eyebrow.

Feeling like the biggest idiot, Lucy then quickly agreed, "Oh, right! Yes, you sure will!"

Winking at her, he opened the door to the coffee shop.

Shaking her head, Lucy hurried back to the apartment, wanting to hide. Of all the days to venture out in her pajamas, she had to pick the one day when she would meet the hottest guy in town. How embarrassing, and he obviously went to the coffee shop often if he said he'd see her around. "This was just perfect," Lucy thought. At least she had a closet full of cute clothes. She'd just make sure whenever she left the apartment from now on she was dressed to the nines.

Thankfully, the guys in the lobby just waved hellos to her as she passed through. If they thought it was odd or unseemly that she was in her pajamas, they didn't act like it when she was within earshot, so at least for that she was grateful.

As she walked into the kitchen where Opal was still sitting, reading her paper and drinking tea, Lucy announced, "Wow, well that was utterly embarrassing!"

Opal looked up, smiling, and asked, "Oh really? Do tell, dear. I so love an embarrassing story now and then."

Giving Opal a look, Lucy told her about Mr. Scary at the coffee shop and all the freaky drink names. That gave Opal a good laugh, and then Lucy added, "Oh, and *then* I wasn't watching where I was going, you know, trying to get the heck out of there, and I bumped hard into *the* hottest guy I have ever seen in my life. Of course, I can't shut up at that point because I'm way too nervous, and I basically tell him my life story."

That gave Opal an even bigger laugh. When she was finally able to catch her breath, she offered, "Life story? Oh Lucy, I wish I could have seen that."

"The worst part is, he is a coffee shop regular, so I'm pretty sure I'll be seeing him most days I work." Even though what had happened had been a little embarrassing ... okay a *lot* embarrassing, she was too excited about her new job to let it bother her too much. Being able to walk back to the barista and ask about the job, and actually get it, was huge! Someone else might say, "It's a job, so what?" but for her, it was more than that. For a moment there, Lucy had felt fearless. Lucy smiled to herself—Summer was going to love this, which reminded Lucy that she still needed to call her. She'd do that when she got back to her room.

Looking at Lucy, Opal explained, "You know, Lucy, you don't *need* to get a job."

Lucy knew she didn't need to work while she stayed with Opal, and if worse came to worse, she might have to quit whatever job she had, but she wanted to test the waters a little bit when she could, see what she was good at, what she liked, and also get experience putting herself out there.

"I know, Opal, but I kind of want to. I want to figure out what my niche is, and I'll never be able to do that if I don't try new things. Plus, if I totally suck, I won't have to worry about walking away and trying something new!"

Opal smiled, thinking that Lucy was a lot more like her then she'd thought. She wasn't a person to sit around and let others do the work for her. She was motivated and open to doing new things, even if she was a little unsure of herself at times.

"I agree, Lucy, you should try to find yourself while you are here, and I would like nothing more than to help you with that. You have all the freedom you need here, and I'm always here for anything."

"Thank you, Opal, I honestly can't believe how lucky I feel right now. Even making the biggest you-know-what of myself, I still feel great! Now, what are the plans for today? I'd love to see or do whatever you planned." Seeing Opal's face, Lucy added, "Well, within reason."

Opal rolled her eyes and announced, "Oh, you're my hostage today. So get ready! I have a doctor's appointment at 4:30, but otherwise I'm free. I'd love to take you around the city to some of my favorite places. I might not have enough energy to walk around at every stop, but we should be able to see enough from the car."

It was the first time Opal had mentioned her doctor, or in any way how she was feeling, to Lucy. Lucy wanted to make sure Opal wasn't overdoing it, but she hadn't been sure how to bring it up to Opal before. Now this seemed like the perfect opening.

So Lucy told Opal, "That sounds perfect! I'd love to sightsee, and please let me know if you get tired. I really don't want to push you, so you overdo yourself. I would feel horrible if that happened."

"Oh come on! That's just what I need, a push! Don't worry about me. I'll let you know if something's bothering me," Opal assured her and then added, "Let's leave in an hour. Will that give you enough time? Unless you wanted to continue with your pajama-ed adventure."

Shooting Opal a look, Lucy explained, "An hour is just fine, thank you."

Then Lucy stood and tried to do her Summer strut down the hallway, her Whipped B in hand, but hearing Opal's laugh made her think she might have overdone it, just a bit.

* * * * *

Sitting down on a huge, comfy chair in the corner of her room, Lucy picked up her phone to call Summer. She had wanted to talk to her right when she had retreated to her room, before she had taken a shower, but she knew talks with Summer could be long, and Lucy needed at least a few minutes to get ready.

Lucy had taken a luxurious shower, even if it had been a tad short, and then she explored her closet. She decided to go with something cute but comfy since they would be sitting in the car and possibly walking a bit. She had chosen a pair of black leggings and a flowing, brown tunic with a black pattern on it. She then spotted a pair of the cutest brown boots that matched her shirt. Thankfully they were flat, barely any heel, so they would be just right for walking in. Completing her look, Lucy put a little something in her hair and let it air dry, so it would have a little curl to it. She threw in a few bobby pins to keep it out of her face, added a longer necklace, and she was done.

Lucy wasn't going to lie—she loved this new closet and all the clothes in it, which all fit perfectly, by the way. It was like shopping for a brand-new outfit every day. She was pretty sure the clothes she had packed would never get touched.

Waiting for Summer to pick up, Lucy marveled that just yesterday she had been nervous—not sure what to expect of Opal—and today she was comfortable and excited to see what would happen next.

"LUCE!" Summer yelled into the phone, "You totally suck by the way! Since when is it okay to text someone who has been waiting *all day* to hear *everything*, that you'd call them *tomorrow sometime?*"

"I know, I know. I was so exhausted, though, if I would have called you last night, you probably would have made me call you back today. I would have been totally worthless in describing to you the amazingness of this place."

"So? I can't wait any longer—spare no detail. I've got time here, lots of time, baby!" Summer urged, waiting impatiently to hear all the details.

"Okay, Sum, I've only got about half an hour, and then Opal is going to show me around the city, so you'll have to be happy with that."

Sighing, Summer responded, "Half an hour is all I get?"

Lucy laughed and started in from the very beginning, knowing that Summer didn't care how much time Lucy had. She'd take whatever she could get, and if she didn't get all she wanted this morning, she'd keep calling Lucy until she was satisfied.

* * * * *

Stretching as she walked down the hall to meet Opal for their day, Lucy rubbed her eyes, neck, and ears. Summer had screeched so loud when Lucy had told her about bumping into Hot Guy that Lucy had to hold the phone as far away from her ear as she could until Summer quit. Then she proceeded to tell Summer that if she ever screamed like that through the phone again, Lucy would put a stop to all the info. At that Summer had profusely apologized. Then she had asked Lucy to describe Hot Guy again, "in just a little more detail."

Lucy had been gone for only a day, but she missed Summer more than ever. She grinned at how much fun the two of them would have here together. She might just have to invite Summer for a little visit.

Opal appeared around the corner, inquiring, "Ready for a day of seeing the sights?"

"Ready as I'll ever be," Lucy told her grandmother with a smile and then proceeded to link her arm with Opal's.

Shaking his head as he saw them dancing toward the elevators, Bowden asked, "You two, lovely ladies, ready?"

"Yes, sir!" Lucy sang, grinning at him, stepping into the elevator as Bowden pushed the button for the lobby.

Opal just looked back and forth at each of them and then shook her head while Bowden looked like he wasn't sure what to make of Lucy. Opal piped up and said, "Don't worry, Bowden, she's just as crazy as I am."

The comment just about earned her an elbow in the side, but Lucy decided against it, saying, "Hey! I'm not crazy, I'm … mysterious. Yup, that's what I'm told anyways."

"Ha! Very, dear. Very mysterious," Opal laughed, wiggling her fingers in Lucy's direction.

Stepping out of the elevator and walking toward the doors leading outside, Bowden advised, "Okay, ladies, let's get you two into the car before you scare anyone."

Lucy just glared at him, which made Opal smile and Bowden chuckle as he opened the doors of the SUV for them.

They drove around, showing Lucy the sights. Opal pointed out all the places she liked to go or just interesting places in general—restaurants, bars (Lucy was surprised, a few of them were some of the "IT" places in Minneapolis), clothing and jewelry stores, fashion designers' offices, PR firms, beaches, parks, ice cream parlors, coffee shops.

They didn't get out of the car much because Opal had admitted to being a little tired, but they did stretch their legs some at one of Opal's favorite places—Lake Calhoun. It was a lake in the heart of what Opal called "uptown," with a path the entire way around it.

There were kids swimming, and people wind surfing and paddle boarding—something Lucy had always wanted to try. It was a great place for people-watching, and since it was such a beautiful day, the three of them found a bench after Opal had tired of walking, and they sat to enjoy the sights.

Rollerbladers, runners, moms with strollers, and couples with dogs all passed before them, everyone enjoying the day in their own way. Opal sighed as she watched them. "I'm going to miss this," she murmured to no one in particular, a small smile playing on her lips.

Lucy didn't know what to say that would comfort Opal, so she just grabbed her hand and leaned her head on Opal's shoulder. Bowden seemed to be in the same boat because Lucy saw him reach over and gently pat Opal on the arm, resting his hand there for a while, as if to say he understood.

* * * * *

There were so many places and things to do in the city that Lucy's head was spinning by the end of their journey. Lucy would definitely need to consult Opal again if she was going to plan an outing anywhere, as there were many places she had seen that she'd wanted to visit again, but she couldn't remember them all off the top of her head.

As they were heading home, Opal asked, "So, Lucy, what do you think of my city here? Pretty amazing, isn't it?"

"Um, yeah! I don't know where to start, what to do first! I could probably spend my whole life in this place and not see everything. It makes me even happier to be here, knowing that I have all of this to explore!" Lucy leaned her head back against the headrest, closing her eyes, thinking of all the places they had seen.

Seeming a little run-down, Opal told her, "That's good to hear, dearie. I have to head to the doctor now, just some little checkup. Would you like to have dinner with me tomorrow night? We could get all dressed up and go someplace swanky?"

"I would love that! But, are you sure you don't want me to come with you to your appointment? I'm good with doctors, I'm not freaked out or anything like that, and I'd like to be there for you if you want someone." She didn't want to push Opal who seemed pretty private about her health so far, but Lucy wanted Opal to know she was there and would do that for her if needed.

"Oh, no thank you, dearie. It's just a little checkup, is all, and Bowden will be there. I'll see you back at home in a bit." Opal waved her away, smiling, as they pulled up to their building.

Again not wanting to push, Lucy waved good-bye as she stepped out of the car, declining Bowden's offer to walk her to the elevators.

Once upstairs, Lucy drifted into the kitchen, thinking about looking for a snack when one of Opal's staff walked in.

Opal had several people working for her. Bowden was one, and he was obviously her driver and helper of sorts. She then had a personal chef, a housekeeper, and a few other people that Lucy wasn't sure what they did. She had met them all last night but still wasn't sure who was who. It was a little weird for her to get used to these people doing things for her. Opal had told her to just ask anything of them for anything she needed.

Thinking it was going to take a while for her to do just that, Lucy smiled at the older woman walking in.

"Oh, hello, Lucy," the woman greeted her, smiling back.

"Hi," Lucy said, then she quietly added, "I'm sorry, I forgot just who you are again. I'm not always the best with names."

"Don't worry about it. I'm Lila." The woman then asked, "Are you hungry? Would you like something to eat? I was going to get started on supper, but if you'd like something—maybe a glass of wine or some cheese and crackers, just to tide you over?" She smiled encouragingly at Lucy, reminding her a little of Bowden.

"Actually, that sounds prefect. Thank you so much, Lila." Lucy sat down on a bar stool in the kitchen to watch Lila. "So, how long have you known Opal?"

Lila smiled while she sliced some cheese. "Oh, let's see. I've worked for her for about twenty years now, I'd say."

Surprised, Lucy replied, "Wow! That's a long time! I guess I've never thought about how long Opal has lived here and had everyone around to help her. That's pretty cool. I bet you guys are all like family to each other."

Looking a little surprised herself, Lila looked up at Lucy and shared, "You know, that is exactly how we are. Most of us have been here for at least as long as I have if not longer. We really are a big family here."

Pausing and looking at Lucy again, as if try to figure out what all she should say, Lila continued, "Opal is very kind and compassionate. I think she might have lost her way here or there in the past, but when it comes right down to it, she cares deeply for all of her family, those by blood and those who are not."

Lucy, having taken Lila's comment as a compliment, responded, "Thank you. Honestly, I might not have always thought that was the truth, but I am coming to believe it now. And that's really all that matters to me anyways. Getting to know who she really is, really, honestly, getting to know her. It means a lot that she's given me the opportunity."

Setting Lucy's tray of cheese and crackers down in front of her and pouring her a glass of wine, Lila quickly wiped away a stray tear and explained, "Opal really cares for you, Lucy. She was over the moon when you agreed to come and stay. You really are changing her life by doing this."

Touched that someone who worked for Opal would have such perspective—they really were family Lucy thought. She replied, "You know what, Lila? I might be doing something nice for her, but she's the one giving me a chance to start again. So I'd have to say that she is changing my life, too." Looking at the food and wine Lucy added, "Oh, and thanks for this. I'm starving!"

"Enjoy," Lila said, as she smiled and turned to get started on supper.

After her delicious snack, Lucy hung out in the living room, watching TV and relaxing, waiting for Opal to get home, so she could see how the appointment had gone. Lucy was starting to get a little worried when finally the door opened and Opal walked in.

Deciding to ask how it had gone, Lucy was about to stand up. Then Opal glanced her way, and she changed her mind. Opal looked wiped out, like she'd spent the entire day running a marathon. Lucy wasn't sure what to do or say, but Opal beat her to it.

"Hello, Lucy. I'm absolutely beat right now, I think I'm going to go lie down. Let's plan on catching up tomorrow." She then turned to walk toward her room as Bowden softly took her arm and guided her down the hall.

Worried, Lucy walked into the kitchen where Lila was just finishing dinner and asked, "Is she going to be okay? She looked, well, not so good."

"She'll be okay. Those appointments just take all of her energy. Usually by the next day she's back to her normal self. Looks like she'll be skipping dinner again tonight," Lila explained with a worried look, as she twisted a dishtowel absentmindedly in her hands.

Stopping suddenly, as if just realizing what she was doing, Lila put the towel gently down beside the sink and asked, "Would you like to eat at the dinner table, or would you like me to make you a plate here at the island?"

"The island is fine with me, but would you and Bowden join me? It feels weird eating by myself. It's more fun with friends around," Lucy replied.

Looking at Lucy, Lila smiled, "I would love to join you, Lucy. It would be my pleasure. I'll set a place for Bowden, too. I doubt he'll refuse a good dinner with us girls, huh?" Lila dished up three plates and set them on the island. Then she pulled out silverware and a couple of more wine glasses.

Lucy took a deep breath, closed her eyes, and smiled, "Yum, that smells delicious! I'm not sure if I'll be able to wait for Bowden before I start!"

Laughing, Lila pointed down the hall, "I don't think you'll have much of a wait, here he comes now."

Bowden walked in, a frown on his face, but when he saw Lucy, he forced a smile, saying, "Hello, Lucy, I hope you enjoyed your day with Opal. This looks amazing, Lila, thank you." He settled himself down on a stool, looking longingly at his meal.

Sitting down and picking up her fork, Lucy asked, "How is she? She really hasn't said much to me about what's going on. I'm not sure if I should ask or just let her tell me if she wants to. I don't want to step on her toes, but I want her to know I care."

"Ah, yes. Well, Opal is a very hard person to read. She's private at times and not at others. I think with all that is going on with her health, she doesn't want anyone to worry about her. The thing is, with Opal, if you really want to know what's going on with her, you have to make her tell you."

Looking at a startled Lucy, he laughed and went on to explain, "I know how that sounds. She's a hard nut to crack, but if you want to know what's going on in there, you've got to give her a little nudge."

"So it's okay if I ask her about … things?" Lucy asked, playing with her food.

Smiling at her, Bowden urged, "I think you should ask away, Lucy. That's what you're here for, isn't it? Don't worry so much about what's right or wrong, just do what feels right."

"Thanks, Bowden. Lila, this is the best chicken masala I've ever tasted. You're going to have to make this again, and soon!"

"Just wait until you try her lasagna and her fried chicken and her shrimp jambalaya. You're going to want her to make everything again soon, and then you'll be eating and eating, and then look what happens." He pointed to his stomach that looked a little like Santa's and laughed.

Smiling and laughing, they enjoyed each other's company long after they had finished their dinner and wine. It was later than she'd thought when Lucy thanked them both again and headed towards her room.

Walking into her closet, she found another pair of comfy-looking pajamas and tossed them on. These were grey and purple flannel and the softest things ever.

Smiling, she slipped into bed, reflecting on her day. All in all, it had been pretty good. She could have done without the embarrassment of the coffee shop this morning, but the coffee had been great, and she did have a job lined up for tomorrow. She only hoped her working wouldn't be precious time missed with Opal. She'd make sure it wasn't by spending her free time tomorrow morning with Opal, and they did have dinner plans as well. Lucy closed her eyes, and before she could think another thought, she was asleep.

CHAPTER FIVE

Opening her eyes, Lucy smiled. Then, remembering she was starting her new job that day, she felt butterflies fluttering in her stomach. She wondered if Summer ever got butterflies. Probably not, darn Summer.

After a long hot shower, Lucy dressed herself in a pair of Hudson jeans, a black tank top, and an open black-and-white cardigan. She thought she looked cute but casual, just right for her first day at work—a lot better than the pajamas she had worn the day before.

Finding Opal resting on the couch in the huge living room, Lucy leaned down and gave her a hug. "I hope you're feeling better today, Opal. I was worried about you last night."

"Thank you, Lucy, dear. I'm still a little tired, but better nonetheless. What are your plans for this morning?" Opal asked, her voice sounding strained.

"I was going to ask you the same thing. I'd love to spend some time together before I try my hand at the coffee shop."

Opal laughed and said, "That's right, I'd forgotten you were doing that. Ha! That should be interesting. If you wouldn't mind, I'd like to take it easy today, just stay home. Should we get our coffee and tea and sit out on the balcony? There are a few things I'd like to tell you."

Nodding her head, Lucy went to the kitchen to make her coffee and put Opal's teapot on the stove. When their drinks were ready, they headed out to the balcony to watch the activity going on below.

Setting her drink down on the small circular table and slowly lowering herself into a chair, Opal stated, "Of all my years here, I never tire of watching people. Everyone has a story in them, don't you think? Maybe you don't always see it right away, but if you take the time to get to know someone, you find out so many interesting things about them and their life." Opal smiled, looking at the view.

Sitting as well, Lucy smiled and nodded, waiting for Opal to say more. It was a beautiful day out, and she didn't mind relaxing and enjoying the view.

Wrapping her hands around her warm mug, Opal sighed and continued, "Like I've said before, I've always regretted what happened between your mother and me, Lucy. Looking back, I should have bit my tongue and let her live her own life, but I thought I was helping her."

Lucy looked at Opal, confused, admitting, "I have no idea what you're talking about. My mom has never told me what happened between the two of you. It's been one of the mysteries of my life."

"Well, for some people, some things are better left unsaid. But I'd like to tell you my side of the story anyway, if you'd want to hear it." Opal glanced at Lucy, and at Lucy's slight nod, Opal continued, "After your mom graduated from college, she came back home, here. Your grandfather and I thought she was going to start looking for a job, something she could do to make use of that shiny new degree. Instead she surprised us with some jaw-dropping news. She was pregnant!"

Opal paused, squeezing Lucy's arm, telling her, "Don't get me wrong, I had always wanted to be a grandmother, and I am and always will be extremely thankful for you, but your grandfather and I thought it was the worst possible timing. Newly graduated, the ink barely dry on her diploma, and she gets herself knocked up? I'm sorry if that seems harsh, dear ..."

Unsure of what to say, Lucy just shook her head, adding, "No ... no, it's okay, so what happened next?"

Opal gave a small, sad smile and continued, "Well, your grandfather and I weren't pleased. We weren't even aware of her having a serious boyfriend at the time, but we knew these kinds of things happen. When we questioned her about who the father was and what role he would be playing, she threw another curve ball at us. 'There is no father, not really,' she revealed." Opal looked at Lucy, trying to gauge what her reaction might be.

Lucy smiled and admitted, "I think I know where this is going. I know this part of the story, at least."

Looking relieved, Opal took a deep breath and finished, sadness rushing through her, "So she said there was no father, that she had decided to get pregnant on her own. She had said it was her deepest desire to have a child, that she felt she wouldn't be complete otherwise. 'What?' we asked, 'No father? But how?' 'I did it by myself. I just made up my mind, went to the sperm bank, and that was that,' your mom told us." Opal paused for a while, seeming to be caught up in that long-ago conversation.

Lucy was about to speak when Opal held up her hand, asking for one more minute. "Your grandfather and I, we weren't very understanding. We were livid. Yes, livid is the perfect word to describe us at that moment, and cruel. We told her she had made a mistake. That she had wasted our money, sending her to an Ivy League college only for her to come home pregnant and without a plan. She told us she had a plan, and she did.

She had things all planned out. But the problem was, she was counting on living here, at home with us, for a while anyway, but we refused. You should have heard your grandfather yell. Oh boy, was he fired up. I don't think I had ever heard him raise his voice before that day. He told her to get out, to leave and not come back. That was it," Opal said sadly, raising her hands and letting them fall back onto her lap.

This was all news to Lucy, but it all made sense. Well, it made sense why her mom had never really spoken to her parents again. It made sense why her mom had such horrible guilt about never setting things right with her father before he had passed away.

"I just don't understand why this situation, why having me, would come between you all, how could a baby push you all apart so completely?" Lucy questioned, feeling unwanted and almost responsible for something she had no control over, no choice in.

"We thought your mother should have been more responsible. We wanted her to find a job, get married, be settled and secure before even thinking about having children. We couldn't fathom why she would just go to a sperm bank and pick out someone who sounded good on paper. How could that work? We thought it was a horrible idea, and if she were going to go through with it, it wouldn't be with us standing by watching. So she just up and left. She found a place a couple hours away, found a job she loved, and had you. Your mother was always so different from your grandfather and me. She was a free thinker, someone who looked at things in an entirely different light than we did. The sad thing was, that was the way we had raised her to be, that was what we wanted for her—to think for herself. To be different and make beautiful things in her own way, it just wasn't what we wanted, the way that we wanted, and that wasn't fair to her. Her father never forgave her, not really, but despite that I should have just kept my mouth shut and been supportive of her. That's what you both needed, and I can see now that I let you down. I think if he would have been alive to see you, Lucy, he would have done a complete one-eighty and come to his senses. I know I did, even though it probably didn't seem like it."

"Thank you for telling me all that. It's nice to finally understand what was going on between Mom and you. She told me when I was little about why I didn't have a dad around like most of my friends so that part I've always understood, but it's nice to get some perspective on what happened with you and my grandpa and mom. My only question is, why were you so crabby all the time?"

"That's a good question, Lucy. I think, even in the recent past, I could be very judgmental. If someone was doing something that I didn't think was appropriate, I would make it known. I was upset with your mother and, therefore, always in a bad mood when you two were around. For a long time, I was angry with her for what she put her father and me through, I blamed her for the pain we felt. Years after his death, I began to see things in a new light, began to realize that we had a choice, her father and I. We could have accepted her for who she was and what she wanted, but we didn't. Maybe she made a choice that we didn't approve of at the time, but we made the choice to cut her out of our lives and be angry about it. I feel horrible about that now, thinking about what all your memories of me from back then must be, but I'm here to make up for it now. I hope the memories we make now will make up for the ones from back then."

Putting her hand on Opal's arm, Lucy assured her, "Those memories have already been made up for, Opal. Your kindness at inviting me here, your generosity and the support you have given me in such a short period of time more than make up for any mistakes in the past. Now that I understand what went on back then, I'm more than ready to move forward."

"Me too, Lucy. Me too." Sighing, Opal turned away before Lucy could see her eyes misting over. She still wasn't good with emotions; sometimes you really couldn't teach an old dog new tricks.

Until Lucy had to leave for work, she and Opal sat outside, eating, drinking and sharing both happy and sad stories from the past. When their time together that afternoon was over, they both had a better understanding of the other and felt a kind of kinship that neither one had felt before.

* * * * *

As she walked in the door to Grinder, Lucy was on the lookout for Scary Guy. She hoped she wouldn't be so intimidated today since she actually had clothes on.

"Hey!" she heard someone call out.

Startled, she turned to her left to see a skinny guy clearing some mugs off of a table. "Oh hi, I'm here for the job. I talked to someone yesterday. He said I could start today. He, um, had lots of tattoos all over his arms."

"Oh yeah, that's Cash. He's the manager ... but he kinda owns the place, too," the guy informed her with a smile.

Even still, Lucy she eyed him cautiously. The guy seemed friendly enough, but you never could be too sure since he worked with this Cash guy.

"Anyways, I'm Teddy, I'll train you in today. We usually don't start newbies on the bar right away, but we're gonna be totally jammed later today, and I'll need you to know as much as you can in case I need you to help me out. Plus, the whole cash register thing is easy. It'll take, like, two minutes to show you that," he explained, all the while smiling and squinting at her.

Hesitantly, Lucy stepped behind the bar, which was the place where they actually made the coffee. A little freaked out she inquired, "Are you sure I should be doing this?"

She made a face as she looked at the big machine before her, which made Teddy laugh. He answered, "Yeah, it's fine. Just don't blow anything up or, you know, anything like that, right?"

Lucy wasn't sure if he was joking. Was it possible to blow up an espresso machine?

The look on her face had Teddy shaking his head, reassuring her, "Don't worry, I'm just messing with you. You'll be good. You probably won't have to touch this thing at all today. It's just in case there's an emergency or anything. You know how people get about their coffee." He grinned at her and then added, "You never told me your name, by the way."

"Oh," embarrassed and feeling like an idiot again, she said, "It's Lucy. Nice to meet you."

Teddy nodded. His blond hair, which was a little longer on top, with shorter sides, flopped into his eyes. He looked young, probably younger than Lucy, maybe twenty at the oldest. He smiled again and started showing her how to run the espresso machine. "So, you put the espresso in here, right? The decaf is here and regular here, then you push this button and wait for a second."

Lucy watched, nodding, as the espresso came out into two little cups.

"So depending on which drink people order, and what size, that's how you know how many espresso shots to put into a drink. But then they can add extra shots, or ask for less, or whatever, so you need to pay attention to that, too. Then here is where you steam your milk. Watch this temp gauge because the milk has to be exactly right, unless they ask for extra hot, or not so hot. Okay?"

Lucy nodded. She really hoped she wouldn't have to use this beast today. It was a little overwhelming. Okay, a *lot* overwhelming.

"So when you're done steaming the milk, always clean the steamer with this towel right away. It takes like half a second, but just do it. Then you pour the milk into the cup. Now remember, depending on which drink they order, you either do froth or none, and add whip, or sometimes no whip. It just depends on what the drink is. Also, if the drink has any chocolate or syrup in it, those things always go in first, before the espresso or milk. Got it?"

"Um, no, but I'll try to remember," admitted Lucy, giving her best smile. She decided she'd channel Summer today to see if that helped her get through her first day of work.

"Right on, Lucy. That's the best we can hope for, right?" Laughing, he showed her where the cups and covers were kept, then he told her, "Alright, I know this is like a total crash course today, but it's gonna get crazy here in a bit, so let me show you the register."

Taking a deep breath, Lucy repeated (more to herself than to anyone else), "Okay, I can do this, I can do this!"

"That's right, you can! I'm loving the attitude, girl! Okay, so it's all touch screen here. See? So each drink is on here, the size and if there are any add-ons, or other specific thing they want. I mean, it's pretty simple. Then the drawer opens when you push "cash" and put in how much they are giving you. Sometimes it gets stuck, and then you just need this key here," he explained, pointing to a key dangling from a chain that was hooked to the register, "and you can open it that way. Don't worry though, I'll be here the whole time, and most people are pretty cool. They'll know you're new." He smiled again, holding his thumbs up.

"Okay … I'm a little freaked, but I'm hoping I'll get the hang of it as the day goes on. I just hope Cash doesn't come in. Then I'll totally freak and mess it all up. He was a little, well, intimidating yesterday."

"Ha-ha, yeah, he can be like that sometimes. But he's pretty cool once you get to know him. Plus he hired you, so he can't be that bad right." He smiled again and nodded at her like she knew what he was talking about.

Lucy looked at Teddy, lowering her eyebrows, and added, "I don't know about that."

"Yeah, just you wait though; he'll totally have your mind changed in a few months. Then he'll be like, the funniest person you know, and you'll be like, wondering why you ever thought otherwise."

"We'll just see about that, Teddy. I'm highly doubtful, but never say never, I guess."

She was just about to ask Teddy how long he had worked at Grinder when the door opened and in walked the cute guy from yesterday, the guy she had bumped into in her pajamas.

"Hey, Teddy, what's up, man?" Hot Guy said, giving Teddy a silly salute.

"Oh hey, Jax," Teddy responded, nodding his head.

Lucy was trying to avoid eye contact with Hot Guy/Jax (seriously, Jax? Couldn't his name have been something more, well, boring, like

Harold or Cleveland? Or something? Summer was going to have a freaking heyday with this). She was still embarrassed from yesterday.

It wasn't working, though. Jax was quickly approaching, his eyes on her.

"Hey, you. Honestly, I'm a little disappointed. I was hoping to see what kind of PJs you'd have on today," he joked as Lucy's face turned bright red.

"Thanks for reminding me, thanks a lot," Lucy responded, as Teddy looked at the two of them, confused.

Seeing Teddy's face, Jax explained, "You should have seen this girl yesterday, smashed right into me when she was running away from Cash! Should have seen her face, Teddy, terrified of Cash! Oh yeah, had some pretty happening PJs on too."

Not sure if she was feeling even more embarrassed because he remembered her wearing pajamas or just plain flustered, Lucy responded with as much dignity as she could, "Seriously, if you two would have been in here and seen Cash, you'd have run away terrified, too."

Studying her with a small smile on his face, Jax said, "I never did get your name pajama girl, but … I kind of like the way 'pajama girl' sounds. What do you think, 'pajama girl' or … ?"

Mouth dry, Lucy tried to act cool (which can be a little tricky when the hottest guy you've ever met is asking for your name), offering, "It's Lucy."

Tilting his head to the side, he squinted at her, stating, "Lucy, huh … Yeah, I'd say that's just a little bit better than 'pajama girl.' "

He gave her a heart-stopping grin, and then he turned to Teddy to ask, "So, what do you have for me, Teddy? Today feels like an original day, got anything?"

"Yeah, man, I came up with a new one yesterday. I call it the Vanilla Gorilla. It's your basic vanilla, white chocolate mocha, but there are an added three espresso shots," Teddy told Jax, shrugging.

"What the heck, I'll give it a whirl man, sounds good." Then Jax looked at Lucy and added, "Lucky girl, getting to work with Teddy. He invents the best drinks this place has. He's a genius. Serious coffee master!"

Widening her eyes and making a face at Teddy, Lucy replied, "Oh, I'm in the midst of a coffee master genius here, huh. Out of all the coffee shops in the entire city, the master genius works at the one that I happened to walk into yesterday. I am lucky!"

Laughing, Teddy shook his head, explaining, "Nah, it's just this thing I do when it's slow. But, okay I am a *little* bit of a genius, just don't tell Cash, though. He'd totally throw me out—no geniuses allowed, man!"

"I'm confused, I thought you said Cash was superbly cool once you got to know him," Lucy said, looking at Teddy out of the corner of her eye.

"Yeah, well he is, but he also wants to believe he's like the smartest person around so ... yeah, that's pretty much it." Rolling his eyes, he pointed to the register, saying, "Okay, Lucy, show me how it's done, girl."

"Great," Lucy replied, a little nervous. Of course Jax had to be her first costumer. "Okay, let's see here. Yeah, so that'll be $20.95 please." She looked up expectantly at Jax and then, realizing what she just said, added, "Wait, that can't be right. Or Teddy really is a genius and figured out how to make a twenty-dollar cup of coffee. Let me try again."

She pushed a few more buttons and the register started buzzing and dinging repeatedly. Lucy looked over anxiously at Teddy while Jax tried not to laugh.

Teddy walked over cheerfully, pushed a couple of buttons, and the buzzing stopped. "Okay, man. So it'll be three ninety-five."

"Breaking the bank, Teddy, sheesh!" Jax laughed, handed over a twenty-dollar bill, looked directly at Lucy, and said, "Keep the change." Then, grabbing his Vanilla Gorilla, waved good-bye and walked out the door.

"Wow," Lucy remarked when he was gone, "He is like the hottest thing I've ever seen."

Shaking his head again, Teddy agreed, "Yeah, I don't think I know of any girl who wouldn't agree wholeheartedly with you. I kind of think he has a thing for you."

Lucy's head snapped up, inquiring, "What? Why?"

"He comes in here every day. He has for as long as I've been here, and I've been here forever, but I've never seen him really interested in anyone. Sure, he's a bit of a flirt, but, yeah I'm pretty sure he's got a thing for you."

Lucy smiled, admitting, "Well, if he *did* have a thing for me, I don't think I'd object."

"Ha, right on girl!" he said smiling.

Lucy sighed, thinking about Jax. He was the first guy since her divorce that she'd actually been into, but she wasn't sure he really was into her. They'd just met, and she really didn't want to get ahead of herself. "A girl can dream," she thought, "A girl can dream." She sighed again.

"Lucy!" Teddy called out, elbowing her and breaking into her thoughts.

"Oh sorry, just thinking about Hot Guy," she told him, dreamily.

"Hot Guy?"

"Oh, well, I mean Jax. That's what I called him before I knew what his name was, and it's a pretty accurate description," she said happily.

Nudging her, he suggested, "Okay, let's go over this register thing again before the crazy comes."

They huddled over the register for a few more minutes, until people started pouring in. And then, like Teddy said, the crazy definitely came.

People kept showing up, and things didn't slow down until it was 4:00 and almost time for Lucy to leave. She was exhausted and flustered and not sure she wanted to come back the next day. That dumb register had beeped and buzzed and jammed up on her way too many times to count. So many that Teddy had tried to do both making the coffee and ringing people up, but Lucy had felt bad just standing there watching him dash back and forth. So she finally pushed her worries and embarrassment aside and stepped up to that annoying register and did the best that she could. She banged on it, swore at it, and even pleaded with it to give her a break. Finally it had when it was time for her to leave, dumb thing.

As she and Teddy walked out, he remarked, "I'm thinking you should try bar tomorrow, I don't know what it is with you and that register, but I think the two of you need a little breather."

"You can say that again, we definitely weren't getting along today. How much time did it take you to get the hang of that piece?" she asked, hoping there was a big learning curve.

Teddy just looked at Lucy and answered, "I don't think you want to hear my response." He stopped next to a shiny silver car, and leaning against it, rattled his keys.

"Great, you were totally rocking it within the hour, weren't you?" she asked, and when he just nodded, she added, "Jerk!"

"Don't worry, Lucy, I'm sure you'll be a rock star at bar tomorrow." When she just glared at him, he asked, "So what's up tonight?"

"Tonight, my grandma and I are hitting the town. She's taking me out to one of her favorite spots for dinner. What about you?" Lucy asked, leaning against his car, still worn out from the register.

"Ha, sounds rad, girl. Me? Well, I'm really into mixing music, so I'm just gonna chill and do that tonight. I need a little stress reliever tonight. You and that register man, that sucked!" He shook his head and laughed.

"Thanks a lot, Teddy. So if you're into mixing music, do you ever DJ parties or anything like that?" Lucy asked, interested. She always thought being a DJ would be pretty fun, getting everyone dancing to the music.

"Oh yeah, all the time, love it! There is this one huge party coming

up, in about two months, you should totally come, bring a friend or ...
bring Hot Guy! Ha yeah!" He smiled, giving her what she would come
to know as his famous thumbs up.

"Right, I'm sure that'll happen. Me and Hot Guy," noted Lucy,
rolling her eyes but smiling at Teddy.

"We'll just see tomorrow, Lucy, how he acts when he comes in. It'll
be interesting, for sure." He nodded, unlocking his car and tossing his
water bottle that he'd had stuck in his back pocket onto the passenger
seat.

"Thanks, Teddy, now I'm more nervous for tomorrow than I was
already, and that's saying a lot! I need a stress reliever, too. I think I'm
going to go lie down and cry myself to sleep." She looked at Teddy who
just rolled his eyes and smiled. "See you tomorrow, Teds," she added,
slowly turning around and starting to walk back home.

"Bye, Lucy," he said, walking over and ducking his head as he got
into his car, but not until after shooting her an air high five.

CHAPTER SIX

Going out to dinner with Opal was a whole different experience than Lucy had thought it would be. She was expecting quiet, calm, laid back, but it turned out to be just the opposite.

When Lucy had arrived home, Opal asked how her day had gone. Shaking her head, Lucy said she wanted to forget all about it. Opal laughed and pointed Lucy towards her room, telling her to get ready for a night out on the town. Lucy had opened the door to her room and seen an amazing dress lying on her bed, just as Opal had called out to her, "Put it on!"

It was a little black dress, and well, it was *little*. It was probably the shortest dress Lucy had ever worn. It was more like something she'd seen Summer wearing, and it was strapless. Lucy opened the door, calling out to Opal, "I have no idea even how to—"

Opal appeared in the doorway, insisting, "Just put it on, Lucy, it'll look beautiful on you. I've got shoes and jewelry when you're finished. Oh, and Tia is here to do your hair and makeup." Then she turned and walked away before Lucy could argue.

Lucy slipped the dress on. Looking in her mirror, Lucy realized, a little grudgingly, that Opal was right. It looked great on her.

Opal then reappeared with Tia. She was probably one of the most beautiful people Lucy had ever met, dark skin, big brown eyes, and a friendly smile. What Lucy liked best about her, though, and what she thought made her even more beautiful, was that her looks hadn't seemed to give her a big head; it was like she had no idea how beautiful she was. Lucy also was realizing she was amazing at hair and even more amazing at makeup.

"Wow! You really need to come over every morning and do this, seriously, Tia. I don't even recognize myself!" Lucy exclaimed, as she checked herself out and watched Tia put the final touches on. Lucy was amazed as she looked in the mirror. She didn't think she'd ever looked as good as she did at that moment.

Opal appeared once again, declaring, "Now you know why I keep her around, she can make an old lady like me look half my age!" Opal teased, "Ready, Lucy? We have a reservation at Blush at nine sharp, so we'd better get a move on."

Waving a good-bye to Tia as she packed up, Lucy looked at Opal. "Blush?" she asked excitedly, "That's like the it place to go around here, isn't it? I can't believe we are going there! Summer is going to die, just *die* when I tell her!"

"Why are you so surprised, Lucy? I'm old, but I'm not boring, not yet anyway. I still like to go have some fun!" Opal explained, grabbing Lucy's hand.

Looking at Opal, Lucy laughed, announcing, "Blush! Here we come!"

The rest of the night was a blur to Lucy, an amazing kind of blur. They got to Blush and were directly escorted to the VIP section, where a bottle of the most expensive champagne was brought to them, and it was from the owner, yes the owner of Blush!

"What?" Opal asked Lucy when she saw her expression.

"The freaking *owner* of Blush, Opal?" Lucy inquired, eyeing her grandma suspiciously.

"Oh that." Opal waved her hand like it was no big deal.

Wanting the scoop, Lucy urged, "Yes, that! Do tell!"

Flushed, Opal replied, "I don't think you want to hear that story, do you, Lucy? Who wants to hear about an old lady and her younger male ... friend."

"Opal! Did you just blush? Summer was right, you do have some stories in you," Lucy said, wiggling her eyebrows, and Opal laughed.

Lucy was able to get a little bit more of the story out of Opal, but not much. Then their dinner came, and, of course, it was amazing, dessert even more so. After dinner, Lucy and Opal sat at their table talking, laughing, and keeping watch for cute boys.

The champagne going a little bit to her head, Lucy was convinced by a few cute guys and even some older handsome gentlemen to hit the dance floor. Even Opal joined in the fun, after Lucy kept calling out to her to come shake her booty on the dance floor.

By the end of the night, her feet hurt from dancing, and her stomach hurt from laughing. It was the best night that Lucy could remember having in a long time, and it was all thanks to Opal.

* * * * *

Opening her eyes, Lucy was prepared for the mother of all headaches, but after sitting up and blinking a few times, she realized there wasn't one. That's when she remembered that Opal had made Lucy her signature "no hangover" drink. Lucy had no idea what had been in the thing. She just remembered plugging her nose and chugging it after Opal had told her she'd be sorry if she didn't drink it.

Thinking of all the fun she and Opal had had the previous night made her smile, they really did get along well. She honestly couldn't believe that Opal was such fun! Lucy was beginning to see another side of Opal, the side that Opal had promised she would show Lucy, the side that was fun and loving and full of life. Lucy was just worried that all that life, that energy was going to be gone before she could discover all that she wanted to about her. She hoped she was wrong, but Lucy had a feeling that there was more to what was going on than Opal was telling her, and with Lucy, when she had a feeling, she was usually right on.

* * * * *

Lucy opened the doors to Grinder with dripping wet hair, feeling more than a little flustered. She hadn't realized that Opal's hangover cure would also cause her to sleep most of the morning. She woke with only half an hour to get ready, eat, and rush to work. She had skipped the eating part, and now her stomach was loudly protesting.

"Wow, girl, what happened? Is it raining out there?" Teddy asked, grimacing and glancing outside.

"Ha. Ha. Ha. No it's not *raining* out there, I just slept in a little bit. Thanks for making me feel like I look like a drowned rat," replied, Lucy pushing her wet hair back, frustrated. At least her clothes were cute, that was always something she could count on these days, cute clothes if nothing else.

"Hey, hey, simmer, girl. You look fine. Plus, by the time anyone stops in I'm sure your hair will have dried ... a little. How was your night out?" Teddy asked, wanting to change the subject. Lucy looked a little peeved right now.

"Oh, my gosh, Teddy, you won't believe where we went! Blush!" Wet hair forgotten, Lucy was smiling ear to ear.

"Whoa, did you just say Blush? That's like the place to be, dude. Wait, didn't you say you were going out to dinner with your grandmother?" Teddy inquired with a skeptical look on his face.

"Yeah, we did. We ate at Blush. You don't know my grandma, Teddy. She's like the life of the party even at seventy years old! She knows the freaking owner of Blush. He even reserved the best table in the place for us and sent over a bottle of champagne!" Lucy's eyes were huge as she told Teddy about the previous night.

"What the heck! You're kidding, right, Lucy? Otherwise, you have, like, the total most kick-ass grandma I've ever heard of."

Teddy looked impressed, and Lucy thought she'd have to have him over to meet Opal. He would love her, who wouldn't?

"She's pretty amazing. You'll have to come on over one of these days and meet her."

"Sure, girl, I'd love to. So, okay let's talk work here for a second. You ready for bar?" he asked, patting the big silver machine like an old friend.

"Do I have a choice?" Lucy asked sullenly.

"Nope," Teddy asserted, and eyeing the door, he added, "You're up, girl, and good luck. Looks like Jax is your first customer of the day again. Oh, and you look fine, so chin up, Lucy, you got this." He flashed his thumbs up and pretended to be busy filling the bakery case as Jax walked in.

Weirdly, Teddy's last remark gave Lucy the boost of confidence she needed. She gave Teddy a goofy grin and turned to watch Hot Guy walk into the shop.

"Hey, Teddy, what's up man?" Jax smiled, doing his silly salute again. Lucy wondered if it was something he did all the time, or just to Teddy. Spotting Lucy, Jax called out, "Looking good, but I'm still missing those PJs." He winked after saying the last bit.

Trying not to blush, Lucy told him, "Well, I was good until you mentioned PJs, *again*. Don't you remember we were forgetting about that?"

"Those were some nice pajamas though, I'm not sure I want to forget," Jax remarked, sending her a look that made her heart pick up speed.

Feeling her face flush, Lucy looked away, embarrassed. "Thanks, I guess," she managed.

Laughing, Jax noted, "You're kind of cute when you're embarrassed. Don't you think, Teddy?"

Lucy was about to die. Was he actually flirting with her, or was he always like this? She obviously had no idea because she'd never seen him around anyone besides her and Teddy.

"Yeah, man, she's pretty cute. But then I remember that I'm the one who had to run back and forth between bar and register yesterday, for, like, way too many hours, and that takes some of the cuteness away. Man that sucked!" Teddy divulged, all the while shaking his head and smiling at Lucy.

"Hey!" Lucy called out, elbowing him in the ribs as he came over to restock the cups.

"Nope, still cute. Don't think you'll be able to change my mind, dude," Jax reported, making a what can-I-say? look at Teddy.

"Okay, so what do you have for me today, man? That Vanilla Gorilla was just what I needed yesterday, but I'm going for something stronger today," Jax informed them, rubbing his hands together.

"Stronger, huh? Right on. Well, basically, if you want strong and nothing else, I've got just the thing for you. I call it Gut Rot. It's six shots of espresso and a splash of milk and that's it, man."

Teddy was passionate about his coffee.

Lucy laughed at his expression and sneaked a look at Jax. He was still looking up at the menu, deep in thought, so she took that moment to check her hair. Yeah, still wet.

Shrugging, Jax decided, "Sounds a little intense, but do me up, bro."

Nodding, Teddy said, "Okay, Lucy, let's do this. Come over here and pull the shots." He watched as Lucy slowly did what he told her.

Teddy continued instructing, "Right, nice work. Okay, now just add a splash of milk, just a—well, I didn't literally mean to splash the milk in. Here, I'll take care of it." Teddy rubbed his temples and set the overflowing drink aside to make another.

"Um … sorry, Teddy," Lucy replied, embarrassed and then quickly went to work cleaning up the espresso shots and milk she had so clumsily spilt all over the floor and counter. Of course, she would have to mess up the easiest drink and dump milk all over the place in front of Jax.

As Teddy was finishing Jax's drink, Lucy looked up to see Jax studying her. He made a come-here motion with his hand. Wondering what he could want, Lucy walked slowly over to where he was standing and looked up at him, blowing a strand of hair out of her eyes.

"Hey, don't worry about it. That was your first time ever making a drink, right? You're doing fine, don't look so sad," he advised her.

"Dude, drink's up," Teddy called to Jax from the other side of the counter.

Grabbing his drink from Teddy, Jax nodded, then he looked down at Lucy.

Brushing some hair back from her face, he confessed, "I don't know what it is about you, but I'm intrigued. Could I take you out to dinner sometime this week? How about Friday, does that work?"

Baffled that Jax was asking her out to dinner, she simply nodded and agreed, "That'd be great."

"Great, see you then, Lucy," Jax said with a smile and then turned, calling out to Teddy, "Dude, thanks for the Gut Rot. Later."

Turning to leave, he stopped, turned back to Lucy, and stuck something in her front pocket, saying, "Just in case you miss me." Then he walked away.

"Wow. I was so totally right, Lucy!" Teddy exclaimed, grinning at her when she spun around.

"I, uh, I think I'm in shock," Lucy uttered, pulling whatever it was he had put in her pocket out. It was his business card with his number on it. "Yeah, I'm definitely in shock, did that just happen?" she asked, holding up the card to show Teddy.

"I told you, girl, chin up. It works every time, babe." Teddy winked at her, then added, "Yeah, so about the coffee, we need to work on that." His face serious, he motioned her over for more lessons.

Teddy spent the rest of their shift, in between costumers, trying to teach Lucy the tricks of the trade, but she just wasn't getting it. After she sent one of their favorite customers running to the ER from accidentally burning him with the milk steamer, Teddy decided she needed to go back to the register where she couldn't spill, burn, or spray anyone else. By the end of their shift, she was even more miserable than she had been the day before.

Walking out the doors of Grinder, Teddy divulged, "I hate to say this, Lucy, but you really suck at this job. I mean, like bad, like total suckage. Like maybe this isn't for you … "

"I know, I totally suck! I don't know why I'm so bad, but it's only my second day, I'm thinking I might make some improvements tomorrow?" Lucy suggested, lifting an eyebrow.

Stopping at his car, Teddy shook his head and responded, "I don't know. I've never seen anyone this bad before. It's like Grinder doesn't like you, you're totally coffee shop cursed right now. It's bad, Luce." He swallowed, Adam's apple bobbing, eyes serious.

"So, you're saying … I'm not sure I want to know, but I don't think you have high hopes of me being a coffee genius master like yourself." She smiled at him as she leaned against his car. She did really suck, but she'd had fun getting to know Teddy.

"Yeah, no master genius coffee girl in the works for you, Luce. You should probably try something else. Entirely." He paused, took a deep breath and stated, "Oh, so what I'm saying is … you're way, so much, totally fired." He glanced at her, not sure what her reaction would be.

Sensing that he felt horrible about what he had just done, she replied, "Hey, it's okay! I thought as much. I think after I burned that guy with the milk steamer, I pretty much knew I was a lost cause." She made a face at the way too recent memory.

"Yeah … I had no idea that was even possible, you know, to burn someone like that," Teddy admitted, making a confused face, "Wow that was such an epic fail. But, you're cool, though, so that makes up for most of it." He smiled and gave her a thumbs up.

"Thanks, Teddy, you're the best. See you tomorrow, but this time I'll be buying some coffee, not spilling or spraying it," she told him, punching him softly in the arm as she turned to walk towards home.

"Yeah, see ya tomorrow, Lucy," he responded, getting into his car and driving away.

* * * * *

When Lucy got home, Bowden informed her that Opal was taking a much-needed rest, but he assured her things were fine. Having nothing better to do, Lucy wandered into her room and decided to check her email, wondering if Drew had emailed about any other mishaps. She sure could use a good laugh right about now.

Opening her email, she smiled and started reading, then silently thanked Drew. He had given her just what she wanted and most definitely needed.

> Dear Lucy—
> I hope things are going better for you then they are for me … I am actually very embarrassed to even think about what I am going to tell you, but I can't think of anyone else who I can tell, and I need to get this off my chest if nothing else.
> In my hopes to try to free myself and backpack around the world, I was actually hoping to do just that, go around the world! My expectations have been very high, but that's just me, I expect and only want and usually get the best. We have been in New Orleans for the past few days. Normally I wouldn't mind being here, but I want to see the world, Lucy! I'm not sure why Corbin, or any of the other buddies who agreed to this, don't want to as well. I am getting off the topic, I apologize. I am having a difficult time putting into words what happened two nights ago. I haven't even been able to eat since this happened, and you know me Lucy, I need to eat. Here goes—
> So Corbin came back to this scummy place we are staying at (Lucy, I'm not sure I can do this much longer, I need my pedicures and other essentials, you know how I am), and he told us he had a big night out planned, he

promised us it was going to be amazing. So I was very excited, even in New Orleans, a night out can be something out of a fantasy.

I took my time getting ready, though there wasn't much for me to do since I don't have all that I need here—hair products, all my lotions, cologne—I think Corbin sold it for cash—but I looked good, Luce, I looked decent.

We arrive at this nightclub place, a little dingy but, well, what can you do, Corbin doesn't have the best taste, walk in and are directly rushed into the back. I was very confused at this time, until Corbin threw something small and black at me and told me to get dressed. You will never believe, Lucy, what it was. It was a dress! Right when I realized what it was, he walked up to me and said he enrolled us in a cross-dressing competition! I was about to run out of there when he told me if we won, we would each get $100, well ... you know me, Lucy, I can't pass up a competition. So I did it. I put on the skimpy black dress and a short black wig, and I even let Corbin put some 'fire engine' red lipstick on me. I was then pushed out on to the stage and had to 'shake what my mama gave me' to the song "I'm Sexy and I Know It."

I was so thankful when it was over, all I wanted to do was see if we all had won and then go back to the motel. I was at the bar, waiting for Corbin and the others, when a guy came up to me ... here's where it gets sticky, Lucy. This guy, he said he liked my show and he wanted more, then he leaned in and kissed me! I tried to push him away, but he was very strong. When he finally backed away, I ran outside and vomited. I feel sick, Lucy.

I am worried, do you think this means I'm gay? Help me! I feel so, so ... violated!

Drew.

Lucy couldn't believe what an idiot Drew was. She actually felt sorry for him, even though he kind of deserved everything that came his way. After she wiped the tears from her eyes, she felt a lot better. After that long, hard laugh, she clicked "reply."

> Drew—
> All I can say is—wow. It took me awhile to stop laughing at the picture in my mind of you dancing in a little black dress and wig ... I wonder if Corbin put it on YouTube, could you check? Anyways, to answer your question about being gay, well ... seriously, Drew, come on! I can't believe how ignorant you sound in your email, and I'm hoping this trip will teach you a few things about life and about other people who are different than you are. Just because another man kisses you, doesn't mean you are gay. I'm sorry that happened to you, but you need to realize that maybe he thought you were. People make mistakes. I think you just need to chalk it up to another crazy night and move on, go get something to eat. It's really not that big of a deal, I promise you are going to be okay!
> Hope things start to look up for you from here on out though. Oh, I have recently moved in with my Grandma Opal, remember her? She's actually really amazing, I'm so thankful I've had the chance to get to know her. Anyways, good luck on the rest of your freeing vacation.
> Lucy

Logging out of her email, Lucy shook her head. Drew could be amazingly smart, but he could be so dumb, too! He was definitely one of those people who had no street smarts, but he could kick your booty on anything academic. She really couldn't remember now what she had ever seen in him before.

It was like she was a totally different person today than she was only a few short months ago. She wasn't sure how she felt about that. Was it normal or okay for a person to change so much that they could barely recognize who they used to be? All she knew was, normal or not, she was starting to really like the person she was now because she was beginning to feel more and more like herself.

Deciding she needed to find something to eat, she made her way to the kitchen and was happy to see Opal, laughing at something Lila had just said. Opal looked over as Lucy entered the room, and her eyes light up.

"Lucy! How was your day? Mastered that coffee bar yet?" Opal inquired.

"Sorry to let you down, Opal, but word on the street is that I really, totally suck at it, and they fired me," Lucy confided, plopping down beside Opal at the bar.

The look on Opal's face went from surprise to anger in a millisecond. "What? How dare they fire you! I have half a mind to go down there and tell them just what they are missing! What were they thinking?" she growled, then slammed down her drink, and was about to head towards the door when Lucy grabbed her arm.

Trying not to smile at Opal's reaction, Lucy simply stated the truth, "Oh, I think they know exactly what they are missing Opal, and it's a good thing, too. They were probably thinking they should do the right thing for their customers. It's never good when you go in to grab a quick pick-me-up, and leave with a third degree burn because the bar girl can't control the extra hot milk she's trying to steam for you."

Opal gave Lucy an odd look and stated, "I'm confused."

Lucy looked at Lila, who was trying to cover a laugh, and continued, "It's okay, go ahead and laugh. Yeah, I totally burned a guy today, Opal. Oh, and I couldn't for the life of me operate that darn cash register, either. I almost got whiplash yesterday from watching Teddy, the guy whom I was working with, run back and forth from the bar to the register because I was having … difficulties."

Clearing her throat, Opal offered, "Well … well they hardly gave you a chance! I'm sure in a few days … maybe weeks, a month—you'd have it down."

Lucy had to laugh. Opal was really trying to make her feel better. "Thanks Opal, but nope, I honest to goodness sucked. I think I got the better end of the stick with that deal, though."

Opal raised her eyebrows as Lucy continued, "You see, I made a good friend, Teddy, who is really great. He's like this master genius coffee maker. The best part, though, is that I have a date!" Lucy shared, biting her lip and waiting for their reaction.

"What?" Opal and Lila both screeched at the same time.

"Yes! Hot Guy totally asked me out, and we're going to dinner Friday night!" Lucy exclaimed.

"Hot Guy? Oh! Hot Guy!" Opal exclaimed, remembering Lucy's

story of how she had bumped into him in her pajamas.

"So does he have a name?" Opal asked.

"Jax," Lucy reported, adding, "Isn't that like the most perfect name, too?" Lucy smiled dreamily at the two of them.

Lila shook her head, noting, "Uh-oh, sweetie, looks like you've got it bad." Turning, she started to put some stuffed chicken breasts on plates, along with green beans and potatoes.

"Well, I think it's great. You need to get out there and start meeting other people. I never thought Drew was right for you anyway, he was too, what's the word ..."

Sighing, Opal looked at Lucy and divulged, "Sorry, dear, but I just have to say it. He was always so selfish, always thinking about himself when he should have been paying more attention to you. I think your mother told me you had to schedule him weekly pedicure appointments?" Opal inquired.

Lila spun around to face Lucy, and looking distraught, she exclaimed, "He should have been making you pedicure appointments and pampering you!"

"So true, girls, but the sad fact is that never happened. I was just wondering what I ever saw in him to begin with, but then I realized I am a different person now than I was then."

Looking at Opal, then Lila, she asked, "Do you think that's a bad thing? That I feel like I have changed so much?"

Rubbing Lucy's back, Opal assured, "Everyone changes, Lucy. That's how life is, and isn't that the point? Every experience you go through, good or bad, forces you to grow a little bit. Especially the bad experiences, I'll admit. Those seem to show you who you really are. The more you go through, the more interesting and beautiful your life is." Opal smiled at Lucy and continued, "Think about someone who has never had any big challenges, someone who hasn't had to overcome anything. Yes, their life might look easy and great from the outside, but it's not. That person hasn't had near the experiences compared to someone who has had to struggle and learn and grow."

"I agree," Lila said, nodding and placing a glass of wine in front of Lucy, "When you go through hard times, you do change. Those hard times make you change, but most of the change is good. You stop taking things for granted, you start to appreciate people or things or ways of life like you didn't before. Going through that and changing helps you understand who you are and what you want, what you like and don't like."

Opal nodded, grabbing Lucy's hand, and stated, "If there is one thing I can tell you, it would be—please don't ever let anyone define who you are, don't let anyone else steal your sparkle. There is a saying I love, by Francis Bacon, and it goes, 'There is no excellent beauty that hath not some strangeness in the proportion.' Perfection isn't beauty, Lucy, it's the differences that make us who we are, that make us beautiful. If someone can't see that, if they tell you you're not whatever, it's not you that's lacking, Lucy, it's them."

Opal squeezed Lucy's hand, continuing, "I mean that, Lucy, I've been through a lot in my life. That is something I've learned, being different, being who *you* are is the most beautiful thing there is, and you'll never be truly happy until you accept that and yourself."

Feeling so thankful that she could blurt out whatever her insecurities were and feel so enveloped in love and understanding, Lucy hugged Opal and then got up and ran around the bar and hugged Lila, saying to them both, "Thank you. Thank you for understanding me. That is just what I needed."

Taking a breath to calm her emotions, Lucy confessed, "I'm starving. Looking at that chicken breast stuffed with goodness, I think I'll pass out if I have to wait any longer!"

Laughing, Lila pushed Lucy's plate towards her as Lucy sat back down and urged, "By all means, Lucy, eat!"

CHAPTER SEVEN

After dinner, Lucy called Summer to fill her in on all the details of her day. As expected, Summer totally freaked when Lucy told her that Hot Guy (she should probably start calling him by his real name) had asked her out on a date. They spent the next twenty minutes talking about what Lucy would wear, and Summer was insisting on Lucy asking Tia to do her hair and makeup. Just so she could get off the phone and go to sleep, Lucy agreed to ask Tia. Feeling satisfied, Summer finally said good-bye. She supposedly had a hot date with her own hot guy, and she was itching to get out the door.

The next morning, after taking her leisurely time in her shower, Lucy got dressed and wandered out into the kitchen. She loved Opal's kitchen. It was open to the living room and bright with natural light. Lila, with her short brown hair and ready smile, always seemed to be whipping up some magic whenever Lucy passed by. This morning it was blueberry pancakes.

"I've just died and gone to heaven," Lucy remarked to Lila, as she pulled out the bar stool and sat down, breathing in the delicious smells.

Looking at the thick pancakes stacked on a plate in the center of the bar, along with fresh blueberries, strawberries, raspberries, and sliced bananas made Lucy's mouth water. There were also pitchers of what looked to be fresh-squeezed orange juice and lemonade, and a steaming pot of coffee on the counter.

"I could wake up to this every day. Thank you so much, Lila," Lucy said, eyes wide.

Lila placed a plate and some silverware in front of Lucy and smiled, telling her, "Sure thing, Lucy. I like doing it. It's one of my favorite things to do. Would you like some coffee?"

"Do you even need to ask?" Lucy responded, grinning as she reached for a pancake.

At that, Lila grabbed a mug, poured in some coffee, and handed it to Lucy, along with some cream and sugar, inquiring, "So what are you up to today?"

Lucy took a heaping bite of pancakes and rolled her eyes. After her first bite, she uttered, "These are the best. I think I'll probably go to Grinder this morning. I got a text from Teddy. He said he wanted to show me something. After that … probably sit around and worry about what I'm going to wear tomorrow night."

Setting down her bowl of oatmeal and raspberries and taking a seat next to Lucy, Lila suggested, "You could always ask Tia to help. She is amazing when it comes to that type of thing. That's what I do when I'm worried about how I'll look or when I want a second opinion. When Bowden first asked me to dinner, well, I was a nervous wreck. But after Tia was done with me, not so much."

Lucy stopped mid-chew, syrup dripping down her chin. As she slowly wiped it away, she questioned, "Bowden? You and Bowden are a—couple?"

Pressing her lips together to hide her smile, Lila replied, "Don't be so surprised, Lucy, us old folks like to have fun, too!"

Lucy squeezed her eyes shut. She'd just gotten a mental picture that she really didn't want to have. Taking a gulp of coffee, Lucy continued, "No, it's not that … but thanks for the image now burned into my brain. It's just that I never, well, I had no idea you two were together. I guess I never thought of it."

Nodding, Lila explained, "Well, we've been together for almost ten years now. It was interesting at first, working together, seeing each other during the day, not sure how to act towards each other when anyone else was in the room. Of course, we were worried about what Opal would think, but, you know her, she was overjoyed at the idea."

As if on cue, Bowden walked in and kissed Lila on the head, "You've done it again, Lila, made the most delicious breakfast. How you do it every day, I don't know, but I love it, even if you are making me fat." He smiled down at Lila and then over at Lucy, adding, "So, Lucy … I heard about … yesterday. Don't let it get you down, sweetie, you'll find your way." He ruffled her hair like she was a six-year-old as he walked by.

Finding the gesture endearing, Lucy smiled and replied, "Ha-ha. Thanks, Bowden, no worries, though. I tried, but it just wasn't my thing, so on to the next, I guess, whatever that'll be. I guess I have time today to figure that out."

Standing up, she brought her plate and mug to the sink. How she managed to get her fingers all sticky every time she ate something with syrup she had no idea. Washing her hands off, she turned her head to Bowden and asked, "Have you seen Opal today? I was hoping we could spend some time together before I go out tonight."

Frowning, he shot Lila a quick glance and then explained, "I'm afraid she's not feeling the best this morning, Lucy. Maybe later on she'll perk up, though." Looking like he wasn't sure what else he should say, he rubbed the back of his neck and stated, "I don't know how much she's told you Lucy, about what's going on ..."

Feeling her stomach drop with worry, Lucy braced herself against the counter. "Not much, Bowden, practically nothing. I'd like to know more but ... it's her choice to tell me. I just want her to feel like she wants me to know, I guess," she explained.

Looking back and forth between Bowden and Lila, Lucy felt her stomach knot. She had a feeling things were worse than she had been led to believe.

Sitting down beside Lila, Bowden took his time answering, almost like there was a battle going on inside of him that no one else could hear. Finally, he told her, "I promised myself I wouldn't get involved, but ... you need to know. It's bad, Lucy, it's real bad."

Feeling as though her legs were going to give out on her, Lucy slowly sat down opposite Bowden, asking, "How bad is bad, Bowden? I know next to nothing about cancer."

Rubbing his forehead, he took a deep breath and then revealed, "She has stage four lung cancer, Lucy. That's the worst it can be. She's been through chemo, well, is going through chemo, but this is her last round, and the doctors ... well, they're not exactly hopeful that she'll recover."

Drawing in a breath, Lucy shook her head, inquiring, "What? Why didn't she say something to me? I ... How long—do you know how long she has?"

Lila reached across the bar and took Lucy's hand as Bowden answered, "They aren't sure, Lucy. Not long, especially if this round of chemo doesn't show any improvements. I think ... it's probably best if we expect ... if we expect that things aren't going to work out ..."

Seeing Bowden struggle, Lila quietly chimed in, "I know, that sounds horrible, right? Almost like giving up, but ... it's not, *we're* not. We'd never give up on her, but you can't deny that her... leaving us is a possibility. It's important to know what you are faced with, to have all the information, so you are ready if or when something happens."

Trying to hold it together, for the moment anyway, Lucy swallowed a few times and then said, "No, I don't think you are giving up on her, I know you're not. I agree that you can't deny what might happen, what very possibly is going to happen ... I just ... I really wanted more time with her, I just don't want to lose her so soon after we finally found each other." Staring down at the granite countertop, Lucy steadied herself, deciding, "I'm just going to have to make sure all our time together is perfect ... I might not have control over the quantity, but one thing I can control is the quality."

Lila stood up and walked over to where Lucy was sitting. She pulled Lucy up to her feet and told her, "I'm so sorry this is happening, Lucy, for you and for all of us, and mostly for Opal. She loves you so much. No matter how much time she has left, just your being here is making it quality for her. I want you to know, whatever happens, that we are here for you. Although we are still getting to know each other, you're family to us too, don't ever forget that."

Lucy was about to give Lila a hug and thank her for her kind words when Opal walked into the kitchen. Looking at each of them, she declared, "Well, hell, you told her, didn't you?"

When no one said anything in response to Opal's question, she sighed and said to Lucy, "Come here, girl. We need to have a chat." Then she slowly walked out to the balcony and sat down, waiting for Lucy to follow.

Lucy looked from Lila to Bowden and said in a whisper, "Nice work, you two. Now I don't know who's in more trouble, you two or me."

Her smile lightened the mood a little as she walked out to meet Opal and to hear what she already knew.

"Sit," Opal commanded when Lucy stepped outside into the sun and beautifully fresh air. Lucy sat down, folded her legs under her, and looked to Opal.

"There's no easy way to say it, Lucy, and I really don't like talking about it anyway because what can talking solve? It can't stop what's happening from happening. I'm in my last round of chemo, but it's not working—I know it, the doctors know it, and Bowden and Lila know it. Damn doctor had the nerve to tell me I could go on hospice if I wanted. Hell if I will, I'm not giving up yet," Opal confided with a sigh and then sat back to take in the beauty around her. She was going to miss it here.

"So it's true, that you're … you're dying?" asked Lucy, barely able to look at Opal. It hurt too much to think about the pain Opal was going through and that she had tried to keep in inside, so no one else would have to bear that burden.

"Yes … it's true," Opal affirmed, almost defiantly, lifting her chin.

"Does it … does it hurt?" Lucy asked quietly while looking out towards the Mississippi River. It was easier to breathe that way, not looking directly at Opal, at what she would be losing.

"No … well, not all the time. I have medicine. I take it when I remember and that helps with … it helps," Opal answered.

"Are you scared?" Lucy asked Opal, as she started to softly cry.

Opal was quiet for a long time, taking slow, steady breaths, looking out over the city that had been her home for years. She saw the river and all the buildings, the way the sun shone down on everything around her. It was so breathtaking, even the simplest things—how could anyone not find beauty in it?

Opal wished she had spent more time simply *being*, just like this, just breathing, taking things in, taking life in. How different would her life have been if she hadn't worried as much? If she had let the insignificant things go and just enjoyed the little things, the little moments that can so quickly pass you by. Taking one long, lasting breath, she stated, "Sometimes I wonder why it's at the end of our lives that we see things so clearly. Why not earlier when we can use it to our benefit? Of course, I'm scared, Lucy, but ... when I think about it, honestly think about it, I feel ... at peace. I guess I'm more scared of the process than actually being gone from this world."

Leaning forward, her elbows on her knees, Lucy just nodded.

Opal, sensing Lucy needed more time to absorb everything, assured her, "It's going to be okay, Lucy, I promise. I'm never really going to leave you. You know that, right? When I'm gone, I'm not really going to be ... gone. I'll be all around here, in your memories of me, of us."

Thinking about what she had said, Opal looked at Lucy, her beautiful eyes full of heartache, and wanted to make it better, wanted to see those eyes sparkle again, so she added, "You do know I'm going to be even more of a pain dead than alive, don't you?"

A small smile played across Lucy's face as she inquired, "Oh really, and how's that?"

"I'm going to be keeping my eye on you. If you do something I don't like, you're gonna hear about it, from me—one way or another I'll get through to you!" Opal told Lucy, figuring, somehow, she would make sure Lucy would be okay.

"Promise?" Lucy asked.

Noting Lucy was getting her glow back, Opal nodded, affirming, "That's a promise, Lucy. And one that I'm betting you're going to regret from time to time. Now, shake a leg." Opal stood up and was motioning for Lucy to do the same, adding, "I need to rest, and I don't need you running around the place waking me up. Well, I give you permission to wake me up before your date with Jax tomorrow if I'm not up when you leave, so I can see how pretty you look. Until then, get out and do something fun, if not for you, then for me!"

Lucy watched Opal walking slowly back inside and sitting down at her grand kitchen table. She looked so small sitting there by herself, the table that could easily seat twenty, dwarfing her. Walking over to where Opal sat, Lucy leaned down and gave Opal a gentle hug, then she whispered quietly, "Love you, Opal," and then she stood up to leave.

* * * * *

Lucy opened the door to Grinder and smiled. Even though her morning had been emotional and a little draining, seeing Teddy's grin as she walked in lightened her mood and was just what she needed.

"Lucy! Hey, girl, I'm glad you're here. I have something for you that I'm hoping you are going to love," Teddy called out in greeting. Holding some plates and mugs that he had cleared from some nearby tables, he nodded his head toward the bar as he went to set down the dishes to be washed.

Lucy walked towards the espresso machine, glaring at the bane of her existence, and leaned against the counter, waiting for Teddy. He came back and immediately started making a drink, adding a little of this and a little of that at top speed. When he had finished, he topped the drink off with a little whipped cream and handed it to Lucy with a flourish. "For you," he said, "I call it the 'Lucky Lucy.'"

Lucy looked at Teddy in surprise. "You named a drink after me?" she squeaked.

Shrugging, like it was no big deal, he responded, "Yeah, girl. Try it, tell me what you think."

Lucy closed her eyes and took a sip. What she tasted was amazing, probably the best coffee drink she'd ever had. It was a little sweet, but there was also some spice too, something that gave the drink just a little kick.

"Okay, wow, I'm not just saying this because it's my drink, but this really is awesome! What's in here?"

Grinning widely, Teddy told her, "So last night, after I sadly fired you, I wanted to do something to make up for it. I felt bad, even if you did suck at the job. Plus, you're super cool, so I decided I'd make a drink for you, so you could be eternally remembered at Grinder. I wanted to make the drink a little bit like you, so even though it's called the *Lucky* Lucy, and we know you haven't been so lucky here, that something about it would be similar. Thinking about your personality a bit, I decided that you are sweet—but you have a little hidden spice in there that comes out and surprises people. So I messed around with drinks a little and came up with that." He pointed at her drink and then continued, "It has chocolate, obviously, but then I added some crushed cayenne pepper to add the spice ... I have to say, I think it represents you perfectly."

Lucy took another drink and nodded, declaring, "Thank you so much, Teddy! This is awesome. I actually have a drink named after me!" Lucy started dancing around Teddy, chanting "Lucky Lucy, Lucky Lucy! I am feeling lucky, lucky, lucky today!"

As she was doing her final spin around, she lost her balance and almost fell on her face, that is, until someone caught her at the last minute. Looking at the hand on her arm, she felt her face redden. She knew that hand, and she knew it wasn't Teddy's.

"Careful, sweetheart, don't want you bumping into the customers again, do we?" he asked, looking down at her with a grin on his face.

"Hello, Jax," Lucy said, looking up at him. Why did all the embarrassing things happen when he was around? Trying to recover, she quickly held out her drink and announced, "Guess what Teddy did last night? He made a new drink."

"Oh really?" Jax asked, eyes on Lucy, causing her to bite her lip and look away. He stepped closer to her and took the drink out of her hand, taking a sip. "Wow," he said, eyes wide as he handed Lucy her drink back, "that's great, Teddy, a lot better than Gut Rot, I have to say. I'd love one of my own. What's it called?"

He was standing incredibly close to Lucy, causing her heart to flutter. She tried to breathe normally, but it was hard. She was surprised at her reaction to him. Ever since Drew had dumped her on her butt, no one had made her feel close to how Drew had made her feel during their brief good times, and all Jax was doing was standing there.

She really hadn't had many opportunities to try to see if anyone would make her feel that special way. She really hadn't been interested in anyone. There was a time where she hadn't even wanted to think about being near another man. She had just wanted to get through each day and figure out what had gone wrong between her and Drew.

Now though, with Jax standing so close and possibly interested in her—he *had* asked her out—she thought she'd like the opportunity, with him. So the idea of being around another guy was … welcoming.

Despite her best intentions of staying away from the opposite sex, Lucy was beginning to feel herself opening up to the possibility that she might find someone who could make her feel amazing, someone who would love her for her, someone who would let her shine.

Teddy's voice brought her back to the present when he answered, "Ah … it's called the Lucky Lucy."

Hearing Teddy's newly coined drink's name made Jax roar with laughter, "It's perfect, perfect!"

Turning to Lucy, he grabbed her hand, spun her around, and asked, "How does it feel to have a drink named after you, lucky Lucy? I've been coming in here for years and haven't had that honor yet. I guess you really are lucky."

Smirking at Jax, she replied, "Well, there's a first time for everything, I guess."

Giving her a smoldering look, Jax answered quietly "True, very true."

He continued to stare at her until Teddy yelled out loudly, "Lucky

Lucy!"

Jax then turned and walked over to where Teddy had placed his drink, grabbed it, did his funny salute, and walked back to Lucy. "What time works for you tomorrow night? Oh, and you need to give me your address, so I can pick you up."

Still a little breathless, Lucy answered, "Um, any time after six works." She walked to the window and pointed down the street toward the building she lived in. "See that building down there? That's my place, so it should be pretty easy to find."

"Wow, high class! All right, I'll be by tomorrow to pick you up at seven. See you then, Lucy." He smiled and walked away whistling.

Sighing as she watched him walk away, Lucy sat down at a table by the bar where Teddy was refilling coffee beans and stacking up the cups. "So, who's going to be here to help you during the craziness? You fired your star employee yesterday, so you're totally out of luck, unless you hired someone else already?" Lucy asked with a pout, making him laugh.

"Nah, girl. Your bestie is coming in. He'll be here in a few," explained Teddy as he finished replenishing supplies and was wiping down the counter.

"My bestie? And that would be?" Lucy asked, a crease forming in her forehead.

"Cash, of course!" Teddy replied, nodding at the door.

Lucy looked over to see Cash walking towards Grinder. He didn't look too happy. In fact, he looked pretty pissed off. "Wow, he looks ..."

Lucy wasn't able to finish her sentence before Cash stomped in, glaring at Lucy. "What are you doing here? Don't tell me you've come to ask for your job back because I'm not going to be so nice this time around. I don't do well with employees who can't operate a simple machine and end up hurting the costumers. You are a lawsuit waiting to happen, my friend."

Tensing in her chair, Lucy thought about making a run for it but decided against it. If she was going to come in and visit Teddy while he was working, she should probably get used to Cash. Teddy even had said he was pretty cool once you get to know him, so maybe ... she should try.

"Hi, Cash. Uh, no actually, I just came by to see Teddy. I'm sorry about what happened yesterday, and I know I am totally worthless when it comes to working here. I'm hoping to find something else that I'm a little ... better at," she told him with a smile. Well, she tried to smile, but it felt more like a grimace.

"Huh, okay then. Well, as long as you promise to be good, I'm fine with it," Cash offered in response. He turned to walk back behind the counter, stopped, and turned back to Lucy, sharing, "Actually, my brother is looking to hire someone. He has this office supply store and needs someone part-time. The job he is hiring for is pretty foolproof, and the pay is good." He took out his phone and started typing something.

Eyebrows lowered, Lucy looked at Cash, "What kind of job is it, exactly? Because I am totally not doing the whole cleaning toilets thing ... I mean I've tried that before, and well ... yeah, not a good idea."

Lowering his phone, Cash explained, "Then lucky for you, that's not the job he's looking to fill. His office supply store logo is this funny-looking computer with legs. He's been wanting to get the word out about his place, and he's looking for someone to dress up in a costume as 'Zippy Computer' and stand outside on the corner waving to people."

Lucy heard Teddy laughing behind the bar, and she shot him a look before replying to Cash, "So all I need to do is put on the costume and wave at people? Does this costume cover my face?"

It wasn't the ideal job, but it was something. Lucy was willing to give it a try if she could be incognito. Maybe it would lead to her working in the actual office supply store, which would be okay until she found something more permanent.

Looking at his phone again, Cash laughed and told her, "Yeah, it's like this fuzzy computer. No one would be able to tell it was you."

Lifting up his phone, he called out, "Say cheese!" and snapped a quick picture of Lucy.

Trying to duck out of the way, but failing, Lucy declared, "Hey, what the heck, Cash? What are you doing? Haven't you heard of, well, I don't know, asking a girl for her picture first?"

Glaring at him, she proposed, "If no one can see my face, then I'm in, but only if you delete that picture."

Strutting back behind the counter while texting, Cash explained, "Sorry Lucy. My brother just wanted to see who was applying for the job. He's weird like that, something about not hiring psychos. I don't know. Anyways, good because you're hired. You start on Saturday, at eight in the morning. Think you can handle that, champ?" He looked at her with eyebrows raised. Then he fake coughed to cover up his laugh.

Standing up and stretching, Lucy looked thoughtfully at Cash, "Interesting that he can tell by a picture if someone is a psycho or not. I'm glad I passed the test." Picking up her cup, she took one last sip and threw it in the trash, then turned to leave, "See you, Teddy. Oh, and thanks for the job, Cash."

Lifting his hand in a small wave, Teddy smiled, saying, "Have fun tomorrow, Lucy."

Cash, squinting at Lucy said, "Yeah, you're welcome. Just don't mess it up. If that keeps happening, you're going to have to find some other chump to line up all these awesome gigs."

As Lucy started her retreat, she heard Teddy laugh out loud at Cash's comment. Quietly to herself she muttered, "I can't believe he isn't even polite enough to pretend to be coughing!"

Lucy just shook her head, opened the door, and walked out into the sunshine. Walking past street venders, restaurants, and other pedestrians, Lucy felt good. She was leaving Grinder in a better mood than when she had arrived there this morning. She had a new job already lined up for next week, and all she had to do to get it was agree to try it. And the following day a smoking hot guy would be picking her up for their date.

Life, well *this* part of her life, was pretty awesome right now—at least at this minute. Lucy knew that with all the tough times ahead with Opal, she needed to find the bright side of life. Right now, looking around and appreciating the beauty that surrounded her, being able to spend time with Opal, her luck at finding a good friend so soon after moving here, and meeting someone she was willing to open up to were the bright things.

She hoped that whatever happened with Opal, however much time they had left together, that she would always remember to be thankful for what she had. Because doing that gave her hope, hope that things *would* be okay, no matter what life threw her way.

* * * * *

When Lucy got home, Opal was still sleeping, so she decided to check her email. Again.

When her email loaded up, Lucy shook her head and groaned when she discovered another one from Drew. This time the subject line was in all bold, and it definitely sounded more like him.

Subject: COME HOME IMMEDIATELY!!!
Lucy—WHAT ARE YOU THINKING? YOU CAN ABSOLUTELY, POSITIVELY, NOT STAY WITH YOUR GRANDMA OPAL!!! I AM ABANDONING THE EXCURSION AND COMING TO TAKE YOU HOME RIGHT AWAY. PACK YOUR THINGS, I WILL BE THERE WITHIN THE WEEK. LISEN TO REASON AND PLEASE DO WHAT I ASK!!!
Now, that that has been taken care of,

Lucy, and you better listen, I can tell you what has been going on with me. We have been traveling around Mexico, and it has been horrendous. I have no idea why I agreed to have Corbin arrange this part of our trip, but I will think better of it next time.

You will never believe how we got here, Lucy! You see, none of us had our passports ... Yes, it was a slight misstep on all of our parts, seeing as we were supposed to be world traveling, but Corbin thought of a way to get us through the border from the US to Mexico. He told us he knew someone famous in Mexico, someone with super celeb credibility! You know me, Lucy, famous people, celebs, the most wealthy, are my kind of people ... I just connect with them because we are on the same frequency.

So we all agreed that, yes, he should contact this person to help us get to Mexico. I was very excited to lie on the beach in Cancun and look at all the sights. Well, one night he comes blaring in at around 3 in the morning, yelling for us to get up! It's time to go to Mexico! He has found us a way to get there, but we need to GO NOW! So we pack up our things and go. I, of course, am expecting a private plane or Lear jet, but NO! There was only an old, junky El Camino parked out front.

I asked Corbin, what's going on? What is this? He said it was our ride to Mexico, and that we had to get in back. I tried to resist, but NO! I was tossed in the back with everyone else and told to lie as flat and as still as possible, as to not "upset" the "supply" beneath us. Then we were all covered up with an old, stinky blanket and a bunch of stuff that the driver uses to make churros!

I was NOT HAPPY, Lucy! Not at all! I asked him why his famous friend hadn't helped us, but he said he had! He said the guy driving worked for his friend. I was a little suspicious, so then I asked, who was his famous friend? What did his famous friend do? Lucy, you will never believe what he told me! He told me his famous friend is a DRUG LORD! The biggest one in Mexico! That we were helping him bring bails and bails of cash across the border in exchange for him getting us in! When I asked what the cash was for, he looked at me like I was crazy, telling me it was obviously for drugs that he had sold in the US! We were helping to transport DRUG MONEY!

I think I might have had a little accident in my pants then Lucy—but I can't recall, I must have blacked out—because then Corbin was yelling at me, saying we'd be "dead meat" if we got the "supply" dirty. I cried the entire way there, and Corbin had to hold his hand over my mouth when we drove past the border, so they wouldn't know there were people in the back of the car.

It was horrible, Lucy! It still is! Needless to say, we got past the border and are now in a small house/shack in some town whose name I can't pronounce, and we are not even by the water!

I woke up today, Lucy, and I saw Corbin's "famous friend" with my SILVERWARE! You know how I bring my own silverware whenever I go anyplace, because I don't trust anyone else's ... but you know mine is REAL SILVER! Well, this "famous friend" was MELTING MY SILVERWARE DOWN! When I told him to stop immediately or else! He just laughed and said it was my payment to him for the nice ride! How am I going to eat now, Lucy???

I don't know how, but I will be there in a weeks' time. Be packed and ready to go home and get back into the swing of our normal life. DREW.

Lucy had to read the email a few times through to really understand what he had said. He had been stuck in the back of a car that was transporting drug money? Despite Drew being a jerk, she was beginning to get a little worried about him. Of course, he was still being his normal controlling, bossy self, and she wasn't too worried about him actually showing up. She wasn't sure how he was going to get back into the US without a passport … not that she wanted him to. But still, she didn't really want him getting into trouble either. She wondered how he was getting access to a computer to email her. Shrugging her shoulders, she typed out a response.

> Drew—Wow … well, I don't even know what to say! I hope you are okay, but you are a grown man and can make decisions for yourself. That is really too bad about your silverware. I guess now you will have to eat like the rest of us, with whatever utensils are available! You'll be fine.
>
> As for your coming to get me … forget it! I love it here and am having a great time getting to know Opal. In case you have forgotten, you asked me for a divorce, so you could be free and explore … and it seems that is exactly what you have been doing! To be honest, I actually appreciate you doing what you did, even though at the moment I was so angry and hurt that I couldn't see that it was the best thing for me.
>
> I hope you are able to enjoy Mexico, even for a little bit, and if you are ever to get back to the US, do not, I REPEAT, DO NOT try to find me. We are over and done, and I am moving on with my life.
>
> Lucy
>
> PS—If you really do need help, let me know. I think my mom knows someone.

Shutting down her computer, Lucy rubbed her eyes and sighed. She hoped she hadn't been too harsh with her reply to Drew, but it was true. He was a grown man, and he made his own decisions. She would help him if he really needed it, of course. She was pretty sure her mom had dated someone who worked border patrol or something like that. In any case, it really wasn't her problem … Plus, she had a date to think about!

Climbing into her cozy bed, Lucy leaned back against her pillows and pulled out her cell. She was going on her first date since Drew, and she needed Summer and needed her now.

* * * * *

After getting dating advice from Summer and catching up with her mom, Lucy headed down the hall and into the huge, open family room. She was hoping to find Opal and see how her day had been.

It was quiet in the apartment, and Lucy was about to step out onto the balcony to enjoy the early evening sunshine when she spotted a note on the island. It was written in Lila's loopy cursive, telling her they had taken Opal in for an appointment and would be back later on that night.

Hoping everything was okay, Lucy grabbed a bottled water from the fridge. She also spotted some chicken salad sandwiches wrapped up in plastic wrap, so she grabbed the one with her name on it, deciding to enjoy her light supper outside on the balcony.

It was a beautiful summer evening, the kind you dream of in the middle of winter when you are stuck in the house, not wanting to venture outside for fear of instant frostbite.

Lucy ate her supper slowly, enjoying watching people walk or ride or skate by on the street below—their voices floating up to where she sat, snippets of conversations making her laugh or smile.

As she watched the setting sun turn the sky a vivid pink, she thought of how her life had changed in such a short period of time. Looking back just a few months ago, she never would have thought she'd be where she was. She wondered what the future would bring, what would happen with Opal. She knew she had to be realistic and face the fact that Opal might not make it. When that time came, if it came, she knew she'd find sorrow, but she hoped she'd be able to find a little bit of happiness too.

When Lucy finally went back inside the apartment, it was still quiet and dark. She decided to head to her room, snuggle into her bed, and binge watch *Revenge* on Netflix until she was too tired to keep her eyes open.

CHAPTER EIGHT

Looking in the mirror and admiring Tia's handiwork, Lucy had to admit she looked pretty good. Lila was right—having Tia do her hair and makeup had calmed her nerves a little bit. At least she knew she looked decent. Tia was amazing at what she did and seemed like someone who would never let Lucy leave the house if she wasn't satisfied.

Tia had chosen a pair of red skinny jeans with a white t-shirt and a black leather jacket over it. And, of course, she had picked out the highest heels—in black. And Lucy, wobbling a little in them now, was hoping she wouldn't have to walk too far. She loved the outfit, though. It was something she wouldn't have chosen for herself, and she was excited to try out something new tonight.

Then Tia had taken and twisted Lucy's long dark locks around a flat iron and surprised Lucy by making the prettiest curls. She had then taken a section of hair from the right side of her head and added a kind of messy side braid that fit right in with the messy curls.

After making sure the braid was secure, she started in on Lucy's makeup. Lucy liked this part the best, watching the magic Tia could work. She had lined Lucy's eyes with a thick black eyeliner, all the while smudging away, and then added a little shimmery eye shadow and mascara. The result was the perfect smoky eye, the kind Lucy had tried for hours to create on herself, but could never get it right. Yeah, that kind. Then she added a few coats of mascara, some tinted lip gloss, and some more shimmer to Lucy's cheeks and brow bones, making Lucy look fresh and glowing.

The end product was something Lucy only wished she could recreate every morning, or whenever she wanted to look like a million bucks. Twirling in the mirror one more time to check herself out, she smiled. She did look amazing. Grabbing her black studded clutch off the bed, Lucy took one last glimpse at herself and headed to see Opal.

Walking down the hall to Opal's room, Lucy pretended she was walking the runway. She liked the way she was able to strut Summer-style in her heels. It made her smile, thinking about her best friend. Lucy knocked on Opal's door, and she slowly opened it when she heard Opal's voice.

"Come in, Lucy," Opal called out, sitting up in her bed, "Let's see you all dolled up! I've been waiting to see you. Tia said she's done her best work tonight."

Opal smiled and looked Lucy up and down, pushing herself up in bed to get a better look, declaring, "Wow, you look stunning! Your hair and that outfit! If he isn't speechless when he sees you, well, then he's got other things to worry about."

A blushing Lucy twirled for Opal, saying, "Thanks. I'm really thinking Tia needs to do this for me every morning ... or at least teach me some of her tricks! Do you really think he'll think I'm ..."

Lucy looked down at Opal, confessing, "Drew never, he never really told me I was pretty ... He was always telling me how I should be more like this girl or that girl ... It pretty much sucked."

Lucy paused and then continued, "I just wanted him to like me for me."

Not sure why her old issues with Drew were popping up now, she hadn't really thought about them for a long time. It must have been the recent email.

"Drew was an idiot, don't you see that?" Opal stated, grabbing Lucy's hand. "You are beautiful just the way you are, Lucy, even without all the glamour I'm seeing here tonight. It's getting more and more clear to me that he never really saw you. He just took you for granted, and that breaks my heart."

Opal stopped, as if considering whether she had said something out of place. Then she added, "I'm sorry if that's harsh, but there are so many good qualities that you have, and it makes me angry to think that he didn't appreciate them."

Taking a deep breath, Opal slapped her hands down on her bedspread, announcing, "So! Tonight is the night you get to forget all about him. Tonight you go have the best night of your life with this nice young gentleman. And know that when he tells you you're beautiful and funny and all those other things—that he is telling you the truth, Lucy."

Opal smiled, leaning back against the headboard of her bed.

"Thanks, Opal. You're right, you know. Tonight I am going to go and have the best time I can. I'm not going to waste all of Tia's hard work!" Lucy promised and then, turning to grab the doorknob, she looked back at Opal and blew her a kiss. She was about to leave when Opal raised her finger, indicating for Lucy to wait.

Wiggling her eyebrows at Lucy, Opal added, "Oh, and a goodnight kiss never hurt anybody either, make sure to get one of those."

Surprised, Lucy's mouth fell open. "Opal!" she screamed. Then, regaining her composure—she was an adult after all—Lucy slowly closed the door to the faint sound of Opal's chuckling.

* * * * *

Stepping out of the elevator, Lucy waved at Oliver, the doorman.

"Looking good, Lucy!" he called out.

Giving him a quick smile, she walked as fast as she could in her heels toward the door, hoping Jax was out there waiting for her. She was nervous and didn't feel like making small talk.

Stepping outside, she saw Jax leaning back against an expensive-looking black car. He raised his eyebrows at her as she walked up to him and declared, "Damn, girl—looking good! Wow, really, Lucy, you look amazing." He held out his hand to her and pulled her into a hug.

"Thank you," she responded, smiling at him as she pulled away.

He opened the car door for her, which just made her smile more, as she sat down on the sleek black leather seat. Drew had never opened a door for her.

Jax slid into the driver's side seat a moment later and shut the door. Giving her the once over again, he stated, "You really do look great tonight. I'm a lucky guy to be going out to dinner with the likes of you."

She smiled and felt her cheeks heat up. She really wasn't used to compliments like this, but she *could* get used to it, and fast. She looked over at Jax and saw that he was wearing dark jeans and a white t-shirt. His dark hair was spiked up a little in the front, and he was grinning at her with that smile he had that always seemed to make her breathless. He pretty much had the bad boy look going on.

Looking over at him, she offered, "You're not so bad yourself."

Shaking his head, he put his beauty of a car into gear and asked, "So, do you like sushi? There is this great place, not too far away … I thought we could go there. But if you're not a fan, then I know of a few other places we could check out. What do you think?" He looked from her to the road as he drove.

"Sushi is perfect. I haven't had it in forever," Lucy answered, glancing at Jax from the corner of her eye, and biting her lip. He was so cute, was this really happening right now? He was someone she could see with Summer, one of her model guys she would rave about. Lucy wished she could snap a quick picture and text it to Summer. Too bad, she was pretty sure he'd notice if she just whipped out her phone and starting taking pictures, and she was pretty sure he'd turn the car around, drop her off, and drive away never to return again.

Smiling at her thought, she glanced at him again, and this time he caught her eye.

Jax asked, "What're you thinking about? You look like—I don't know—like you have some kind of bad idea … or … " He trailed off.

Before she could catch herself, she answered, "I'm just reminding myself that I need to be good tonight." Slapping her hand over her mouth, she shut her eyes and shook her head.

Trying not to laugh at her reaction, Jax said, "Um … okay."

"Okay, that sounded … weird, but it isn't what it sounded like," she tried to explain, all the while partially opening one eye to gauge his reaction.

Smiling, he said, "Oh, really?" Pulling his gaze from the road, he smirked at her squirming in her seat.

Thoroughly embarrassed, Lucy thought that, of course, this would happen to her when she was with Jax. Didn't something embarrassing always happen when they were together? What did she have to lose in telling him the truth?

Lucy decided to put it out there, be brave, break lose from her typically cautious self.

"Okay," she said, smiling, and continued when he elbowed her, "So, I was just thinking about how … good you look and thinking that I'm a little surprised you asked me out … and thought about what my best friend from back home would say if she saw you."

Lucy's face reddened, and she chanced a look at Jax.

Grinning at her again, he urged, "Go on …"

Rolling her eyes, Lucy continued, "So then I was kind of laughing to myself thinking about how freaked out you'd be if I just broke out my phone and took a picture of you driving. So that's what I mean by 'being good,' as in—no unapproved picture-taking going on tonight, I promise." She smiled over at him as he laughed.

Slowing the car down, he turned into what looked to be a strip mall parking lot. He found a parking space and turned to Lucy, asking, "Ready?"

Looking around, confused, Lucy questioned, "Are we here?" She didn't see any sushi sign. Actually, the whole place looked like it was closed.

"No, we're just going to take a quick picture together, and then we'll get back on the road. Almost there, though," he said with a smile and held out his hand for Lucy's phone.

Her grin slowly spreading across her face, she handed the phone to him, stating, "I can't believe we're doing this … Summer is going to freak. I can't believe you are game."

Leaning over to her, he pulled her as close as he could while sitting in his car, and together they said, "Cheese!" Then he snapped their picture and handed the phone back to Lucy. "How does it look? I hope I look good enough for your friend." He winked at her, and she laughed.

Quickly pushing the "send" button, Lucy put her phone back into her clutch and set her hands in her lap, waiting for Jax to put the car into gear.

When he wasn't moving, Lucy looked over to see him watching her. "What?" she asked, wondering what was going on in his mind.

"You are something else, Lucy. Something else," uttered Jax, smiling and shaking his head.

Wrinkling her nose, she asked hopefully, "Is that a *good* thing?"

Laughing, he replied, "Yes, Lucy, it is definitely a good thing." Then he put his hand on her shoulder, slowly slid it down her arm, and grabbed her hand. Lacing his fingers through hers he asked, "Ready?"

She only nodded. She really couldn't speak at the moment, not when he had just grabbed her hand in the best way. He smiled and put the car into gear, driving them toward their future.

* * * * *

Sitting down at a table by the window, Jax eyed Lucy's phone and finally asked, "Are you sure that thing isn't going to blow? I'm not sure any phone can handle that many texts coming in."

Sitting down and making a face at Jax, Lucy assured, "Don't worry, my phone is used to it. It's just Summer going crazy—that happens when I don't text her back, and she knows something is going on. She can't stand it."

Lucy smiled just thinking about it. Summer was fun to drive crazy. Yes, she loved her like a sister, and loving her like a sister included loving to drive her nuts.

"You look like you're having a little too much fun ignoring her texts," Jax noted, leaning back and looking down at his menu.

Laughing at Summer's insistent texting, Lucy explained, "That's just how it is with Summer. She's fun to mess with, and … she wouldn't pass up an opportunity to do the same to me. It's all in fun, though. She's the best friend I could ever ask for."

Then Lucy quickly shot Summer a text saying she'd call her later, put her phone in her clutch, and picked up her menu. "So, what do you recommend, sir?" she asked.

Smiling up at her, Jax answered, "The California roll is always a good choice, and if you like eel, the unagi roll is good, or … the Alaskan roll is good too. Whatever you're in the mood for, I guess." He shrugged, looking up at her, and smiled.

Placing her menu back on their table, Lucy decided, "I'm going with the good old California roll, my standby and always delicious!"

Jax placed their orders when the server came back. "So," he began, when the server had walked away, "tell me about yourself. What don't I know about you? You said you just moved here, right?"

Lucy smiled at him and began her story, of her visits to Opal's house when she was younger and how they had always been at best, awful, and then her surprise at reading Opal's letter.

She was surprised at how easy Jax was to talk to. She felt herself opening up to him in a way she never thought she could with a guy. She didn't hold anything back, telling him how she and her mom had had a heart to heart for probably their first time since she was a little girl and how great it had felt. She told him about Drew—why he had split up with her, what he had said on that fateful day, and the emails that had been coming in ever since. That caused a look of disgust and then a huge belly laugh from Jax. Lucy was beginning to love that laugh.

She told him of Opal and how welcoming and loving she had been since she'd moved here, how happy she was that Opal had asked her to visit. That she was extremely thankful that she was able to spend these last moments with her grandmother, realizing what a special person she was. She even told him how Opal had opened up to her that very morning, talking to Lucy about life and death.

While Lucy was worried it might be too much for him, heavier than he might have wanted to go on a first date, she also didn't want to be her typically overly cautious self. She wanted to be real, and Jax seemed to respond well to her openness. He seemed to understand completely, and he wanted to know more.

The conversation slowly turned to Jax, and he also opened up. Lucy learned that he was one of three boys, that he and his brothers were all extremely close, and they saw each other every Sunday when they had dinner together at their parents' house, the house they had grown up in. He told her about his love for baseball and trying new things—hence his appreciation of Teddy's daily new drink. He told her that he had been engaged before, but never married, that they had been high school sweethearts. Over the years they had changed and grown apart; even though they loved each other, both knew things just weren't going to work out. They had parted as friends, going their own ways.

When Lucy asked him what he did for work, he cleared his throat and said that he and his brothers had started a graphic design company a few years back, and it was finally taking off. It was something they had dreamed of ever since they were little—working together, having their own business—and now they were doing it, and it was going really well.

Lucy was impressed, but also curious because for some reason he seemed to be downplaying things. She found out why a few minutes later when Jax excused himself to the men's room. She quickly googled the name of his company and found several articles about it being the "next big thing" in graphic design. It was projected to be included as one of the Fortune 500 companies within the next two years. Lucy laughed to herself, thinking that "finally taking off" was definitely an understatement.

Lucy was surprised at how great the night had been going. There were no awkward pauses in conversation. Nothing that he had said had worried her, and he hadn't seemed weirded out by anything she shared, either. She hoped that was the case, anyway! She was having an amazing time and really wanted this date to lead to another. She sighed as she thought about spending more time with him and smiled.

Clearing his throat as he sat back down, Jax queried, "What's going on in that head of yours, Lucy? You sometimes get this faraway look, and it makes me so curious to know what it is you're thinking of."

Blushing a little (he always caught her off guard), she admitted, "I was thinking about how much fun I'm having … and I hope we can do it again." She looked up at him and bit her lip; she wished she knew what *he* was thinking.

Studying her for a second, he responded, "I'd love to do this again, too."

Smiling at him, she looked back into his eyes. They were the darkest brown, almost black, and she felt like she could stare into them forever. The longer she did, though, the harder it was to keep her breathing normal, so she finally pulled her eyes away.

Grabbing her hand from across the table, Jax asked, "Ready to go? There's some place I'd like to take you if that's okay?"

Lucy nodded, and Jax quickly paid their bill.

"Thank you," she told him as he pulled her up from the table and led her out to his car.

Smiling and opening her door for her, he replied, "It is my pleasure, Lucy."

When he shut the door, Lucy closed her eyes and tried to make her breathing return to its natural state. She hadn't felt this way about a guy in, well … probably ever. It was never like this with Drew. And before Drew … well, there were guys, but they paled in comparison to Jax.

Sliding into his seat, Jax looked over at her and shook his head.

Wondering what he was thinking, Lucy asked, "What? What's going on in *your* head?"

Jax looked over at her as he put the car in gear and slowly pulled out into traffic, saying, "I'm not sure I should say it." He smiled at her.

"Oh, come on! I've been telling you all the embarrassing things that

I've been thinking. It's your turn now, Jax."

And boldly for her, Lucy grabbed his hand as she looked over at him.

Scrunching his eyebrows together, thinking for a minute, finally he confessed, "Okay, I guess I do owe you a little inside info." He gave her his grin and continued, "It surprised me that you were surprised that I'd ask you out."

Raising her eyebrows, Lucy urged, "Okay, go on." She laughed at using his earlier remark back at him.

"Well, for one—you're gorgeous. I'm sure you never have to look far to find someone who would drop anything to go out with you. And two—wasn't it obvious from the first time I laid eyes on you that I was interested? If not, then I need to work on my game!" he shared with a small smile that made Lucy think he looked the tiniest bit nervous.

"Really, Jax? Do you not remember how we met? Me almost spilling my coffee on you while I was trying to run away from Cash … Oh, and I almost forgot, I was in my *pajamas,* too. I'm really trying to block that incident from my memory, in case you were wondering. The next time I saw you, I couldn't for the life of me make your drink right. So, no, it wasn't obvious to me probably because I spent most of the time you were around feeling extremely embarrassed."

Lucy then stopped talking and took a deep breath. She needed to stop talking.

Halting the car at a red light, Jax looked over at Lucy, took her chin, and turned her to look at him, declaring, "You are so damn cute when you're flustered. I don't know what it is about you, Lucy, but I like it."

He let go of her chin and smiled as he gunned his car, making Lucy scream and grab onto his arm. He drove for a few more minutes, finally pulling into a small parking lot surrounded by trees with a lake glistening in the distance. Opening his door, he looked over at Lucy and said, "Stay there."

He then ran over and opened her door. "Thank you. I didn't want you opening your door. I like to do that for you," he told her, smiling, and gave her his arm.

She linked her arm through his and asked him where they were.

It was cool out, but not too cold, and she was happy that she could have an excuse to snuggle a little closer into him. Looking around, she saw a trail that lead to some worn-looking benches that overlooked the lake. The spot was surrounded by trees, and if you didn't know about it, you would miss it. By the looks of it, that's where they were walking to.

"I love this place. It's kind of a hidden gem around here. Hardly any tourists know about it, so it's mostly just locals. I used to come here whenever I needed a break from life, just to think, you know. There's something about being almost submerged in nature that does something to you, don't you think?" he explained, then sat down on one of the benches, and pulled her down beside him.

Taking a minute to appreciate where they were, Lucy closed her eyes. She could hear the water rushing in and out, back and forth, the traffic a distant enough sound that it was almost calming. She heard Jax's slow, deep breaths and smiled. He was right, there was something about being out here, and she had only been here for a few minutes.

Opening her eyes, she quietly stated, "You're right, it's beautiful here. I can see why it would be the place you'd come to find some peace." Feeling Jax's eyes on her, she turned her head to look at him.

Smiling, he pulled her closer so that they were only inches apart. Then he slowly ran his hand through her hair, pulled her mouth to his, and kissed her softly.

The kiss only lasted for a few seconds, but Lucy was breathless when it was over, her forehead resting against Jax's.

They sat like that for what seemed like forever, until he shifted her over a little and told her, looking into her eyes, "You're pretty perfect, you know that?"

Surprised and taken aback by his comment, Lucy wasn't sure how to respond. Her usual defense in instances like this would be to make a silly joke. She was about to do just that when Jax cut her off.

Shaking his head, like he knew what she was going to do, he murmured, "Sh-h-h, don't … tonight was, well, better than I'd expected, and I want you to know that I mean it, what I said … You never have to doubt what I say, Lucy." He looked at her, eyes serious.

Feeling like the luckiest girl in the world and hoping against hope that he was telling the truth, Lucy smiled, replying "Thank you." Then she touched her lips to his.

Grinning at her, he wrapped his arms around her waist, stood up, and flipped her over his shoulder. "Time to get back, Lucy," he announced over her screams as he started walking up the path to his car.

"Jax!" Lucy screamed, kicking her feet, "Put me down!"

"Nope," he said, laughing, "You can kick and scream all you want, Lucy, but I've got you right where I want you. I'm not letting go now."

He carried her all the way up the path, set her down beside his car, and then opened the door. Grinning at the glare she sent his way, he stated, "Ladies first."

Then he shut the door and walked around to his side of the car.

Watching him slide into his seat, Lucy couldn't help but smile. She definitely felt like the luckiest girl in the universe right now. Teddy just might be on to something, calling her "Lucky Lucy."

Leaning back against the seat, she looked over at Jax and reported, "You know, I could have totally kicked your butt back there, right?" When he simply raised an eyebrow, she added, "Just wanted to let you know, I'm pretty tough, despite my size. I've been told I'm scrappy." She looked at him and raised her chin an inch.

Hearing that made Jax laugh, hard. When he caught his breath, he said, "Yeah, I guess I could see that." Then he laughed again, starting up his car and turning towards home.

Shaking her head, Lucy glanced at the clock, seeing it was a little after eleven, and remarked, "I hope dressing up as a computer and waving to people all day isn't something I need a lot of sleep for."

Jax gave her a confused look, questioning, "What are you talking about?"

Suddenly wishing she hadn't opened her mouth, so Lucy shook her head. She hadn't wanted to tell anyone, especially Jax, about this silly new job. That way even if anyone she knew happened to drive by, they wouldn't know it was her inside the costume.

Quickly glancing at her, Jax ordered, "Let's hear it. This sounds too good for me to just let it go." He reached over and grabbed her hand, insisting, "Spill it."

Looking at their fingers together, feeling his thumb rubbing the side of her hand, Lucy decided she didn't care if she was embarrassed about this new ... adventure. As long as he wouldn't let her hand go, she'd tell him whatever he wanted to know, so she explained, "As you know I'm jobless. Well, I was until Cash got me the job dressing up as 'Zippy Computer' for his brother's new business. All I need to do is stand on the street corner and wave at cars as they pass by. Not too difficult, right?"

Looking over at her, Jax revealed, "I know what I'm doing tomorrow! Driving past the hot girl dressed as a computer!" He flashed her his quick smile.

Putting her head down and covering her eyes with her free hand, Lucy said, "Great, I was trying to keep this on the down low. I didn't want anyone to know it was me!"

After kissing her hand, Jax told her, "You know, Lucy, no one will be able to see you in there, so it really doesn't matter, and the people that do know it's you—they don't care if you're dressed as a computer or burning people with coffee. That stuff doesn't matter. You don't need to be embarrassed." He paused, then chuckled, adding, "but I'm still doing a drive-by tomorrow."

"Gee, thanks," Lucy muttered, rolling her eyes.

She did feel better, though, knowing Jax didn't care that she was dressing up as a silly computer. It was a job, and right now Lucy was looking for something to inspire her. She doubted it would be a computer costume, but you never know, inspiration could strike at any moment. You had to put yourself out there, she knew, if you wanted to find what you're looking for.

Pulling up in front of her apartment, Jax pulled her in for another kiss. "That," he announced, after he pulled away from her, "will never get old. Wait right there." He then opened his door and walked around to open hers. Walking her up to the doors to her building, he offered, "I'm not sure what you're doing after … work tomorrow," he gave her his heart-melting grin, "but if you're not busy, would you like to grab a coffee?"

His gaze gave her butterflies, just being around him did, so she should be getting used to it now since they'd been there most of the night … but the way she was feeling was something she had never felt before. It was more than just butterflies, it was like some part of her had woken up, been brought to life, just from being around him. It almost hurt, but in a good way.

Biting her lip, she looked up into his eyes and tried to take a breath— why was it sometimes so hard to breathe around him? Nodding at him, she quietly agreed, "That'd be good."

Smiling at her in that way he had, he leaned down and whispered in her ear, "See you tomorrow." He kissed her cheek and walked back to his car, grinning.

Ducking her head, Lucy turned and walked into the building. She really didn't want to have to talk with any of the guys working the front door. She wanted to enjoy her good date high a little longer before anyone brought her back to reality.

Glancing over at the desk as she walked towards the elevators, she saw that Oliver was pretending to be deeply engrossed in whatever was on his desk, but she did see him look up once she got on the elevator and give her a little wink. She wouldn't hold it against him tonight, though; she was in too much of a good mood.

All was quiet as she entered the apartment. As she walked through the huge entry hall and into the kitchen, she saw a note on the counter from Opal.

> *Lucy—*
> *I hope you had a fantastic night with Jax. I wanted to wait up for you to see how things went, but I'm a little drowsy at the moment. My hopes are tomorrow we can catch up. Sleep well, Lucy.*
> *Opal*

Smiling, Lucy tossed the note in the trash and walked toward her room. She'd had an amazing night and couldn't wait to tell Opal all about it tomorrow. She was pretty sure Opal would be proud of her; she'd even gotten her goodnight kiss.

Lucy quickly washed face, brushed teeth, and got into her jammies, the nightly routine. She was wiped out.

Snuggling in to her amazingly comfy bed, Lucy's heart felt like it had grown two sizes over the past few hours. She couldn't believe that she had met a guy as attractive as Jax who was also sweet, courteous, and romantic. That she was able to tell him anything was huge because she'd never been able to do that before, never with a guy and rarely with anyone else. Summer was the only other person she'd ever felt comfortable enough with to say everything that was in her heart, and now she had Opal and possibly Jax.

Thinking back over the night, Lucy felt like she could burst with love and excitement. She couldn't help but replay in her mind, over and over, the time they had shared on the bench when he had kissed her and after when they had just sat, foreheads together, enjoying the moment. It was the sweetest thing to think about. And think about it she did, until she fell asleep with a smile on her face.

* * * * *

Waking up with a start, Lucy looked at the clock and swore. It was 7:30—she had just enough time to get dressed and get her booty over to where her new job was. Stumbling into her closet, Lucy located a pair of boyfriend jeans, a white Billibong t-shirt that had a bike on it and said, "Ride on," on the front, and a pair of Toms.

Throwing her clothes on, she looked in the mirror and noticed her hair was a little crazy. She shrugged. She would probably have some kind of computer head thing, anyway. She also noticed that she hadn't done the best job of washing off her makeup either. It looked okay though, the way it sometimes can if you're lucky. She had to wipe a little smudged mascara off from under her eyes, but other than that, she looked good to go.

Grabbing her bag, she flew out the door and had almost made it to the elevator, when she heard Opal's voice, "Hold it right there. Where are you off to in such a rush?"

Bouncing on her feet, Lucy rushed over and gave Opal a hug where she sat in the kitchen, explaining, "I'm off to my new job!"

Raising her eyebrows, surprised, Opal urged, "Oh? Do tell."

Lucy quickly explained to Opal what had transpired the other day with Cash and his finding her the job. How Lucy thought she'd try it, but hoped no one would know it was her, but how everyone knew because she had told them all … or they had overheard her and Cash.

"Oh, Lucy! You are so adventurous, and right now I'm living vicariously through you! I'm going to have to get Bowden to drive me by, so I can see you in action!" Opal laughed a real long laugh, one she hadn't in a long time.

"Well, if nothing else, at least I know that everyone had good laughs over this." Giving Opal a quick kiss on the cheek, she stated, "I gotta jet, but when I get back, I'll give you all the details about last night." She winked at Opal and had her grumbling.

"You know an old bat like me can't wait that long. It's torture, pure torture!" Opal responded, shaking her head, sadly.

"Sorry, Opal, see you soon! Or maybe not … yeah, I think you should probably take a nap this afternoon instead of driving by," Lucy proposed, looking pleadingly at Opal.

"You know, I'm feeling surprisingly chipper today, Lucy. I think a nice drive is just what the doctor ordered," Opal insisted with a smile as the elevator doors closed on Lucy's frustrated face.

Walking through the lobby, Lucy kept her head down, hoping Oliver wouldn't be at his usual post. Peaking up to see who was there, she realized at the last second she was out of luck.

Seeing her eyeing him, Oliver smiled, calling out, "Hey Lucy, where you off to?"

Not feeling up for another new job mocking, Lucy huffed out a reply, "Don't even ask."

She stomped out of the building and looked around for a cab. Seeing one, she jumped in. At least in that department she was lucky today. She quickly rattled off the address Cash had texted her late last night, then leaned back, and closed her eyes. It was going to be a long day.

* * * * *

Closing the door to the cab, Lucy slowly walked up to the doors of the office supply store, all the while looking around. Her hopes were that the place would have been in a quieter part of town, someplace not many people would be driving by. She was out of luck.

The store was in the heart of uptown, surrounded by cafés and restaurants, bars and boutiques, and other unique stores. There was a steady stream of traffic and people walking past. She could understand why Cash's brother wanted to get the word out about this place, with so many other stores around. It could easily get lost in the hustle and bustle, being just one piece of the puzzle in this funky uptown area.

Pushing open the door, she shook her head wondering why she'd agreed to do this. At least she would be hidden beneath the costume. It couldn't be *that* bad, could it?

The ringing bell of the door opening alerted the guy behind the counter at the front of the store, and he slowly looked up. He looked to Lucy like a carbon copy of Cash, except this one didn't have tattoos all over his body. He smiled, saying, "Hi, can I help you? Wait—are you?" He held up a finger, glanced down at his phone, and then continued, "Yeah, are you Lucy?"

Cursing Cash and his stealth photo-taking skills, Lucy admitted, "Yeah, I'm Lucy. If the picture is bad, well ... Cash totally surprised me. So ... yeah ... "

Feeling awkward, Lucy shifted her weight from foot to foot, waiting for him to look up from his phone.

Putting his phone down, he laughed, saying, "Nah, it's fine, just this thing I have." He looked at Lucy, who just raised her eyebrows, and continued, "See, I have this really crazy ex, and she keeps applying for all the jobs I post. So I always make sure I see the person before I have them come in. It's a lot less ... it's a lot easier that way."

He shrugged, then remembering what Lucy was there for, rubbed his eyes and cracked his neck, as if clearing any memories of his ex from his mind. Then he said, "I'm Carson, by the way." He held his hand out to Lucy.

Shaking his hand, Lucy responded, "Nice to meet you. So what exactly will I be doing today?" Lucy just wanted to get on with it, so she could get it over with and get home without being seen.

"Well, we need someone to get the word out, and instead of handing out flyers or something boring like that, I decided having you dress up as our mascot, Zippy Computer, would be more fun and more memorable, as well. So, all you need to do is put on the costume and stand out there, on the sidewalk by the road, and wave to everyone driving by. It's pretty straightforward. I'm fine with you listening to your phone out there, too. You might get a little bored after standing there for a few hours."

Looking at Carson while he was explaining to her what he wanted her to do, Lucy started to see more differences between him and Cash. Carson was more clean-cut whereas Cash was more rough. Carson was definitely more well-spoken and polite. If you had to pick which one would be the businessman, you'd pick Carson every time, but by looks only. Cash was business savvy, possibly more so than Carson, but he just didn't look the part. He didn't think about what he said, he just said it and didn't seem to care what you thought. Besides those few differences, they looked a lot alike, and she wasn't sure who was older.

Lucy wondered if there were any more brothers in the family who could offer her jobs if she messed up in some way today. She wasn't sure she'd take up the offer, though. She'd be too embarrassed. Plus, Cash told her this job was foolproof, so she really didn't need to worry about a thing, *right*?

Leading Lucy back to the bathrooms where she could change, Carson stopped when he came to a small storage space. He opened the door and pulled out a fuzzy heap of material, saying, "Here you go. The bathrooms are back there." He pointed toward the back right corner of the store and continued, "Just put on the white tights you brought first and then this baby, and I'll meet you at the front of the store."

Confused, Lucy slowly took the fuzzy mess from him and asked, "White tights? What white tights?" Taking a deep breath, she sent up a prayer that Carson was only messing with her.

"Ah … didn't Cash tell you? You were supposed to bring a pair of white tights. The costume is supposed to have these white leg things, but they got lost somewhere along the way, so whoever dresses up as Zippy needs to bring their own white tights …" He trailed off as he noticed her horrified expression.

"Nope, Cash did not inform me of that," Lucy said shortly, unsure of how to proceed.

Carson eyed her for a few short seconds, then decided, "Well … it should be okay, this time. I mean, no one will notice if Zippy's legs are more of a … flesh tone. Don't worry about the tights, just stash your jeans and purse behind the counter. When you finish changing, I'll meet you out front."

He then turned and walked away quickly, not waiting for a response from Lucy.

Lucy quickly walked into the bathroom before anyone could see her bright red face. How awkward! She was going to kill Cash, really kill him! She had a feeling he had purposely forgotten to tell her about the stupid white tights. Locking the bathroom door, she shot Cash a scathing text about supposed white tights and then grudgingly turned herself into Zippy Computer.

The only problem Lucy could see about being Zippy Computer, well aside from the missing white tights, was that the computer screen had a cut-out square in the front, so she could see out and yes, people could see her. The only thing she was actually thankful about was that there was also a fuzzy keyboard attached to the costume. If not for that, she would have felt inappropriately exposed without the dumb tights.

As it was now, the entire costume came down to about mid-thigh, which was a little on the short side with only her skivvies on underneath. The costume had built-in arms made of a white t-shirt material. They were a little stiff, causing her arms to kind of stick straight out instead of fall to her sides like normal. She was a little worried that if something happened to make her lose her balance, she wouldn't quite be able to catch herself. She hoped nothing would happen to cause her to really regret trying Zippy on for size.

Walking out of the bathroom with what she hoped looked like confidence, she spied Carson out front waiting for her. She stuffed her jeans and purse under the front counter as he had asked and walked outside to meet him.

Turning to see who was approaching, Carson did a double take at Lucy/Zippy Computer. He looked at her legs, then up at her face, and then down and up her legs again. Seemingly unsure of what to say, he cleared his throat.

Finally he remarked, "Well ... you're definitely the most interesting Zippy we've ever had. I think the whole no-tights thing actually works for us in this instance."

Lucy wasn't sure if she should feel appreciative or appalled. She was pretty sure her new boss was complimenting her in a weird kind of way. "Um, thanks, I guess" was all she could think of in response.

Clearing his throat again, he said, "Yeah ... follow me. I'll show you where I want you to stand." He led her through the parking lot to the sidewalk that lined the busiest street and then explained, "So, all you need to do is stand here and wave as people pass by. Like I said, I'm fine with you listening to music or whatever, as long as you wave and look friendly. I have a feeling that won't be a problem for you."

Nodding, Lucy looked around at all the traffic whizzing past. People were gawking at her already, and she'd only been standing there a few seconds.

"Great. So when is my shift over?" she asked desperately, as a car full of guys drove past shouting, "Woo-hoo! Zippy is *back*!"

"At one," he replied, trying not to laugh at her expression. "Don't worry, it'll go by fast once you get into the groove of it."

He gave her arm a gentle pat and started walking away.

Sighing, Lucy looked around. People were pointing and laughing and waving at her. She definitely wasn't going unnoticed, which would have embarrassed her even if her face had been covered by some kind of mask. But, of course, with her dumb luck, everyone had a clear view of exactly who the new Zippy was, and they were taking full advantage, some even snapping a few pictures.

Thinking about Summer and what she would do, Lucy knew she

should just try to enjoy it, maybe try to set some sort of record—like being the Zippy who brought in the most business or something. Deciding that trying to have fun with it would most likely make the time go by faster than moping, Lucy started waving back and smiling for the pictures.

"This isn't so bad," she thought to herself and fell into a rhythm of waving, turning, turning, waving.

The morning flew by, and before she knew it, it was almost noon. Excited at the prospect of her shift ending soon, not to mention the fact that she was kind of enjoying all the attention she … well, Zippy was getting, Lucy pulled out her phone to text Jax.

She hadn't seen him or Teddy or Opal the entire time she'd been standing outside, which was definitely a bonus. Seeing people she didn't know laughing at her was one thing, but seeing your crush cruising by while you were rocking a non-flattering computer costume was definitely not something Lucy wanted to experience. Even seeing Opal or Teddy would have embarrassed her. She didn't want them to ask her what had happened to her pants, which they most definitely would have wondered.

Shooting Jax a text that said, "Almost done with work, when do you want to meet?" Lucy was about to stuff her phone back inside Zippy (yes, surprisingly Zippy had one pocket on the side, bonus!) when a loud honking caught her attention. She looked up to see Jax, Teddy, and Cash driving by, all waving at her and shouting. She couldn't make out what they were saying, though.

Seeing Jax's heart-melting grin flustered her, and instead of carefully putting her phone back into the one small pocket Zippy had, she tried to stick it back inside very quickly. But the pocket was just a little too small and tight for quick phone stuffing, so the phone bounced off the fuzzy material and flew into the street. Thinking only of her embarrassment and clumsiness, Lucy stepped out into the street to grab it. She was met again with a loud honking. This time though, it wasn't from a friend driving by, it was from a guy in a car who was about to hit her if she didn't get her fuzzy self out of the street.

Quickly grabbing her phone, Lucy jumped back up on the sidewalk to sounds of tires screeching and then to cars smashing. Not wanting to look at the scene she had just caused, Lucy slowly opened her eyes. She wondered if causing a car accident would warrant getting fired. She was pretty sure it would, especially since the reason she had stepped out into the street was for her cell phone. Dumb.

Looking at the two drivers who were quickly approaching her, she grimaced. This was not going to be good.

"What the heck?" the one who had almost hit her yelled.

"What were you thinking, lady? Can't you see out of that costume?" the other guy screamed.

"What were you diving out in the street for, anyway? Sheesh, I almost hit your sorry self!" shouted guy one.

She didn't respond for a few seconds, but realizing they actually wanted an answer, she squeaked out a reply, "Um, my cell phone?"

"You've *got* to be kidding me!" guy two yelled, flinging up his arms in frustration.

"I'm sorry …" Lucy replied to the two of them, as they started walking back to survey the damage of their cars, from where guy two hit guy one when guy one was trying not to hit Lucy. "I'm really, really sorry!" Lucy called after them again.

Shaking their heads at her, the two men exchanged information and got back into their cars and drove off, one of them giving Lucy a not-so-friendly good-bye gesture.

Hearing footsteps behind her, Lucy turned to see Carson running over. Jax, Teddy, and Cash weren't far behind. And to her embarrassment, Lucy was pretty sure she saw Opal and Bowden pulling into the parking lot just then.

"Are you okay, Lucy? What just happened out here?" Carson panted, stopping in front of her, examining her, or maybe he was just making sure the costume was still in okay condition.

"I dropped my phone and kind of forgot to look before I tried to grab it …" Lucy started to explain but trailed off. She was beyond embarrassed and pretty sure she was going to get canned again.

"Yeah, that probably wasn't the best idea, but I'm glad you're okay. Damn, I hope neither of those guys call me to complain. That's not really the attention I was hoping for." Carson eyed her and added, "We need to talk after you're changed."

Nodding, Lucy started walking with him to the store but was stopped by Jax, Teddy, and Cash.

"Giggity girl, what happened? That was brutal!" Teddy looked her up and down, a look of concern on his face.

Jax pulled her in for a hug, "You okay, Lucy?"

Leaning against Jax, Lucy tried to smile. "Yeah, I'm okay. Just completely mortified and pretty sure I'm going to be jobless again in a few."

Looking at Cash she asserted, "You know, you did tell me this job was foolproof!"

Smirking at her, he responded, "It is! But I guess I should have taken into consideration who I was talking to. I did say you were a lawsuit waiting to happen."

Slowly raising his phone, Cash then proceeded to snap a picture of her and Jax, remarking, "Ha, this is the best one yet! I'll see you guys back at the car!" He walked slowly back to the car, his head shaking as he looked at his phone.

"I. Am. Going. To. Hurt. Him. Really, really hurt him!" Lucy stated, glaring after him.

"Oh, come on, Lucy … It'll be okay. I'm sure Carson will be … understanding, but, don't take it too hard if he's not," Jax somewhat comforted her and then kissed her cheek. "I'll see you at Grinder later, okay? Two o'clock work?"

Her heart warmed, and her nerves calmed a little as she thought about spending some quality time with Jax. Even if she was about to get fired, at least she had that to look forward to.

"That works, see you then. Bye, Teddy," she said with a half-hearted wave as they walked back to their car.

"Later, Luce. I'll have a Lucky Lucy ready for you when you get there," offered Teddy as he slowly loped back to join Jax and hopped into the car.

"Wait," Lucy called after him, catching him before she shut his door, "Who *is* at Grinder? If you're here, who's there?"

"We closed up shop," he called, "to see you in action! Gots to get back!" He then slammed the door.

Lucy waved good-bye and steadied herself for whatever Carson had to tell her. She was almost to the store doors when she heard someone calling her name. Turning, her cheeks flushed again when she saw who it was—Opal and Bowden. Of course, they'd have to be driving by at that exact moment.

Lucy watched as Opal stepped out of the car and walked briskly over to her. "Lucy! What is going on? What happened? Are you okay? Maybe they should ban working in huge costumes like that if it causes people to fall into the street and almost get killed!" Opal reported with eyes huge and rapid breathing. She was trying to check Lucy for injuries, but it was a little difficult with Lucy still being in character.

"I'm fine, Opal, just embarrassed, that's all," Lucy assured her grandmother, grabbing Opal's hands to stop her from pulling the costume off right there in the parking lot. "I promise, you can check me over later."

"Okay, okay, I'll let you be for now." Opal looked at Lucy for a second, then added, "What happened? One minute you're waving and laughing, and the next you're out in the middle of the street!"

Lucy really didn't want to tell Opal the idiotic move she had made, but she knew Opal wasn't going to let up, so she confessed, "It was dumb, Opal. Really stupid. I dropped my phone and went to grab it without thinking. I'm sorry to have freaked you out like that. I don't know what I was thinking."

"Well. I agree, that was pretty stupid, very dumb indeed. But you're okay, and that's all that matters now. Next time, just think before you jump into a busy street, okay?" Opal responded, patting Lucy's cheek.

Giving Opal a quick, awkward hug—Zippy wasn't very conducive to any sort of physical contact with other people, Zippy saved that for streets and oncoming cars—Lucy said a quick good-bye, waved at Bowden, and rushed, as quickly as she could, into the store.

"I'm really sorry, Lucy," Carson told her, "I know you didn't mean to do that, but I don't think I'll be able to keep you around as Zippy anymore. I was thinking about giving you another chance, but that was before I got the phone calls." He looked a little tense at the moment; he kept clearing his throat and wiping sweat off his forehead.

Lucy knew she should just accept what he had told her and go change, but curiosity got the better of her. "What phone calls?" she asked.

Sighing, he said, "Well, one from a man complaining that a giant computer jumped out into the street in front of him, causing him to slam on his brakes, which then caused him to get rear-ended. Another, complaining that he had rear-ended the guy in front of him, who had slammed on his brakes to avoid a giant computer that came out of nowhere. The third was from some weird organization that's against people wearing costumes to advertise because they distract drivers and cause car accidents. Case in point."

Unsure of what to say, Lucy just responded, "Yeah that sucks. I'm sorry."

"Yeah, you could say that again." A crease formed between Carson's eyes as he studied something on his phone. Then he looked up at her with a small smile, adding, "Oh! There was one *good* call though. Some guys called, thanking me for bringing Zippy back and making her so hot. They wanted to know what time you got off, so they could come by and meet you." He laughed to himself.

A little alarmed, Lucy asked, "You didn't actually tell them anything, did you?"

"You'd better go change. If you hurry up you might be able to make it out of here before they show up," he suggested with a cough that sounded more to Lucy like a laugh.

"Thanks a lot, Carson. Oh, and by the way, I take back everything I previously thought about you being cooler than Cash!" she yelled as she shuffled as fast as she could back to the bathroom to get her clothes on.

Pulling off the costume, she cursed Carson and Cash. Those two were more alike than she'd realized. If they *did* have another brother, she was steering clear.

Stepping out of the bathroom and running through the store, Lucy tossed the costume at Carson and grabbed her purse, stating, "Sorry about the bad press, Carson." She eyed the front door and then glared at Carson as a car full of loud, whooping teens idled in front of the store.

"Oops, I guess you weren't fast enough. Think of it as payback, you know, for the bad press and all," he responded and gave her a huge smile as he walked over and opened the door. Then he yelled out to the carload of teenage guys, "Here she is boys, Zippy in person!"

Head down, she stepped outside and took off to hail a cab as the guys yelled, "Zippy! We love you! Zippy, you're hot! Zippy, can we get your number?"

Frustrated, Lucy stopped, and then she stalked over to their car, which only got them more riled up. "For your *information*, my name is not *Zippy*! Now *good-bye*," she growled, then turned, and walked back to see if there were any cabs in sight, all the while listening to them profess their love and holler their well thought-out lines back at her.

"Zippy! We love you! Zippy, you're hot! Zippy, can we get your number?" they hollered from their car that was following slowly beside her, honking and hooting.

Finally, after waiting for at least ten minutes, her saving grace appeared. The cab slowed to a stop, and she jumped in and slammed the door, shutting out the screams.

Looking back at her, the cabbie asked, "What's *that* all about?"

Leaning back, she said, "You don't want to know."

Smiling and turning around, he said, "You're probably right. So, where you headed? Oh and keep your eyes peeled, there are reports of some type of human-sized computer gone rogue."

Telling him the address of Grinder, she sat back and wondered what else could go wrong today; she really hoped that was the last of it.

CHAPTER NINE

Stepping into Grinder, Lucy warmed when she saw Jax. He was sitting at the table closest to the bar, animatedly talking to Teddy. He turned when he heard the door open and grinned at Lucy.

"Hey, Lucy!" he called, patting the seat next to him.

"Lucky Lucy coming up!" Teddy called out to her, smiling as he started the espresso shots.

She smiled at Teddy as she neared the table where Jax was sitting. "Thanks, Teddy, you're the best!"

Standing up and pulling her into a tight hug, Jax inquired, "How's my favorite computer?"

Hugging him back, Lucy said, "Ha-ha, thanks a lot for that. Oh, and thanks for the ride too. Because of you guys I had to wade through a dozen admiring fans, all screaming their love for me while I tried to find a cab."

Looking at her confused, Jax sat down and pulled her down onto his lap to ask, "What's this about now?"

"Wait!" Teddy called from behind the bar, "I've got to hear this, I'll be right there." He finished up her drink, adding the whipped cream and putting the lid on, and walked over. "Here you go, Lucky Lucy."

"Thanks, though I'm not feeling too lucky right now," Lucy shared and took a sip of her drink. She then proceeded to tell them what had happened after they had left.

"I don't know what it is about you, Luce, but you seem to always get caught in the weirdest situations, you know, the best kind for storytelling later on," Teddy declared with a laugh and walked back behind the bar.

Rolling her eyes, Lucy noted, "Well, at least *you* guys are getting some enjoyment out of it."

Jax just squeezed her waist and smiled at her, agreeing, "Yup, best part of the day."

Why he thought her cluelessness when it came to finding a job she was actually good at was so funny, she had no idea. She was about to tell him as much, but she noticed Cash pushing out of the back door that led to the kitchen and walking their way. She hoped he wasn't there to give her more grief over another job failure.

"Hey, Lucy," he said, stopping in front of their table, "So, I don't know why I'm actually telling you this but, a friend of mine is looking for some help at his restaurant. He's desperate and needs someone ASAP. He has this great pizza place with one of those brick ovens. He just needs someone to work the pizza oven. All you need to do is *put the pizza in and pull the pizza out* a few minutes later, simple."

Lucy just blinked at him. She couldn't believe he was handing over another job offer to her after how badly she had sucked at Grinder and at his brother's store.

"You say 'simple,' but you told me Zippy was foolproof. Are you sure you would recommend me to work that close to a fire?" Lucy quizzed him.

"Yeah, I do sometimes forget who I'm talking to … but, you know, Lucy, there has to be *something* you're good at. We just need to find out what it is, right? Plus, my buddy is in a real pinch, and he isn't in a position to be picky, so …" he explained, trailing off and then smirking at her.

Peeking out from the bar, Teddy called, "Live it, girl! Do it up!" He gave her a rock-on sign and went back to perfecting his craft.

Lucy glanced up at Cash suspiciously to inquire, "Are you sure I don't need some sort of training to run one of those? A license, perhaps? I'm not so sure I believe that you're not setting me up. Am I going to need some sort of embarrassing attire that you're not telling me about?"

Laughing a rare belly laugh, Cash promised, "Nope, no white tights at this place, I swear. Sorry about that, Lucy. It was too good to pass up. So, what do you think? Want to give it a go?" He then nodded his head and wiggled his eyebrows, surprising Lucy with a moment of funniness.

Considering Cash's offer, Lucy decided she didn't really have anything to lose, so she agreed, "Alright, but if I totally screw this one up, it's on you, Cash." She sent him a look.

Looking down at his phone, he said mindlessly, "Yeah, yeah, you'll be fine. Okay, I'll tell Benno I have someone for him. The guy who is working the oven now is leaving in a few days, so he'll probably want you to come in tomorrow or the next day to get some training in before he leaves. I'll text you all the details later." He looked up and gave Lucy a small smile and walked back to the doors to the kitchen.

"Hey, Cash," Lucy called after him. When he stopped and turned around she said, "Thanks."

Nodding, he pushed through the doors and was gone.

Lucy heard someone laughing, and she looked over at Teddy. "What?" she asked.

"Didn't he say that last time? That you'd have to find someone else to find you all these awesome jobs if you messed up? I guess you get another chance, lucky girl."

Laughing, Lucy leaned into Jax and replied, "Whatever you say, Teddy."

Even though she didn't feel too lucky on the job front, she felt lucky sitting here with Jax, goofing around with Teddy. She even felt lucky that Cash was nice enough to find another job for her. She hoped she wouldn't screw it up this time.

Lucy spent the rest of the afternoon and some of the evening hanging out at Grinder with Jax and Teddy. When Teddy's shift ended, he joined them at the table, bringing a new drink over for Jax to try. This one was called the "Michael Jackson."

Lucy was surprised that Teddy even knew who Michael Jackson was, and when she told him so, she received a killer look and a long lecture about how age doesn't matter when it comes to pop culture and icons, and something about how music will always live on.

Shrugging her shoulders, she tried to change the subject to something less evasive, even though Teddy gave in and went with the flow, he tossed out a few good-hearted jabs now and then, making sure she wouldn't question his knowledge of music any time again in the near or distant future.

Later they were joined by a couple of Teddy's friends, Max and West, whom Lucy had never met before. They were both into music like Teddy, and Lucy was more than happy to keep her mouth shut and just listen when the topic of who the best band/artist/musician was came up.

After a while, Teddy, Max, and West stood up to leave. "Later, gators. West is DJing a party in a few, so we're off," Teddy announced, nodding to the two of them.

After they said their good-byes, Lucy stood up and stretched, and then looked at Jax to ask, "Want to walk me home? I'm sure Opal is freaking out, thinking I somehow fell into a coma or something since I'm not home yet."

Jax looked at her and frowned. "I'm glad you're okay, you really need to be more careful. If you're going to be working at Cash's friend's pizza joint, you'd better watch yourself near that oven. I'm not going to be happy if you walk out of there with third degree burns and no eyebrows, Lucy," he stated solemnly.

"Whoa, am I getting a lecture? My first Jax lecture. I have to say, you're pretty good at it, too," she teased and then smiled sweetly while he frowned some more.

Standing up, he put a hand on either side of her face, tilting her head up, so she was looking straight into his eyes. "I'm not joking, Lucy. I don't want you to get hurt." Then he gave her a quick kiss and announced, "There, my lecture is all done. Now let's get you home before

Opal comes to find you, and I miss my chance to kiss you good night."

Straightening up, he tossed their drinks into the trash and grabbed her hand.

She smiled up at him, never wanting the night with him to end. She loved the way he looked at her, how he made her feel like it was only the two of them in the room, even if it was crowded with people. The butterflies in her stomach felt good, and her fluttering heart beat felt even better. How could he do that to her just by giving her a quick peck or even by grabbing her hand? She felt like she could stand there with him all night, just looking into his dark eyes. She could get lost in them … she wished she would.

Walking out into the cool night air with Jax, Lucy thought of how different things had been with her and Drew—it was like night and day. It amazed her how she could be attracted to two completely different kinds of guys. But now that she was experiencing all this with Jax, she was starting to question what she'd had with Drew.

With Drew, in their early years, things had been … comfortable, very safe, bordering on boring, but she thought that was just how things were between two people. Those feelings had changed after they married when he let her in on who he really was. She didn't feel safe or comfortable then. She wondered why she could see things so clearly looking back, but when she was in it, deep in it, things had just been … confusing.

When she had first met Drew, she'd liked him right off the bat, though right now she couldn't really remember exactly why. She'd had warm feelings towards him, but nothing that she would consider hot, nothing passionate. No, there had never been any passion there, and that saddened her now. How could she have been so blind as to think that was normal? That those lukewarm feelings she had towards him from the beginning weren't anything more than that, just lukewarm friendly feelings? She figured it must have been her overly cautious self at play then.

She remembered telling Summer about Drew, explaining her feelings, and being hurt when Summer had said she didn't think Lucy was really in love. Of course she was, she had insisted, how couldn't she be? Why would she continue a relationship with someone if she didn't love him? Or think that love and possibly marriage was in their future? Summer had backed down, saying that if Lucy loved him, then that was all that mattered, that there were all different kinds of love. If what they had was more like calm water on a windless day, instead of the ice caps on the ocean before the storm breaks, well that was just fine, as long as Lucy was happy.

Thinking back, Lucy wasn't sure if she really had been happy. It was almost like her being happy was an afterthought. She wasn't sure if she had really even been satisfied with her life. No, she really hadn't been, and that was because she had spent most of her time trying to please the unpleasable Drew.

Looking up at Jax now, she wondered how she could have ever thought that was enough, the trying to please, the not being really quite happy, the calm and still waters, her just waiting, just dying for something *good* to actually happen. It wasn't enough, and it never would be again, not when she was feeling all of these amazing feelings she was with Jax.

How could she give up the fire that she felt when he looked at her, just *looked* at her? How could she think that those calm waters were enough for her when she'd felt just a little bit of that oncoming storm? Her heart wanted that storm, wanted to see what it was like when it broke, and she was never ever going back to those calm, still, passionless days again. Nope, she knew what she wanted, and this was it. Right now she was going to do what she had been doing since she got here—silence her overly cautious mind and listen to her heart.

Pulling her close and rubbing her arm, Jax asked, "What are you thinking about?"

"You," she replied before she could stop herself. Embarrassed as usual, she shyly looked up at him.

He was looking down at her, his eyes serious, studying hers. "Oh really, what about?" he asked with a small smile.

He took her hand and led her out of Grinder with him, and then down the sidewalk toward her apartment. They walked slowly for a few minutes. When they were almost to the front doors of her place, he stopped short and pulled her with him into the shadows of the building, where it was more private.

"So?" he asked again, looking at her with his amazing eyes, *"What were you thinking about?"*

Her heart sped up a notch at that, and her head was clouded as she attempted to reply, "Ah-h, just that ..."

"It's okay, Lucy," he reassured her, brushing her hair back from her face. "You don't need to be embarrassed. You can tell me."

She gulped. He was standing so close it was hard to think of what she wanted to say. "I like the way you make me feel. When I'm with you, I feel ... alive," she finally confided with a gentle smile. It was true, she really did feel alive when they were together.

He leaned down, so their foreheads were touching, and responded, "Good. I want to make you feel that way, and more. I want to make you feel like you can't live without me."

She struggled to keep her breathing even. She'd never felt this kind of intense connection before, not with anyone, and it was surprising her.

"I don't know what it is about you, Lucy, but you captivate me in a way I've never felt before, it's crazy. We've only just met, but I feel this connection to you. I don't understand it, and in the past, if I didn't understand something, I'd turn away from it. But with you I can't, I can't turn away even if I wanted to. I just want to keep going and see where this goes," he revealed and then let out a breath.

Was he nervous? The thought made her smile.

He was close, really, really close, and it was getting hard to think. Trying to calm herself, she drew in a breath and let it out fast, too fast, making her breath hitch. She could feel him taking deep, even breaths and wondered what he was thinking. She bit her lip.

"What are you thinking? Am I crazy?" he asked in a whisper.

"No, no you're not crazy. I feel the same way, and it's overwhelming to me because I've never, *never* felt anything like this before in my life ..." she voiced, trailing off, and closed her eyes as she felt his lips on hers. She could do this all night. She could kiss him and let him kiss her in his way that made her knees weak, but after a few minutes, she pulled away, declaring, "I really need to get home."

He looked down at her, grinned, and agreed, "All right, I suppose I can let you go home now. I did get my goodnight kiss, and I don't want your Opal cussing me out for keeping her girl out too late. Got to make a good impression and all."

He grabbed her hand and walked with her toward the door. When they reached the front doors, he opened one of them and said, "Have a good night, lucky Lucy."

Then he smiled, and after she stepped inside, he walked slowly away into the night.

* * * * *

Stepping into the beautifully ornate surroundings that formed Opal's entry into her amazing apartment, Lucy felt a little guilty. She hadn't meant to stay out so late. Even though it was only about eight o'clock, she was worried that Opal would be in bed already or waiting up and worried about her. Lucy hoped that wasn't the case.

Turning the corner, Lucy heard voices and smiled when she saw Opal, Lila, and Bowden, all sitting around the coffee table in the spacious living room.

"Hey guys," Lucy called out, walking over to the couch and flopping down beside Opal. Sighing, she leaned her head back to declare, "It's been a long day. I hope I didn't worry you when I didn't come home earlier, Opal."

Looking over at Lucy, Opal patted her hand, assuring her, "Nonsense, Lucy, I thought you'd be spending some time with that young man of yours. I knew you'd be here in due time."

Smiling across the coffee table at Lucy, Lila said, "I hear you had quite the scare today. We're all glad that you're okay."

Stretching her arms up above her head, Lucy tried not to sigh. She really wanted to forget what had happened, but she supposed that wasn't possible until everyone who cared about her knew she was okay. "Yeah, that was embarrassing to say the least. But I'm okay. The more I think about it, the more I realize how lucky I am that I didn't get hurt."

Clearing his throat, Bowden looked over at Lucy, replying, "Well, we're all very glad that you're okay. You're very loved here, Lucy. We hope you know that." He looked away and cleared his throat again.

Lucy was surprised. Was Bowden getting emotional on her? Having someone whom she had only known for only a handful of days tell her he loved and cared about her was something entirely new to Lucy. It made her feel safe and secure. It made her feel like it was okay if she were screwing up, as long as she tried her best. She smiled at him, sharing, "Thank you, Bowden. You don't know how much that means to me, really."

Clapping his hands together, he smiled at Lucy and said, "You're very welcome, now how about some chocolate cake? We've been waiting for you to get home so we could have some. Lila wouldn't let us even look at it until you got here." He looked over lovingly at Lila as she chuckled softly.

Lucy's eyes brightened, saying, "Chocolate cake? Really? If I'd have known that I would have been here a lot sooner!"

Lila smiled at her, and then she went into the kitchen to get the much-desired cake.

Opal softly pinched Lucy, querying, "Would you have really, Lucy? I'm thinking chocolate cake wouldn't hold its own against Jax. Did you have a good time?"

Blushing, Lucy looked up at Bowden who, as if on cue, got up and said he needed to help Lila with the cake. Lucy whispered to Opal, "You're right, Opal. As things are now, Jax would win. Is that bad?" She smiled up at Opal.

Laughing at Lucy, Opal replied, "Oh no, Lucy, that's good, that's really good. That's what you want, right? You want the person you like to rip you away from reality for a moment, don't you? Otherwise, what's the point? Of course, things go back to normal eventually. But if that person is someone you can't live without, your so-called 'normal' changes for the better into something more … chaotic, but in a good way. You need passion, you need to live, you don't want to look back at your life and think it was all … vanilla, do you?"

Opal laughed a loud laugh and then continued, "Looking back, whenever I made a decision that involved love, with my head trying to figure it out, calculated like that, it never really worked out and it wasn't much fun. But when I went with my gut, my heart … whew, what a ride it was then! That's what I lived for, that rush. What's life if you don't get to experience those highs and lows?"

Thinking on what Opal said for a bit, Lucy replied, "You're right, Opal. I think before now, most of my life has been cautious and calculated—me trying to figure out the exact right thing to do at the perfect time. But I wasn't really happy. I've been trying to let go a little though I'm not sure it's working. Look at how things have been going, me getting fired twice in a week? Then with Jax, even though we're still getting to know each other, things are new, so being able to let go has been great … but I'm worried I'm being stupid, that if I let go and just go with my heart and not hold back that I'm going to get hurt … " She trailed off, biting her lip, and then added, "Plus, we've only just met! I must be crazy."

Opal studied Lucy for a minute and then asked, "Are you happy? Even though you haven't found the work you're great at and you're afraid you might get hurt with Jax, are you happy?" Raising her eyebrows, Opal looked at Lucy, waiting for her answer, a small smile on her face.

Lucy's worried expression grew into a big smile as she answered, "Actually, I am … I really am, and that's what freaks me out. Shouldn't I be a mess? Depressed because I can't find a job I can do without messing something up? Worried that Jax isn't being real? Worried that it can't be real because we've only known each other for less than a week? But it's not bothering me, not really, and I trust Jax."

"Exactly!" Opal shouted, grabbing Lucy's hand, "Go with your heart. You don't need to worry about those silly jobs. Of course, you should always do your best, but you just need to find your passion. When you find that, you'll be golden. When you find out what you're meant to do, you'll feel that fire deep inside you, and you'll change the world with it—I promise you. Every person was put on this earth with a specific purpose, something they are meant to do, to be, and once you figure it out, you'll be a natural. As for Jax, don't hold back. Be what you want to be with him, you'll never regret that. But I can tell you, if you hold back and things don't work out, you'll always wonder if things would have been different if you'd been true to yourself. Even if you are true to yourself and you get hurt, you learn and grow, and you become even more beautiful. You only have one life, Lucy. Let go of the worry and just be. That's something I learned a little too late in life." Opal looked at Lucy, a little misty eyed, urging, "Learn from me, girly, nothing is perfect. It is what it is. The sooner you know and live on that knowledge, the happier you'll be, and the sooner things will fall into place for you."

Taking a deep breath, Lucy said, "Thank you so much for that … you have the best advice, and you never make me feel like I'm doing the wrong thing."

"That's because you're not, Lucy. You're just living and learning. What else can we ask for, right?" Opal assured her with a smile and then looked up as Lila and Bowden walked back with the delicious-looking chocolate cake.

Opal gushed, "Lila, you've outdone yourself again! I can tell just by looking at that cake that it's going to be the best thing I've ever tasted."

Sitting down, Bowden plunked glasses of milk in front of everyone, affirming, "That's what I said too—she outdoes herself each and every day, my Lila." He smiled at her and held his hand out for her to take as she sat down beside him.

Waving her hand at him, Lila said, "Oh now, it's no big deal, you know how much I love to do it, it's the thing I'm most passionate about." She smiled at Lucy, reassuring her, "You'll find your way, sweetheart. You're a beautiful girl with so much to offer. Remember that—never doubt yourself. Even if things aren't seeming to go your way right now, they will."

Lila looked over at Bowden, then at Lucy and Opal, and seeing they were about to dig in, she picked up her fork and followed suit.

Taking a huge bite of cake, Lucy closed her eyes, enjoying the decadence of it.

When she swallowed, she opened her eyes, took a big gulp of milk, and reported, "Okay, really? This is *the* best chocolate cake I have ever had! Wow! You guys are my inspiration, do you know that? You're all so confident and comfortable and happy. One day I want to find that, in life and in love."

She looked at Bowden and Lila and smiled, then nudged Opal with her elbow, and took another bite of cake.

If Lucy could be so lucky as to have someone to love her the way Bowden and Lila loved each other, and figure out what she was good at—really amazing at—well, then she figured that should be enough for her.

Was it possible, though? What if she were the one person in the whole wide world that never found her way?

No, she remembered what Opal had told her—to let go of the worries, to live, to just be. She needed to let go and just do what felt right. Go with her heart, wasn't that what she had decided just a bit ago with Jax? She needed to stop second-guessing herself, go with the flow, and trust that whatever was meant to be would be. Jump and fall, as Summer would say.

They spent a few more minutes enjoying the cake and milk and each other's company. When they had all finished the deliciousness that was Lila's baking, Lila and Bowden cleared their plates and glasses, and Opal announced she was headed for bed.

Lucy decided to follow her. She need to make some calls. Summer had been on her all day about her constant lack of communication, and she hadn't talked to her mom as much as she'd planned, so she'd better give her a call as well.

Lucy walked down the plush hallway with Opal and gave her a quick kiss goodnight before heading to her own bedroom to find some comfy pajamas and settling in for the long haul. Lucy knew Summer, so she knew she was in for a long night of spilling each and every detail. She missed that part of her life back home, so she was ready and more than willing to talk for as long as Summer wanted. It was actually just what she needed at the moment.

Taking a flying leap into her bed, Lucy grabbed her phone, found Summer's name, and pushed "call." She couldn't wait to hear what Summer was going to say when she told her about another job mishap and all about her night with Jax. Lucy braced herself when she heard Summer pick up the phone.

"Hello? Who is this? My phone says Lucy is calling, but I'm not sure who that is."

Rolling her eyes, Lucy stated, "Ha-ha, Summer, how are you?"

Sighing, Summer replied, "I'm good, girl. Besides waiting around for you to call, things have been, interesting around here."

Hearing Summer's response, Lucy perked up. If Summer was willing to call something interesting, Lucy knew it was going to be good. "Okay, now you've got me wondering, what's been going on back home?"

"Hmm," Summer said, playing coy, "Maybe I'll just keep you waiting for a little bit, a few days never hurt anyone."

"Oh, come on, Summer! Okay, I promise to call you once a day from now on. Is that better? *Now* will you tell me? Please!" Lucy begged, tapping her feet together, excited for news from Summer.

"Okay, all right, I guess I'll tell you, but only because I can't keep it a secret *any longer!* I met someone, Lucy! A real someone, not a Mr.

Tonight, but an honest-to-goodness someone!" Summer gushed.

Lucy was speechless. Summer had never actually met someone that she considered worthy enough to mention to Lucy, let alone keep secret, whatever that meant. Whoever he was, he must be something amazing for Summer to have fallen for him.

"*What*? What do you mean, *met* someone?" Lucy interrogated. She wanted to make sure they were on the same page here.

"*Met* someone Lucy, as in found *The One*, as in the same guy for the rest of my *life*, someone ..." Summer trailed off dreamily.

Lucy was shocked. She'd never heard Summer like this before, and they'd been friends since, well forever. "Wow, Sum, I mean *really, wow* ... I've never heard you like this before. Time to spill. When did you meet, where did you meet, and what do you mean keeping secret? From who? *Me*?" Lucy blurted out, totally intrigued. She wanted to be sure this wasn't a dream, so she pinched her leg. Yep, it hurt.

Summer laughed, saying, "Okay, okay slow down, Luce, I'll give you all the answers. Just let me tell the story from the beginning. Ready? You're going to *love* this!"

Settling back against her pillows and rubbing her leg, Lucy reported, "Ready, Sum. This had better be good."

"So," Summer started, taking a deep breath, "the day you left, I was a little bummed, you know, to be losing my *best friend* and all, so I—"

Lucy cut her off, "You didn't lose me, Sum. You know that."

"Sh-h!" Summer said, "I *know*, Luce, but that was how I was feeling at the moment. So I went back to the place where we started your test, you know the one where I made you go up to that super-hot guy at the coffee shop? I got a cup of coffee and was just sitting there people-watching and thinking about how much I was going to miss you, when someone walked up to me. Guess who it was?" Summer asked, waiting for Lucy's answer.

"Um, I have no idea. Who?" Lucy replied, as she pulled up the leg of her pajamas and frowned at the bruise now forming.

"Drew!" Summer answered with a laugh.

"Drew? *My* Drew?"

Lucy was confused as to what Drew had to do with the story. Wasn't he somewhere in Mexico or ... well, far enough away for her not to think about?

Lucy narrowed her eyes, declaring, "You'd better not be telling me that Drew, *my ex*, is your *one* because that would just be really, well, weird. Plus you *know* how he was to me, and how the heck did he get back from *Mexico*?"

Summer made a sound that sounded like she was choking, then insisted, "Oh my gosh, Lucy, no! No, no, no! What kind of friend do you think I am? Plus, you know I can't stand *that* Drew, no. I'm talking about the other Drew. The one you went up to that day, that first guy you talked to? Remember?"

Sinking back into her pillow, Lucy relaxed, recalling, "Oh, *that* Drew! Okay, I feel a lot better now, keep going."

Smiling, Summer continued, "So he came up to me and asked me if my friend was the one who had given him her number. I said yes, and then he asked if you'd be open to him calling you. He thought you seemed nice and was surprised because he'd never been approached by a girl like that."

Lucy blushed, "Really? That's pretty cute, actually."

"I know, right?" Summer said. "So then, I told him about how I was making you do it, that you were moving, and that even if a long distance relationship could work, well, he didn't have a chance because you had just gotten a divorce from a real *douche* named … Drew."

"What did he think about your little challenge for me? Was he offended?" Lucy asked curiously. She wasn't sure how she would feel if it had been the other way around and a guy had approached her on some kind of silly dare.

"He didn't really mind, just kind of laughed it off. I think he was disappointed at first because he thought you were pretty cute. Then we just started talking about nothing really. And then all of a sudden it was dark, and the coffee shop was closing, jerks kicked us out … so anyways, he got kind of shy all of a sudden and then asked if *I'd* like to go out with him. He said it was a real nice surprise to have met me and would like to see me again. I think he felt a little awkward because he had first approached me about you, but … I don't know, we just really clicked, and I *had* to say yes. So, you're really not going to believe this, but I broke my number one rule of thumb, and I met him out the next night, we—"

Cutting Summer off again, Lucy screamed, "*What*? Summer Perrier breaking her own dating rules? I just … I'm speechless! I'd never thought I'd see the day."

"Ha-ha, Luce, well I told you, he's totally the one. He really is! All my rules seemed ridiculous when it came to him. They flew right out the window after that first night, girl! So, the next night we went out for dinner at this cute little pizza place. It was so romantic, Luce. Each booth is kind of tucked away and hidden behind these checkered curtains …" Summer trailed off again, leaving Lucy floored. She had not seen her friend like this before. It was big. Really, really big.

"Okay, Summer, you're freaking me out a little bit. I have to admit … if I didn't know better, I'd say Summer, the never-settle-for-anyone-ever is totally and completely in l-o-v-e."

Taking a big breath, Summer admitted, "Totally and completely, Lucy. I'm totally suckered for this guy. I want you to meet him. When are you going to come home? I need to have your approval, you know. Just to make sure I'm not being an idiot about things."

"Summer, I know you, and you're definitely not being an idiot. You wouldn't fall like this for someone if he weren't the real deal. Actually, thinking about it a little more, I'm not surprised. This is exactly the way you *would* fall in love, all passionate and whirlwind-like. That's you, Sum! I'm not sure when I'll be able to come back home. Things are a little crazy here, but … I was thinking that you should come here. You could bring Drew, if it's not too soon for that kind of trip. Teddy is DJing a party in a couple of weeks. You guys should come for the weekend. It would be awesome! Then you could meet Jax, too."

Summer screamed so loud into the phone that Lucy had to hold it away from her ear for a few seconds, "Ah-h! Lucy, that would be amazing! I would love to come and check out your new digs, and to meet Hot Guy and Opal and Teddy. Seriously, I'm like freaking out right now! Yes, I'm in and so is Drew. We're kind of inseparable lately." Summer gushed.

Laughing, Lucy said, "Oh, Sum, I miss you way too much right now. It'll be so fun to see you again and to see you in love. It'll be interesting to say the least." Lucy yawned and added, "I'd better get going, Sum. I still need to call my mom, and it's getting a little late. I'm not sure if she's still awake."

"Oh no, you're not! You're not getting away from me that easy. I need to hear all about Jax! Oh, and Zippy, right? How did that go? Oh, I wish I could have seen you!" Summer's voice was full of laughter.

Sighing, Lucy admitted, "Well, let's just say I'm not really cut out for the whole fuzzy costume thing. Yeah. Not my best moment, Sum."

Clearing her throat, Summer demanded, "Do tell and spare me no details, on both subjects."

Adjusting her pillows behind her to get into a more comfortable position, Lucy settled back into them again. She might as well kiss good-bye talking to her mom tonight. She had a feeling her quick chat with Summer was going to turn into an all-nighter. Leaning her head back, Lucy started in with what had happened with Zippy and continued the story throughout the rest of the day, ending with Jax walking away after he had opened the door to her apartment building for her.

Summer filled in the gaps with oohs and aahs and even some eeks, making Lucy laugh and cringe at herself. When she had filled Summer in on every last mortifying and steamy detail, Summer was even more excited to come visit.

They made plans to chat again in a few days, both knowing the time would come fast when they would see each other again, both minds filled with thoughts of new love and the excitement of the unknown.

CHAPTER TEN

Lucy woke with a start to a strange beeping sound. Confused as to what was happening, she sat up and rubbed her eyes, looking around to see if there was some kind of alarm going off. Hearing the noise again, she jumped; she hoped there wasn't any kind of alarm because the noise was coming from her bed.

Thinking it was just her luck that her amazingly comfortable bed would come with an alarm she had no idea how to turn off, she carefully but quickly stepped out of the bed, glaring at it for deceiving her. It was supposed to be comforting, not distressing!

The noise suddenly stopped, and Lucy relaxed, only for it to start up again, beeping at her. She really didn't want to have to go find Bowden to ask what was wrong with her bed.

Looking around for her phone, she decided to call Teddy. He was pretty savvy when it came to weird techy things like that, so he could probably tell her at least where to look for the shut-off button. Not seeing it on her nightstand, dresser, in the bathroom, closet, or in her purse or clutch, Lucy scratched her head ... slowly she turned to stare at her bed. Stalking over to it, she pulled back the covers to reveal not only her phone, but the so-called "alarm" she had thought was going off.

"Idiot," she muttered to herself, smacking her forehead. She was extremely grateful that no one had been around to see her faux alarm freak out. Grabbing her phone, she glanced at the screen, surprised to see she had six missed calls—all from Cash. Her alarm/phone must have been going off longer than she had realized. She jumped again as it started beeping in her hand. Taking a breath, she held the darn thing up to her ear and said, "Hello, Cash."

"Uh, really, Lucy? I've been calling you like a hundred times, and all you have to say is hello?"

"Yes," she replied demurely.

"Figures. Benno needs you there now, pronto," Cash told her sharply.

Confused, Lucy asked, "Who? What? Who's Benno? What time is it?"

Sighing loudly, very loudly, Cash reminded her. "Benno—the guy who owns the pizza place. You know, the job I got for you? Come on, Lucy, you've got to be on your game here, girl! No wonder you have problems with employment. Get up and get over there," he demanded.

When all he heard was silence coming from Lucy's end of the phone, he added, "It's 8 am, get over there! Now!"

Rushing into her closet to find something to wear, Lucy anxiously said, "Okay, Where? What's the address?"

Sighing even louder—Lucy wondered if that was even possible—Cash rattled off the address and then hung up.

Lucy pulled on mint green skinny jeans, a loose grey top, and some cute flats—no heels today—she didn't want to biff it while trying to get the pizza out of the oven. She threw on her rocker leather jacket and grabbed her black purse and was out the door before she could say, "Pizza oven, baby."

* * * * *

Stepping out of the cab, Lucy looked up at the big red letters of the pizza place and laughed out loud. "Saucy Baby" was spelled out in big letters above the front doors. In the short time that she'd been in the city, she sure had worked at some interestingly named places.

Taking a breath, she pushed open the front doors and wished herself luck—with the way things had been going lately, she was most definitely going to need it. Looking around, Lucy wondered if she had got the time wrong or if Cash had meant for her to get there *tomorrow* morning. The place was dead, no sight or sound of anyone at all. But the doors were unlocked, so there had to be someone around somewhere. Lucy cleared her throat and called out, "Hello?" She waited for a few seconds and again said, "Hello? Anyone here?"

She was answered with silence. She was just about to call Cash to make sure she had the right time and address when someone pushed through the back doors, sending them swinging.

The guy didn't seem to notice Lucy standing in the middle of the restaurant. Instead, he was looking down at something written on a piece of paper and muttering silently to himself. He was tall and skinny and reminded Lucy a little of Cash in the way that he had tattoos all up and down his arms. His hair was jet black and styled in a Mohawk. He also had those kind of earrings in his ears that stretched the lobes out, which made Lucy wince.

As Lucy watched him and waited for him to notice her, he looked around the room and groaned, at what Lucy wasn't sure. He then glanced at her and screamed, dropping his paper. He looked as if he were about to bolt out the door. She hoped he wasn't some robber she had just caught trying to rip off the place. She would for sure get fired on the spot if her new boss found out she had actually seen the guy who had made off with all of his ... sauce? Pizza dough . .? and let him get away without a fight.

Looking at her out of the corner of his eye, he growled, "Who are you, and what are you doing here at eight in the morning?"

Lucy lifted her hand slowly; she didn't want to scare him anymore than she already had. "Hi, I'm Lucy. Um, Cash called me this morning and said you needed help."

The guy just stared at her suspiciously, not blinking.

"You *are* Benno, right?" she asked, her nerves kicking up a notch.

Squinting his eyes at her, he replied, "Who's asking?"

Wondering if this was some kind of prank Cash was playing on her and she was on some hidden camera show, she slowly moved her eyes from side to side, looking to see if there were any sorts of cameras visible. Not seeing anything out of place, she said slowly, "Um ... me?"

Stepping up a little closer to her, he leaned forward and said quietly, almost too quiet for her to hear, "What's the safe word?"

Looking into his crystal clear, almost translucent eyes, Lucy asked, "Huh? What safe word?"

Piercing his lips, he growled again, "The code. What is it?"

Confused, Lucy took a guess, "Pizza?"

Clearly he didn't think this was funny, "Don't mess with the safe word. What is it? Tell me? If you are who you say you are and Cash did send you, then he would have also given you a safe word, so I'd know you're legit."

Feeling her cheeks color, she took a breath and said more to herself than to him, "Of course, he would forget the word. Seriously, Cash? I can't believe you!" Taking another calming breath, she looked up and saw the guy was giving her a strange look.

"Excuse me," he said, "explain yourself please." He stood staring at her, unmoving, reminding her of a weird kind of statue.

"Sorry, it's just that he always forgets things like this when he finds me a job. First the tights, now this. I think he likes to mess with me, actually," she replied and then blew out a breath in frustration.

Eyes squinting again, he questioned, "Tights? What are you talking about?"

Lucy was beginning to wonder if everyone she came across was going to find out about her Zippy experience one way or another, "Well, he got me a job as Zippy the other day, and I was supposed to—"

Before she could finish her sentence, he started to laugh. He laughed and laughed a growly, deep down to his gut laugh, and when he finally caught his breath, he exclaimed, "Oh wow! I forgot about that! All right, all right I believe you now, safe word or not. I'm Benno, welcome to

Saucy Baby." He smiled crookedly and held out his hand.

"Nice to meet you," Lucy said, "and thanks for the job. I'm hoping I can do better at this than I did as Zippy ..." she trailed off, cursing herself for just saying that. It wasn't the best thing to say to her new employer, but it sounded like he already knew about her experience as Zippy, so ...

"Yeah, me too," he agreed, rubbing his hands together as if formulating a plan, "because I really need someone to pick up where Gerald left off, you know. I hope you're a fast learner because you're in for a crash course today. Get ready, babe." He raised his eyebrows at her and smiled.

Staring at his extra white teeth, Lucy let go of her fears and said, "Let's do this!" which earned her a laugh from Benno.

Leading her into the restaurant, he showed her where everything was, even though she wouldn't be working in that part of the restaurant. "The brick oven has its own spot in the left corner of the restaurant, but it is important for you to know the basics of Saucy Baby," he explained.

Benno gave her all the ins and outs of his place, and after they had gone over everything besides her position at the brick oven, he led her right over to it and said, "This is you, where you make the magic happen. I'd say it's the most important spot of Saucy Baby because it's where our signature pies are made."

Lucy looked at him confused, inquiring, "Pies?"

Shaking his head, he explained, "Pizzas, Lucy, pizzas. So this is your one and only job here, when things are super crazy, you are only responsible for getting the pies, the pizzas, in and out of there. That's it. Just putting them in and taking them out. When things are slow, you can help where needed, but only if it's dead in here, and you aren't obligated to do so, unless I tell you. I'm all for teamwork, but our pies are known for their one-of-a-kind taste, and I don't want *anything* interrupting that ... so you are the one person in this place that is off the hook for bathroom duty or whatever else someone tries to fling your way."

Listening to him was worrying Lucy. Cash told her it was a simple job. He made it seem like nothing, but Benno was telling her another story completely.

"Sounds pretty serious. Cash made it sound like, well, *not* as serious," she told him.

"Darn skippy, it's serious!" he said, bouncing on the balls of his feet, "That's because Cash doesn't know pizza from a peanut butter and jelly sandwich. Anyways, today, my little grasshopper, I'll show you all my secrets for getting those pies out in tip-top shape, but pay attention, because tomorrow you're on your own. Do me good, Lucy, *please*, I'm begging you, do me good."

She laughed a little at what he had just said, thinking how inappropriate it could be. But with him, he just seemed so serious and into his work, it was funny, not at all offensive.

He gave her a pleading glance and then started grabbing tools, and explaining to her what each one was and how she was to use it while cooking the pizzas.

There really weren't many tools she needed to use, just a brush with a long handle to clean the oven's inner surface and then a big spatula-looking thing to turn the pizza.

Benno showed her how to light the brick oven by building a small fire in the middle. He pointed to the oven when the smoke was black and again when it was white, saying that when it turned white, it was time to push the fire she had made all the way to the back of the oven, and then it was ready to go.

Sticking a pizza into the oven, he showed her the steps needed for a perfect pizza. When the pizza started to steam, that meant it was time to turn it, so the other side could cook. He showed her how to check the bottom to make sure the crust was just right, not burnt, *never burnt*! When it was done, all you had to do was pull it out and done, perfection!

Asking Benno what his special secret was to getting the pizzas—the pies—to taste so special, he told her it was in the fire. That the fire kind of flavored the smoke, which flavored the pizza, almost like marinating meat. "Also," he added, "it's in the precision of timing and pizza rotation. You know ... getting those babies in and out of the oven *exactly* how it needs to be done."

All in all, it didn't seem too difficult to run a brick oven, but she didn't want to get too far ahead of herself. She thought that dressing up as a computer would be a piece of cake, and look where that had gotten her ...

Despite her odd first impression of Benno, Lucy was actually enjoying her time with him. She wondered why he had been so suspicious this morning, but decided to ask him another time. She wasn't sure what his deal was, and things were going so well that she didn't want to upset him or put him in a bad mood.

She was already on shaky ground with the state of her employment. Due to her inability to hold a job for more than a few days, she didn't want to give him any more reason to not like her than he would if she royally messed up today or tomorrow.

As Lucy tried her hand at working the brick oven and getting the pies just right, other workers started to trickle in, shouting hello to Benno and nodding at her. Some of them wandered over while they were setting up to introduce themselves; others just went about their business.

There was one girl in particular who kept sending her weird looks. Whenever Lucy looked up, she could feel the girl's eyes on her. She only had to look to where the girl was sorting out silverware to confirm that she wasn't just imagining being stared at. Every time Lucy looked up at the girl, the girl was looking at Lucy. And the weird thing was she didn't glance away like most people did when they were caught staring. No, this girl held her gaze until Lucy felt extremely uncomfortable, and then she herself looked away, wondering what was going on.

Confused, she quietly asked Benno, who had just walked over to check on her, "So, who's that girl over there, and why is she staring?"

Benno looked up, and Lucy nodded in the girl's direction. "Yeah, she's going to be a problem, it's about time I tell you about Patrice," Benno told her.

Lucy's forehead crinkled as she looked at Benno. "O-o-o-o-kay," she said.

Benno looked uncomfortable. He quickly looked at Patrice and explained, "She's been working here forever. She was the first person I hired when I started up the place, but she and I, we have history, so no matter how much of a pain she is, I can't fire her."

Still confused, Lucy responded, "I normally wouldn't ask this, but since she's been giving me the evil eye since she got here, I'm going to ask … what kind of history? And why does she seem extremely unhappy that I am here right now?"

Rubbing his chin, Benno continued, "Like I said, she's going to be a problem. She's been wanting this position since I opened up the place, but I'm just not going to give it to her. I just don't trust her, not with this at least. She's spiteful and I wouldn't doubt for a second that if she had the chance to screw me over she would …" Benno trailed off.

Lucy just raised her eyebrows at him, waiting for him to continue.

"We have a kid together, a son. He's six, and I can't in good judgment or bad, fire her and think about the effect it would have on him. She knows this, knows she can get away with just about anything, but she also knows I would never let her run the oven. So she's pissed at me right now, and I'm certain she isn't going to like you." Benno glanced quickly at Lucy and looked away, then back again.

"Great!" Lucy said sarcastically and then asked, "Do you see your son? I'm sure you provide for him right? So you really wouldn't have to worry if he has what he needs because you'll always be there to help."

Chuckling, Benno shook his head, saying, "I *am* there for him, all the time. He *lives* with me, but he sees her and she isn't afraid to make things up, to manipulate him if she wants to hurt me. When we met, she was different, but it was all a ruse. The person who I thought she was wasn't really her. I was even warned by an ex of hers to watch out, that she has a way of 'pulling the wool' over people's eyes to get what she wants. She definitely got what she wanted from me, for the most part." He rubbed his jaw and shrugged at Lucy.

Lucy had no idea what to say; she could only manage, "Wow."

"Yeah, ditto. And I can't believe I told you most of my recent life story. You're really easy to talk to." He smiled at her and laughed at her expression, adding, "Really, it usually takes a lot longer for me to talk about what happened between us. Actually most of the people that work here know about it only because someone else has told them. Probably her."

"Well, thanks, I guess," Lucy offered with a shrug, nudging him with her elbow.

Smiling, he handed her a pizza, gestured to the oven and assured her, "Don't worry about Patrice, though. I'll have a chat with her. Now, we always make a couple pizzas for everyone before we open our doors, and we eat them during our morning meeting. It'll be good. Everyone'll have a chance to meet the new oven master." He winked at her as he handed her the next pizza.

"I'm not sure I'd call myself that *yet*, but I'm really hoping I won't mess this up." She sighed, sliding the pizza into the oven carefully.

Benno laughed, saying, "You're going to be fine, Lucy, despite what everyone might say, I'm really a softie. And I like you. But yeah, don't screw this up." He gave her a meaningful look.

Lucy wasn't sure if his look was meant to scare or if it was just a joke, but either way she was going to do her very best to not mess this job up. She was beginning to like the place, even with the evil Patrice lurking around.

Morning meeting went off without a hitch, and Lucy even got a few compliments on her first official pizza. Sitting around a large wooden table, everyone was eating and talking, laughing and joking with each other. Looking around, Lucy realized these people acted like a big family, where this place was their home where they met to share their stories. Everyone was different in their own way, but they seemed to fit together to make something beautiful, and Lucy hoped she would be able to squeeze in too, to add to it in her own way.

Something about this place called to her, and she felt almost sentimental, which made her feel a little embarrassed. It *was* just a pizza place with a group of people working together to make and serve the best pizza around, but … it was more than that, and just being here with everyone—watching them, listening to them—Lucy was starting to feel it, feel the magic of friendship and family.

When the morning meeting was over, Lucy wandered over to her post and picked up her phone to send a quick text to Summer, Jax, and Teddy before the chaos started.

But before she was able to type a single word, someone walked over and slammed her phone down on the counter in front of her. "Ah-ah-ah, no distractions, remember?" Benno told her, looking down at her and shaking his head at her phone. "You are off the hook when it comes to all the stuff I told you about before, but you are also banned from even *thinking* about your phone until your shift is over, understood? No distractions!" he shouted, clapping his hands at her.

"Yes, sir, no distractions, understood!" Lucy replied in mock seriousness, which caused him to laugh.

Just then Patrice walked by, tying up her light brown hair into a messy bun. Smirking at Lucy, she cautioned, "Watch yourself, girl. You don't want to accidentally set yourself on fire." She stalked away, popping her gum as she went.

"Was that some sort of threat?" Lucy asked Benno, slightly offended.

Getting that suspicious look on his face again, he said, "I'll go talk to her, Lucy, but maybe you should watch yourself. Until I know what's going on in that mind of hers, you can't be too careful." He walked over to Patrice, pulling her aside and pointing over to Lucy.

From Lucy's vantage point Patrice was all innocence, but Lucy knew it was all a show, and she was sure from what he had said before that Benno could see it too.

* * * * *

Lucy held her hand out, getting high fives all around … well, except from Patrice, that was.

"Awesome, girl, and thank you for delivering like I asked this morning. You rocked it today, and I'm hoping this will be a continuous thing," Benno praised her, giving a high five too.

"Thanks, Benno. I hope so too. This place is growing on me, everyone is so nice." Lucy smiled up at him and stretched her arms, they were a little sore from bringing the pizzas in and out, but it was a good sore though, so she wasn't complaining.

Her day had been better than she could have hoped for. She really *had* rocked the oven, not burning even one pizza. Benno had to remind her a few times to turn one or to put it this way or that, but by the end of the day, she had gotten the hang of it. She hoped tomorrow when she was running it by herself, she would remember all the tricks of the trade Benno had shown her.

She was about to go in search of a cab when the door to Saucy Baby opened and Jax walked in.

"Jax, man! What's the occasion?" Benno stated while walking up to him and giving him a quick hug with a slap on the back.

Returning the hug, Jax nodded at Lucy, explaining, "I'm here for your brick oven babe."

Benno laughed, agreeing, "She *is* a brick oven babe! She rocked it today man, hard!"

Embarrassed, Lucy walked over to where the two guys were standing. "Thanks, guys. I hope tomorrow is just as good," she said with a blush as Jax pulled her into a hug.

Benno eyed them and stated, "Tomorrow at eleven, see you then, Lucy. Oh, and you better bring it tomorrow too. I'm not going to accept anything less." He winked and turned to talk to another worker.

Jax gave her her favorite grin and asked, "Ready? I've got something fun planned if you're up for it."

"Sure," she replied, smiling up at him. When it came to him, she'd always be up for anything. "How did you know that I was here and that my shift was over?"

Grabbing her hand and pulling her out the door, he explained, "I was at Grinder this morning when Cash came in. He had this huge grin on his face, which is ... unusual, except when he's up to something. So I asked him about it, and he told me he had sent you here missing some important information. He said he wished he could have seen your face when Benno asked for the safe word, and you wouldn't have a clue as to what he was talking about." Jax walked Lucy over to his car, opened the door, then ran around, and slid into his side, adding, "He was pretty sure you'd be stuck out in the alley waiting for him to text you the safe word, looks like he was wrong though."

Lucy could only shake her head. She was getting used to Cash and his purposely forgetting info. "Yeah, I got in. Benno was a little suspicious at first, but then I mentioned Zippy and that seemed to loosen him up a little bit. I think Cash has it out for me."

Pulling the car out into the street, Jax laughed and suggested, "Nah, I think he has some twisted type of crush on you." When Lucy gave him an unconvinced looked, he added, "He *does* keep finding you jobs, doesn't he? He's never done that for anyone I've known before. I do think he likes to see you squirm, though. He gets some sort of kick out of that."

Deciding she would forget about Cash for the moment, she asked, "So, where are you taking me? It better be good."

Giving her a look, Jax replied, "Just so you know, with me it's *always* good."

Feeling her face heat up, she looked away, trying to regain composure. How did he do that to her? She really needed to practice her poker face.

Laughing, he said, "Don't worry, Lucy. We're just going bowling."

Surprised she said, "Bowling? I haven't been bowling since my sixth grade birthday party."

"Then you'd better get ready. You're in for some fun. Bowling and pizza, there's nothing better," he told her with a smile and pulled his car into a parking lot, where across the street big letters flashed "B-O-W-L-!-!-!" He gave her another long look and said, "Well, I take that back, there are a few things that I can think of that I like better, but we'll just save those for later." He grinned hugely at her and jumped out of the car.

Feeling her heart pumping, she quietly repeated to herself, "Poker face, poker face, poker face." That was the only way she was going to get through tonight without blushing uncontrollably whenever she thought about what Jax had just said.

He could drive her crazy with just one look, just a few words and his amazing smile. She was definitely a goner—she just didn't want him to know it. Not yet.

CHAPTER ELEVEN

The next couple of weeks went by without a hitch, Lucy "rocking" the brick oven at Saucy Baby, not burning even one slice of pizza. She was pretty impressed with herself and secretly extremely proud. It seemed that she had found something she could do without causing some kind of disaster. It was something she was beginning to enjoy more and more each day, getting to know everyone who worked there, seeing how they all worked together as a team. If someone needed help, at work or in their personal lives, most of the other employees would be there in a millisecond.

It was something that Lucy had never experienced before, a big group of people whose only thing in common at first was where they worked, coming together to help, motivate, and even inspire each other. It was something that held a large amount of beauty to Lucy, something most people would look past or take for granted, but Lucy saw it all, and it made her happy to see how much good there could be in people. Even the smallest thing, like someone rushing over to help clean up a spill or giving a small word of encouragement to another, was something that warmed her heart.

Drew had always seen the worst in people, the worst in the world. He had always been so negative, saying that people didn't care, that if they had the choice they would take you for all you were worth. But seeing how this group of people worked together proved him wrong. There was so much beauty and love in the world if you looked for it, if you were willing to give it and to receive it.

Of course, there would always be the person that would prove Drew right too, but Lucy felt that there was more good than bad, that if it came right down to it, good would always win.

Patrice was the one person at Saucy Baby that gave value to Drew's opinion. She was always rude, throwing mean comments out to anyone who crossed her path at the wrong time. She let others clean up her messes, leaving before her shift was over, whenever she felt like it. She seemed to have a vendetta against Lucy, shooting her nasty looks whenever she could. Lucy had her guard up, though, and made sure that whenever Patrice was around, she was extra careful in whatever she was doing. Lucy always kept an eye out for her, always knew where she was.

After her job at Saucy Baby was over for the day, she would usually head over to Grinder or meet up with Jax, and then she would head home and have dinner with Opal. Lila would cook them the most amazing meals, the two of them lounging over their food and decadent desserts long after Lila and Bowden had retired for the night. They talked late into the night about their days or sometimes about memories from long ago.

Other times they would go out to dinner, sometimes places where they could get all dolled up, but other times a hole in the wall that Opal had been waiting to show Lucy. Wherever they went, though, Opal more often than not knew the owner or manager, and they received special treatment, which led to Lucy prying out yet another interesting story from Opal.

There were stories from before she was married, of her crazy single days, or from times when she was married and the adventures she and Henry, Lucy's grandfather, had experienced, meeting all different kinds of people from all around the world. Opal told stories of after Henry's passing, how her world had changed, not for better or worse, just changed.

Instead of sitting around the house, sad that she was now single again, which she had done for a few months, Opal had decided to see the world and her city again, from her new, older perspective. Surprisingly to Opal, she was still able to have fun, and she had been able to gain perspective on her husband's passing without sitting around the house, pining for something that would never be again. She knew without a doubt that her Henry would have wanted her to continue on loving life, and she had done so, with a vengeance.

Lucy loved Opal's stories, loved trying to picture her in all of the adventures or embarrassing situations she told Lucy about. She could see where Opal got all of her character and life experiences. She had definitely been through some tough times and witnessed some amazing things.

Lucy hoped one day that she could have a story like Opal did; that she could know without a doubt that she had lived a good life, one full of love and laughter. She even wanted loss because Lucy was beginning to realize that without the hard times in life, the good ones wouldn't seem as great, as sparkling.

* * * * *

Lucy woke the morning of Summer's arrival with a smile on her face. It was one of her much-cherished days off, and her plan was to head over to Grinder after breakfast with Opal. She could hardly remember the last time she was able to relax in the morning with Opal and then just sit around joking with Teddy while he whipped up a new concoction.

Since she had time to spare this morning, she decided to check her email. She hadn't heard anything from Drew for a while, and against her better judgment, she was beginning to worry about him. Yes, he had been a jerk and should look into getting help for himself and the way he treated her when they had been together, but she didn't want him in serious trouble for something Corbin had done. She maybe shouldn't care, but she did, that was just the way she was.

Logging on, she saw she had received an email from him just a few minutes prior.

> Lucy—
> Please read this!!! I know you said not to contact you again, but I just had to. Thank you for your offer of help from your mother. Even though I am sure she is not my number one fan right now, I appreciate the fact that she probably would help if I needed it. But ... I AM OKAY!!! Everything has been straightened out! Corbin got into some hot water with the authorities in Mexico, but thankfully he told the truth and the rest of us are back in the USA!!! Don't worry, I will not be coming to look for you. I realize that was wrong of me and that you were right. I did ask you for a divorce, and I don't have any say in what you do or where you go anymore. It's good to hear that you are enjoying your time with Opal. I hope she is doing well, and I hope you are also.
> The guys and I are—as we speak—renting a place in LA! We are loving HOLLYWOOD! I don't know how long we will be here or where we will go next, but let me say I am finally enjoying myself! It seems that Corbin was the "wet blanket" all along!
> Drew

Surprised by what she had just read from Drew (was the email actually *from* Drew or had someone hacked his account?), Lucy hesitantly replied and then shut her computer.

If it was Drew, it was the Drew she knew from her very distant past. He had surprised her … but today was a good day for surprises, she thought.

> Drew—Is this really you??? Anyways, I am glad to hear that you are back in the US! I hope you have fun in Hollywood, maybe you'll spot some celebs while you are there. Don't forget the sunscreen …
> Lucy

Lucy took her time in the shower and then skipped into one of her favorite places, her closet, to pick out yet another outfit that she hadn't yet tried out. Looking around, she noticed a bunch of new stuff, as in— Opal had been shopping for her, *again*. Shaking her head, Lucy looked through her recent gifts.

Opal really did have amazing taste. No matter how many times Lucy told her that she didn't need to do this, to buy her all these things, Opal just smiled and said it was something she liked to do, she wanted to spoil her. Every now and then Lucy would notice new clothes, shoes, or jewelry in her closet, reminding her again of Opal and her never-ending generosity.

Throwing on pink skinny jeans with a black belt and a blank tank, Lucy danced down the hallway and into the kitchen, smelling the mouthwatering smells that was Lila cooking breakfast. Lucy wasn't sure what she'd do when it was time for her to go back to her hometown or move out. She was going to miss Lila and her cooking. She was definitely getting spoiled in more than one way, and she was really liking it.

Sitting at the kitchen table, reading the paper and drinking her signature tea, Opal appeared a little pale, which instantly worried Lucy. "Hey, Opal, you feeling okay?" Lucy inquired.

Looking up with a scowl, Opal replied, "You know, I really dislike when people ask that because it implies that I look horrible. So no, I'm not feeling okay. Thank you very much!" She made a small harrumph sound and went back to her paper.

Lucy, still unsure of how to act when Opal was in one of her moods, tried to ignore it and move on to more exciting topics of conversation. "Oh, Opal, I was only asking because Summer and her man are coming into town today. I was hoping you'd be up for going to Teddy's party with us." Lucy smiled big at Opal, hoping she'd buy it.

Pursing her lips, Opal replied, "I'm on to you. Don't think you can pull a fast one on me!"

Trying not to laugh, Lucy said, "Okay then. So does that mean you're in?" She batted her eyelashes at Opal playfully.

Looking up at Lucy's hopeful face, Opal couldn't help but smile, saying, "Look at that face! Okay, we'll see, I'm not promising anything, but I'll at least be up for dinner somewhere special. We've got to show your friend around now, don't we?"

Lucy shimmied to the kitchen bar and grabbed a bowl of Lila's thick, creamy oatmeal. "Oh yeah, going out Opal style! Summer's going to die!" She shouted and then grooved on back to Opal, making her shake her head, trying to contain her laughter.

They talked about plans for the few days that Summer and her guy were going to be there, Lucy explaining that the only solid plan they had was to go to Teddy's party.

Opal suggested a few places that Lucy could take them to, and then she offered up her home, saying that she was fine if Summer and her boyfriend stayed there. Lucy thanked Opal, saying that she had received a text from Summer yesterday, excitedly saying that Drew had surprised her with a suite at a downtown hotel, and they would be staying there.

Sighing with envy, Lucy added, "One day that could be me." She put her hand to her heart and looked up towards the ceiling dramatically.

"One day?" Opal queried, eyeing Lucy, "Don't tell me you've forgotten about Jax already, girl?"

Blushing at the warm feeling that spread throughout her body at the sound of his name, Lucy clarified, "No way have I forgotten about him. I just meant that one day I hope to be surprised like that. Summer and her Drew seem to be pretty serious already, but that's Summer for you. If she's going to fall in love, she isn't going to be slow about it." Lucy scraped the last bit of oatmeal from her bowl and leaned back against her chair.

Giving Lucy a suspicious look, Opal asked, "Don't tell me *you* aren't in love with Jax?"

Lucy quickly looked away, unsure of what to say. She was pretty sure she was in love with him, but it seemed like they had only just met. They'd been dating for about two months, and it wasn't her style for things to be moving so fast. As she thought about how she felt about Jax, her thoughts were interrupted by Opal.

"Just as I thought. You are in love with him, but you're afraid to admit it."

Opal then finished her oatmeal, and as she put her spoon down, she looked at Lucy, waiting for an answer.

"I just think it's a little fast, that's all. Fast for me, that is. I've never felt this way before about anyone, and I don't want to mess it up. I'm not sure he feels the same way, and I'm not about to go confessing my undying love to him and freak him out."

Lucy's leg was bouncing, the way it did when she was nervous. She quickly stopped it, not wanting to give away her feelings.

Shaking her head, Opal sighed and said, "Have you learned nothing? You have but one life on this earth, and it's a short one. Even if you live to be ninety, it's still short! Go for it, don't be afraid. Don't be crazy either, no one likes a crazy girl, but … if you feel like things are good, and they seem to be from what I can tell, then just don't hold back. You don't need to confess your love, but don't hold back from feeling anything, just let those feelings come and see what happens." Opal shifted in her chair to get a better look at Lucy.

"Sometimes that's hard, though, to let go of being afraid. I want to and I try to, but sometimes I just can't," Lucy confessed, lifting a shoulder and tilting her head to one side, feeling a little unsure.

Smiling, Opal assured her, "I get that, I've felt that way before. What has always helped me is thinking, 'It is what it is,' at times when I'm not sure what to do or am worried about what may happen. You know, you can't control other people and you can't always control every situation, so in those types of circumstances, thinking that it is what it is can help you let go." She paused and then added, "I'm a big fan of the thought that where you are right now is exactly where you need to be."

Thinking about it for a few minutes, Lucy came to the conclusion that Opal's advice probably would make her feel better. Just knowing that it was okay to let go and see what happened sometimes was a relief. Lucy felt silly for not believing this before. She had stressed out over so many things, worried so much, but stress and worry didn't ever make anything better. They only seemed to make things worse for the person who was stressed and worried. Letting go would feel so much better. Looking over at Opal, Lucy stated, "Opal, you always have the best advice."

Smiling, Opal replied, "I know! Now take it and run with it. Use it and learn from me! I'm not getting any younger here, and I want to see you happy and settled before I leave this place."

Getting up and taking her bowl to the sink, Lucy remarked, "Way to put the pressure on, Opal. How am I going to let go now?" Lucy winked at Opal and added, "I'm just joking. Today my mission is to let go and see what happens. I'm going to go see Teddy now. It's been a long time since I've been able to just sit around at Grinder. What are you up to today?"

Shifting in her chair, Opal grimaced and then reported, "Another doctor's appointment, but let's not talk about that. Let's plan on going out for dinner tonight around eight. Does that work for you, dear?"

Hearing about Opal's doctor appointment, Lucy felt guilty. Here she was, talking to Opal about things that really didn't matter in the face of Opal's diagnosis, and she hadn't even been to one appointment with Opal.

"Are you absolutely sure that you don't want me to come with you? I feel guilty ... I haven't been with you once to an appointment. Plus, I am just over here blubbering about my problems when you are over there with cancer. I'm just so *sorry*."

"Now don't you go on feeling like that, Lucy!" Opal replied, her voice strong and sure, "I've told you before and I will tell you again—I would much rather not have you come to my doctor visits with me. I just don't want you thinking about me and remembering that. Thank you for your offer, but I'd much rather you be out having fun, living your *own* life! You aren't blubbering about something insignificant; you are blubbering about something that matters to you! And if it matters to you, if it's important to you, then it is important to me. So from now on, no more talk like that, got it?" Opal looked at her with a look in her eye that said she meant business, and then she added, "Dinner tonight, yes?"

Trying not to worry about Opal and her never-ending doctor visits, Lucy smiled, answering, "That would be great Opal. I'm so excited for you and Summer to meet, and I can't wait to take her out. She is going to love it."

Feeling a little better, Lucy gave Opal a quick hug and dashed out the door. She could tell that Opal was serious, and rather than having another long discussion to make sure of it, she decided to take her word for it. She was off to have some fun.

Now that she was thinking about Summer again, she was getting antsy for her to arrive. She wanted to talk with Teddy about the party tonight and what she should wear. She also was excited to have a few hours just relaxing before Summer got there.

She knew it was going to be a wild ride with Summer in town, meeting Drew and taking them out with Opal, going to Teddy's party, doing whatever else Summer had thought of—which could be anything, really. Lucy knew by the time *that* tornado left town she would be exhausted.

Waving to Oliver and stepping outside, Lucy breathed in the sunshine and warm summer air. She loved it here and never wanted to leave. She hoped she would never have to. The sudden thought startled her. She knew she was having fun with Opal, enjoying their time together as well as her time with Jax and Teddy, and more recently her time at Saucy Baby. But for her to absolutely know, without a doubt, that this was the place for her, that she never wanted to leave, and if she had to do so, would do so kicking and screaming, was a huge deal to her. She had never felt those kinds of ties to a place before. Even her hometown didn't bring out those feelings in her. Something inside of her was changing, evolving, and she was starting to feel a little unsteady thinking about it.

Trying to puzzle it out as she walked down the street towards Grinder, one word came to mind, and that word was—roots. Lucy tried to shove the word aside, shaking her head as she did so. How could she possibly be growing roots here? She only had been here for almost two months. Lucy tried to convince herself that "roots" wasn't it.

You needed history to have roots, you needed time and space and, what? She wasn't sure what all you needed to have roots, and even though she tried pushing that word away because—did she even want to have roots here? She was most definitely confused—that little voice inside her head, which sounded considerably like Opal, kept saying, "It is what it is, and roots it could be."

Lucy huffed out a breath and pushed the door open to Grinder. She was feeling frustrated from her little walk and epiphany. The walk should have been refreshing, and what was so wrong with having roots? Why was the thought scaring her so much? She wished she could just figure it out, make up her mind, and know! Huffing out another breath, she remembered her mission to let go and let things be as they were. She was exactly where she needed to be, right?

Resolving to start over, start fresh, she said quietly to herself, "It is what it is." Then she looked up at Teddy, who was smiling and chuckling at her. "Hey, Teddy," she greeted him.

"Hey, Lucy, having a brutal morning or something?" He grinned at her and made his way from the counter to back behind the bar, asking, "Need a double Lucky Lucy today?"

Confused, Lucy inquired, "Double?"

Shaking his head in mock disgust, he said, "Don't you remember anything from our days together? Dang, girl! Double, you know, extra shot?"

Feeling like an idiot, of course, she knew that. Didn't she? She nodded to Teddy and pulled up a seat at the table closest to the bar.

Watching her flop into her seat and put her head into her hands, Teddy asked, "You okay there, girl? What's the problemo?"

Lifting her head and peaking over her hands at Teddy, she explained glumly, "I think I'm growing roots." Her head fell back into her hands as she groaned.

Teddy looked at her in confusion, his lip curling up, and questioned,

"What are you *talking* about?" He stopped his drink making and added quickly, "Should I be worried?"

"Roots! I'm talking about roots!" she cried, flinging up her hands and shaking them at Teddy.

Teddy walked over slowly and sat her drink down in front of her. Then he bent down to look at her hair closely, remarking, "Nah, girl, don't worry about it! I don't see your roots growing in. I never even knew you colored your hair. Dang! Where do you go? I need that number!"

Taking a drink, Lucy choked. Slamming her cup down and grabbing a napkin from the table, she cried out, "No, Teddy! Not those kind of roots!" She was about to go off on him some more when she realized she was getting looks from the few costumers that were seated around her.

Adding to her embarrassment, Cash stalked out of the back door, hands and eyebrows raised at Lucy, ordering, "Seriously, Lucy? Take it down a notch, okay?" He glared at her for a few more seconds, then slowly turned, and walked back into the back room.

Nodding to her drink, Teddy told her, "Drink up, babe. Obviously, you need it." He looked around at the other customers, smiling radiantly.

"Thanks," Lucy replied. Then she huffed out one last breath. She really needed to get this figured out.

"So, roots, huh? Do tell." Teddy took a seat next to Lucy, keeping an eye out for anyone who might need anything.

"Roots, you know—like when someone says you need to have roots or your family has roots. You know, like ties to a place, I guess," she tried to explain, rubbing her forehead.

Eyebrows lowered, Teddy stated, "O-o-o-o-o-kay. And what's so wrong with that?"

"I don't know!" Lucy shrieked.

When Teddy looked at her, and then nodded towards the back room where Cash was, she continued quietly, "Sorry. I'm not sure what's wrong with that or if anything is. The problem is, I'm confused. This morning, walking here, I was thinking how I never want to leave this city, that I love it here, *really* love it. But, I've never felt connected like this to a place before, even my hometown, where my mom and Summer are. Doesn't that seem weird? Shouldn't my roots be where I grew up, where my family is? Shouldn't they be where I've spent most of my life, where all my memories are? I think something is wrong with me."

Teddy chuckled and told her, "There's nothing wrong with you, Lucy. Like it or not, this place is a huge part of who you are. You *do* have history here, even if you don't remember it. It's in your blood." He smiled at her.

"How do you know? How can *I* know?" Lucy asked, surprised by the deepness of their conversation. She'd always known Teddy was someone she could talk to about anything, but they'd never had a conversation like this before. It felt good to be able to talk to him so freely about what was bothering her.

Smiling slowly at her, he asked, "Can't you feel it?"

Confused, Lucy questioned, "Feel what?"

"That you belong here. You know, that feeling deep inside that tells you this is the place, *your* place." He raised an eyebrow at her and continued, "Just because you didn't grow up here or spend each day waking up in the same bedroom in the same house *here*, doesn't mean that the way you are feeling is wrong. You *do* have family here, and you *are* making memories here. Everybody's different, Lucy, some people stay in one place their whole lives, and others move around until they find what feels right. That's what you're doing, isn't it? Finding what feels right for you?"

Frowning slightly, Lucy replied, "Yes, but, it just scared me, I guess. To have this sudden realization that I might have found that place, and it's here and now. It also scared me that it never was or will be the place where I grew up."

Teddy laughed and explained, "You *do* have roots where you grew up Lucy. They are just spreading out a little bit. You're growing and so are they."

Sighing, as Teddy stood up and patted her on the shoulder, Lucy commented, "You make it sound so simple."

"It is," he promised. Then he walked away to whip up another cup of joy for someone who had just come in.

They spent the afternoon relaxing, well Lucy did. Teddy spent it working. They discussed Summer, her Drew, and the party Teddy was DJing that night. As the day went on, Lucy began to feel more comfortable with her roots realization from that morning. Teddy was right, it was okay for her to feel connected to this place. Opal had been here her whole life, and Lucy herself had visited many times before the ill-fated moment between her mother and Opal. Even if she didn't remember it, it had happened. Some part of this place had stayed with her since then and was just coming to life now. She was starting to realize it was okay to admit that it felt, really, really good.

As early afternoon turned into late afternoon, which was about to turn into early evening, Lucy began to wonder if Jax was going to show up at Grinder. It wasn't like him not to stop by for one of Teddy's signature drinks, and Lucy was hoping to see him before she had to get home. She wanted to freshen up before Summer and Drew arrived, and pick something fun to wear for their sure-to-be exciting night together.

Lucy stood up and stretched, thinking she would see Jax tonight at Teddy's party when the door opened and in walked the hottest guy on the planet. Lucy smiled, feeling her heart speed up. She didn't think she could ever get tired of her body's reaction to Jax.

Walking towards Lucy, Jax sent Teddy a salute and called out to him "Lucky Lucy please, Tedster." He stopped when their bodies were nearly touching, looked down at Lucy, and announced, "Now here's the girl I've been waiting to see all day. You ready for the big night?"

Feeling butterflies in her stomach, she smiled as she looked up at him and replied, "As ready as I'll ever be I guess. You never know about Summer. She's a bit of a wild card, I guess you could say, but in a good way."

She smiled thinking about Summer, her unpredictability was something you could always count on, and continued, "We're going out to dinner with Opal before we head out to Teddy's. Would you like to come with us?" Lucy swallowed, waiting to see his reaction. She wasn't quite sure what Jax would think of dinner with Opal. He still seemed a little wary of her, worried about her protectiveness of Lucy. Lucy knew, though, that once they met, they would instantly get along.

Searching Lucy's eyes, he said, "I'd love that, Lucy. If you think Opal wouldn't mind." He cleared his throat, obviously nervous just thinking about it.

Laughing, Lucy declared, "Well, I believe this is the first time I have seen you nervous! It's actually really sexy ..." Lucy trailed off, a little embarrassed at what she had just said, but Jax just laughed.

"Well, Lucy, you might see a lot of it tonight. I have to admit, I'm a little bit terrified of Opal. She seems very lioness-like, and I'm pretty sure that if she doesn't like me, she won't have any problem telling me then and there." He thoughtfully rubbed his chin, looking at Lucy, as if to make sure it was safe for him to join them tonight.

"Lioness! Ha, that's a perfect term for her, I love it!" she agreed, shaking her head and thinking Jax was right on. When she looked up and saw Jax's worried face, she grabbed his hand and continued, "You really don't have to worry about Opal, Jax. She has always encouraged me to spend time with you. She likes you, well, what I've said about you. Summer on the other hand ..." Lucy grinned as she said this to him.

He squinted down at her, saying, "Something tells me I really don't have to worry about Summer."

"You're right," Lucy said, leaning closer to him to give a quick kiss, "You really don't have to worry about anything."

Jax pulled away and smiled, when Teddy called out, "Lucky Lucy!" Jax walked over to the bar and grabbed his coffee, giving Teddy a grin, adding, "Thanks, man."

"No prob," Teddy said, then nodded at the clock, and told Lucy, "You'd better get on it, girl,"

Looking at the clock, Lucy jumped up and said, "Thanks, Teddy! See you tonight." Then she turned to Jax and offered her hand, asking, "Walk me home?"

"How could I refuse?" he responded as he took her hand into his own and led them out into the magical night air.

* * * * *

"Lucy!" Opal called down the hall towards her room, "They're on their way up!"

"Thanks, Opal, coming!" Lucy called back, as she grabbed her black leather jacket and threw her credit card and ID in the pocket. With the bright yellow dress she had on—super cute, the yellow version of a little black dress, tight, short, and hot—her leather jacket would add a little edge to her ensemble.

Lucy ran down the hall and slid into the entry right as the elevator bell sent out a loud chime. Then the doors opened and her best friend stepped out, followed by a very attractive, perfectly dressed, tall, dark, and handsome guy.

Lucy and Summer took one look at each other and screamed, rushing toward each other into a hug all the while jumping up and down. The commotion caused Opal to laugh and shake her head while Drew smiled and pretended to plug his ears.

Stepping away from Lucy, Summer declared, "Wow. You look amazing! Seriously, Lucy!"

Smiling in response, Lucy looked at Summer, and shook her head, "You too, I mean those shorts? Those are perfectly you. Why haven't I seen those before?" Lucy looked at Summer's short, gold sequined shorts, cream sheer shirt, and cream heels, and pulled her into a hug again. She was so happy to see her. "I can't believe you are actually here! I've missed you so much!"

"I can't believe I'm here either, finally! It's seemed like forever, forever that I've been doing some amazing shopping without you," Summer replied and then grabbed Drew's hand and pulled him towards them, announcing, "This is Drew, but … you've met before." Summer laughed and smiled up at the man she was in love with.

"Nice to see you again, Lucy," Drew said. He surprised her by pulling her in for a quick hug.

Blushing, Lucy regained her composure, hoping nobody noticed her flushed face, and replied, "You too. Sorry about … that thing before." She looked at Summer and shook her head, remembering that day.

"Don't be sorry. If it weren't for that, I would have never met Summer," he responded, smiling over at Summer, putting his arm around her, and pulling her close. "It was the best and luckiest day of my life. Well, until the next day when I got to spend more time with her when she agreed to go out with me."

Summer leaned her head back against his chest and looked up at him, smiling.

Observing the lovebirds, Lucy noticed that they looked amazing together, like a couple out of a magazine. She felt a little ping of jealously but shook it away. She was happy for Summer. She deserved every bit of happiness she was getting right now, and Lucy hoped things would work out between the two of them. So far Drew seemed the perfect gentleman.

Remembering Opal, who was standing beside Lucy, observing Summer and Drew as well, Lucy announced, "This is Opal—my amazing grandma!"

Lucy smiled as Opal rolled her eyes and said, "Hello, Summer, it's wonderful to meet you after all these years of stories. And Drew, nice to meet you as well. Would you like to sit for a drink before dinner or—?"

Bowden approached before Opal could continue, and quietly interrupted, saying, "I'm sorry, Opal, but reservations are for eight, so we really should be going." He then smiled over at Summer and Drew, offering, "It's nice to meet you two finally. Lucy has been talking nonstop about your arrival. I'm Bowden."

After everyone said their hellos, Bowden looked over at Lucy to tell her, "Jax is down in the car. I caught him on the way up and said it was fine if he met us there."

Lucy felt her cheeks redden as she felt all eyes on her. She announced quietly, "I hope you all don't mind, but I invited Jax along."

Summer's eyes popped, and she grabbed Drew's hand, squeezing tightly. "This is going to be good!" she exclaimed.

Opal grinned at Lucy as they made their way down to the car, asking, "You nervous?"

"Terrified!" Lucy admitted.

In response, Opal laughed a throaty laugh, and confided, "I would be, too."

When they got down to where the car was waiting for them, Lucy saw Jax standing beside the car, talking on his phone. When he saw them, he raised a waving hand, spoke a few more words to whomever he was talking, and then ended his conversation. "Hello," he said to the group as they approached. "Hi, Lucy," he added, smiling at her.

Leaning in towards Lucy, Summer whispered, "Oh my gosh, are you kidding me? He is *smokin'*!"

Smacking Summer on the arm, Lucy noted quietly, "I know, right!" Then she walked up to where Jax was standing and said, "Hi, I'm glad you're here." She gave him a quick hug, then turned, and introduced him around.

When it came Opal's turn to say hello, Lucy could tell Jax was nervous, but she had to admit he held it together pretty well, saying, "It's great to meet you, Opal. Lucy has been telling me a lot about you. You're pretty much a legend around here."

"Oh well, I hope she hasn't given away *all* my secrets. A girl's got to have some mystery surrounding her, don't you agree?" Opal replied, giving Jax a sly smile and then continuing, "It's good to finally meet *you*, Jax. This girl here has been glowing for weeks, and I think you're to thank for that." Opal winked at him.

Lucy gave Opal a look. She was starting to think maybe having dinner together wasn't such a good idea after all.

Shrugging nonchalantly at Lucy, Opal went on, "What? It's true. It's about time the boy knows you're hooked. The sooner he knows that, the sooner he can ease my mind that he has no plans of hurting you." She cleared her throat and looked at Jax square in the eyes, "So, boy," she interrogated, "do you? What are your intentions with my Lucy?"

Red-cheeked, Lucy turned to give Summer a save-me look. But when she saw Summer's expression, she knew she wouldn't be any help. Summer was covering her mouth, trying not to laugh, thoroughly enjoying the spectacle before her eyes. Drew seemed to be a little more sympathetic, probably wondering if he would have to go through the ringer with Opal at one point or another. He gave Lucy a small smile and raised his eyebrows, looking a bit unsure of how to proceed.

Looking back towards Jax, who was looking more than a little uncomfortable, Lucy saw Bowden coming to her rescue with his suggestion, "Why don't you continue your conversation in the car on the way to dinner, Opal? I don't want you to be late."

He then opened the door to the car and guided Opal inside. Turning towards Lucy, he mouthed, "Sorry," and made a silly face, making her laugh.

When they were all piled in the car, nice and cozy, Opal looked back at Jax and inquired, "So, have you formulated an answer yet?"

Jax looked over at Lucy next to him, and she gave him a small smile, trying to read his expression.

Lucy began, "I am so, so sorry about this, I—" but before she could finished, Jax gave her his award-winning smile and looked at Opal.

"Opal, I have absolutely no intentions of hurting your Lucy. I think she is an amazing person and have enjoyed all the time I have been lucky enough to spend with her. To be honest, I wish we could spend more time together. I miss her whenever we're not together, when we are apart it actually hurts and that's saying a lot because I've never felt something like that before, ever."

He swallowed and looked at Lucy. He had a look on his face she had never seen before, and it made her heart beat triple time. He continued, "If you're asking me what my intentions are with Lucy, well, she absolutely, positively has all of my heart. I would like nothing more than for her to be mine forever." He grabbed Lucy's hand and squeezed, keeping his eyes steady on Opal.

Summer gasped, Drew smiled, and Lucy's jaw dropped, all at the same time as Opal looked back at Jax, stating, "Well, that, young man, was exactly what I wanted to hear. Thank you. It couldn't have been an easy thing to say to me in front of everyone else. Nonetheless, you've put my mind at ease better than I expected, and for that you have my blessing." She smiled and reached back to pat his hand.

Seeming to have just noticed the reactions of the others, Opal questioned, "What's the problem with all of you? Haven't you ever heard someone confess their love before? Lucy, close your mouth! Summer, stop staring!"

Jax leaned down and kissed Lucy on the head, and then whispered, "I hope that wasn't too much for you to hear. I figured if I wanted her off my case I'd have to give it to her all out. She seems like an all-or-nothing type of lady."

Feeling like her heart was about to burst, Lucy leaned into Jax. She couldn't believe what he had just confessed to Opal. Hearing him say that he felt that way about her was a dream come true, but she was worried that it was happening too fast.

Taking a breath, she shook the thought from her mind, remembering what Opal had told her earlier. Lucy knew how she felt. She was pretty sure she was in love with him. Love didn't have instructions or directions, and it wasn't the same for everyone. Sometimes love grew on you, surprising you with the realization when you least expected it years later, and sometimes there it was, standing right in front of you at a coffee shop, the very first day you set foot outside of your new place.

Lucy didn't want to worry or be cautious about her feelings with Jax. She simply wanted to just let them be and see where they took her. On that thought, she whispered back to him, "No, it's not too much at all. It's perfect, in fact. I feel the same way, and to hear you say it, say what's in my heart too, I don't think this night could get any better." She snuggled in closer, breathing in his scent. He always smelled so good.

Laying his head on hers, he replied, "Don't bet on that, I have a feeling that with you and me, things are just going to get better and better and better." Then he smiled at her, and it took her breath away.

That had been happening a lot lately, and she was really enjoying it.

Finally arriving at the restaurant, everyone seemed to breathe a sigh of relief, even though the rest of the car ride had been confession-free. Everyone had been on guard, just in case Opal tried to pry anymore information out of an unwilling or unprepared victim.

Lucy laughed at Summer's expression when the owner of the restaurant (which was, of course, the best of the best, and was frequented by the celebs who were in town) greeted Opal by name and led them to the best seat in the house.

By the time their main course had arrived, Summer was most definitely in awe of Opal. Opal had regaled them with the story of how she had come to meet the owner of the place they were now in. Her story wasn't without drama or scandal, and Opal didn't hold anything back, making their experience dining at the star-studded place even more interesting and exciting.

After dessert, Opal said her good-byes, leaving for home and bed, whispering into Lucy's ear, "You're one lucky girl. I knew he was one of the good ones right from the start. Don't let that one go." She then waved good-bye, got slowly into the car, and Bowden whisked her away.

"Wow," Summer said when they were standing out in the warm summer air, waiting for a cab, "She's amazing, Lucy! Can you believe her story? You are so lucky, Lucy, she really is a legend!"

Nodding, Lucy agreed, "I know, it *is* amazing, and it's like that everywhere we go, too. I've lost track of the times we've been places and people know her, and all of her stories. It's crazy, she's lived an amazing life, she really has."

Laughing to himself, Drew looked at Jax, saying, "Man, that was intense in the car. I don't know what I would have done if I'd been in your spot. She is definitely something else." Then he leaned over and slapped Jax on the back twice, almost congratulating him.

Shrugging, Jax replied, "Yeah, well like I told Lucy, it's all or nothing with Opal. She wants the real truth. I knew she wouldn't stop until she got it, so … I just gave it to her." He laughed and added, "With an audience."

He grinned at Lucy and then hailed the cab that was cruising down the street.

Jumping into the cab, Lucy scooted over to let everyone else in. She gave the cabby the address to Teddy's party. Looking over at Summer, she said, "I hope you're ready to dance, Sum."

Flashing her megawatt smile, Summer replied, "You know me, baby, I'm always up for some dancing. I might even get a little crazy." She bumped Drew's shoulder with her own and winked at him.

Rolling his eyes dramatically, Drew countered, "Great, I have a feeling it's going to be a long night."

Grabbing his chin, Summer told him, "You know you love it, don't pretend you don't like going out Summer-style." She gave him a quick kiss and smiled back at Lucy, wiggling her eyebrows.

Chuckling, Lucy said to Drew, "I know just how you feel. But now, instead of me dealing with her when her crazy night is over, you get to!" Lucy looked at Summer thoughtfully and added, "Actually, crazy is sounding a lot more fun right about now."

"Oh, yeah! Tonight is our night, Luce! No one will be able to touch us tonight because we are *untouchable*, baby. *Magic!*" Summer declared, shimmying in what small space she had in the cab's backseat.

"That's right, Sum. We're going to shine, baby!"

"Like a diamond!"

The two dissolved into giggles as Drew and Jax sent each other looks.

"Uh, what's going on here?" Jax asked, amused at the sight of Lucy, face red from laughing, tears streaming down her face.

"I'm guessing this is a normal occurrence when these two get together," Drew suggested, shrugging his shoulders and smiling at Summer. "I have a feeling we'd better get ready for—"

Before Drew could finish his sentence, Summer and Lucy cut him off singing together, "It's going to be crazy, baby!"

The only thing that Jax and Drew could do was give each other worried looks before they were dragged into the new and unexplored territories of girls' night with Summer and Lucy.

CHAPTER TWELVE

Lucy woke up to a pounding. Was someone knocking on the door? She lifted her head and immediately regretted it. Nope, no one was knocking on the door, but something *was* knocking around in her head, and it hurt.

She opened her eyes and looked around confused. She had no idea where she was or how she had gotten there. A little worried, she wondered where Summer was and if she was waking up with the same feelings as Lucy. She doubted it though; Summer was probably still fast asleep, snoring away, as usual. If she were to wake up at an unfamiliar location, she wouldn't be aware of the fact for a few more hours.

Looking around, trying to identify anything that would tell her where she was, she jumped when the door opened and a guy walked in.

"Hey, beautiful," he said, smiling. He carried a tray with bacon, eggs, toast, and orange juice on it. There was also a vase with a bright pink daisy inside of it wobbling on the edge of the tray.

Sitting up slowly, Lucy pulled the covers up around her and replied, "Hello, so … where *am* I exactly?" She tried to keep her eyes off of his bare chest but was sadly unsuccessful.

Grinning at her, he answered, "My place, of course." He set the tray down in front of her carefully and then added, "I'll be right back with the coffee."

Lucy nodded and eyed the tray. The food looked amazing, delicious even, but she wasn't sure her stomach could handle it right now. She wasn't sure her stomach could handle the fact that Opal would be getting up and wondering just where she was. At any moment in fact her phone could ring, and she'd have to answer it and tell Opal she had woken up in some guy's apartment.

Of course, it wasn't just any guy's apartment. It was Jax's, so she was hoping that if Opal did call, she might be okay with it. Oh, who was she kidding? Opal would either be totally okay with it or totally not, depending on the mood she was in, but what she wouldn't be okay with was a lack of phone call or any sort of message letting her know where she was.

Feeling guilty, Lucy was about to pick up her phone and call Opal when Jax walked back into the room. "Hey, aren't you hungry? Or do you need your coffee first?" He smiled and handed her a to-go cup with Grinder emblazoned on the side.

"Did you go to Grinder?" she asked, shocked.

"Yes, ma'am," he answered, sitting down beside her and helping himself to a piece of bacon.

"Already?" she asked, taking a much-needed sip of Teddy's magic.

"What do you mean, 'already'? It's almost noon, silly girl." He picked up another piece of bacon and handed it to her.

Shocked, Lucy slowly took the bacon, asking, "Noon? I never sleep this late. What the heck *happened* last night?"

Laughing, Jax explained, "Well, you and Summer definitely had your crazy night! It was great to see you having so much fun, Lucy. Just seeing you smile all night long made my night. Oh, and Drew! Can you believe it?"

Lucy squinted at Jax, unsure what he was talking about, so she asked, "What *about* Drew?"

"You don't remember?" Jax asked, smiling a little.

"Remember what? Opal is going to kill me, by the way. She's probably worried sick right now." Lucy picked up her phone again to call Opal, but Jax grabbed it out of her hands.

"Whoa, whoa, wait. What *do* you remember?" he asked, holding her phone just out of reach.

Not having the energy to try and get the phone back, Lucy sighed and settled back against the headboard to think about last night. "Well," she began, "I remember the cab ride, obviously, and getting to the party. Teddy is an awesome DJ, I remember that part. Then Cash was there handing out some kind of drink, and after that I just remember ... bits and pieces, I guess." She peeked at Jax and asked, "Did I do anything embarrassing?"

Messing her hair, he said, "No, unless you'd call dragging Cash out on the dance floor embarrassing. Or announcing to all the partygoers that you were one of the new DJs 'on the scene' while trying to 'mix some awesome beats' that were, well ... not all that awesome. Embarrassing maybe, but, I'd just call all of that cute." He grabbed more bacon and smiled.

Slapping her hand over her mouth, Lucy shook her head as images started flooding her memory. Yes, dancing with Carson. Trying to DJ while Teddy stood nearby looking amused. She and Summer forcing Teddy to play "Ice Ice Baby" and then doing their high school dance team dance to the song. Cringing, Lucy sighed. "Yeah, *that* was bad. That's why those crazy nights with Summer were always few and far between."

Studying her, Jax offered, "You know, if you ever lose your job at Saucy Baby, I'm sure there are many dance groups that would love to have someone such as yourself join their ranks. What with you being able to do those high kicks and all." Jax couldn't help himself and starting cracking up at the memory.

"Yeah, thanks for that," Lucy told him, punching him in the arm, well aware that her punch had zero amount of oomph this morning.

"Oh!" Jax yelled out, smiling at her again and continuing, "and you don't have to worry about Opal, either. I'm not sure if you remember *that* or not, but you called her a few times to let her know you were 'going home with your man.' You seemed very excited about it too, that is until your head hit the pillow. And then, boom, you were out."

"I didn't!" Lucy cried, horrified.

"Oh," Jax responded with chuckles, "you did."

Mortified, Lucy squeezed her eyes shut, hoping those memories wouldn't decide to come back and surprise her anytime soon. "Well, at least I know she's not worried about me lying in a ditch somewhere."

"Yeah," Jax said as he made a "drink up" motion and gestured toward her coffee. "You definitely *don't* have to worry about that. She seemed amused and wished me good luck. I think she knew by what you were saying that you were long gone, pretty close to snoozeville, if you know what I mean."

Looking at Jax quizzically, Lucy inquired, "What?"

Shaking his head, he responded, "She really is something, that Opal. She told me that I should count on a long night of you snoring away. It was pretty funny, actually, and accurate. I'd never thought you'd be the snoring type, Lucy." He piled some eggs and toast onto a plate and handed it over to her. He was obviously going to get her to eat, whether she liked it or not.

"What? I don't snore. That's all Summer. I never have," Lucy reported, her voice matter-of-fact, digging into her eggs. Even though she was probably never going to live down the embarrassing moments of last night, her stomach was starting to settle and the food was starting to look and smell mouthwatering.

"Sorry, but snore you do. But, it's a cute snore—very girly, so it's okay," he responded with a smile and took a drink of his coffee.

Sending him a look, she disagreed, "Nope, you're wrong. You're just trying to trick me, but I'm not buying it."

"Oh, am I, right? I'm going to have to record you next time to prove it!" A look of triumph crossed his face.

Taking a bite of toast, Lucy asked, "What makes you so sure there will be a next time?"

"Because," he said simply, "you love me, that's why." He then grinned his grin and took a bite of his own toast, all the while trying not to laugh at the expression plastered across Lucy's face.

Speechless, Lucy finally caught her breath and countered, "Oh really, and who told you that?"

Not able to hide his smirk, he proudly revealed, "You did. Last night."

Sinking back against the bed again, Lucy could only lament, "I'm never going to live this down, am I?"

"Nope," he replied, shooting her his ever-amazing grin. "Not while I'm around, you're not."

Then he grabbed her plate, moved the tray aside and said, "Now, about last night … I believe we missed something …"

Lucy's eyes widened as he stopped talking and slid into the sheets beside her. Taking in his amazing eyes, heart-stopping grin and the fact that he had just told a car full of people that he wanted to spend the rest of his life with her, she had to agree.

"You're right," she assented, smiling up at him, "I believe we did."

* * * * *

"Hey!" Lucy jumped in her seat and looked over at Jax. They were in his car on the way to meet Summer and Drew for lunch. Jax had driven Lucy home, so she could shower and change clothes before they met. Thankfully the house had been quiet, so Lucy didn't have to face anyone just then. She hadn't been ready to see Opal or to answer any questions about her previous wild night.

Jax looked over at her quickly, inquiring "What's up?" He put his hand on her knee and squeezed.

Putting her hand over his, she stated, "You said something about Drew earlier. What happened? Something about not believing it?"

"Hmm, you're just going to have to wait and talk to Summer today. I'm not one for ruining surprises." He squeezed her leg again.

Blinking at him, she asked, "Surprises? What kind of surprise are you talking about here, and why don't I remember it?"

Jax chuckled to himself and repeated, "Just talk to Summer, Lucy. I can promise you it's something she's definitely going to be bringing up today."

Pulling into a parking spot, Lucy scoped out the little bistro where they were meeting Summer and Drew, and she spotted them sitting at a table outside. They were totally engrossed in each other, so they hadn't noticed Lucy and Jax's arrival. They probably wouldn't have noticed them even if they were seated next to them at the table. The way they were staring into each other's eyes made Lucy almost tear up. It was nice to see Summer so happy—and to see that the guy who made her so happy had feelings equally as strong for Summer as she had for him.

Lucy was about to open her door when Jax grabbed her hand and urged, "Wait!" He climbed out of the car, shut the door, and ran over to her side to open her door.

Smiling, Lucy said, "Thank you," as he pulled her out of his car and gave her a kiss.

Pulling her close to him, Jax said, "I promise to always open doors for you, Lucy. It will never, ever get old for me." He looked down at her smiling and then quietly inquired, "How did I ever get so lucky?"

Raising herself up on her tippy toes, she tipped her head back, so their lips were almost touching and shared, "I'm the lucky one." Then she kissed him quickly and pulled him up onto the sidewalk and over to where Summer and Drew were sitting.

"Hey, guys," Lucy greeted them, sitting down, interrupting their stare fest. She was about to mention something of the sort, but she had to close her eyes because something on the table was blinding her. Opening them slowly and squinting down at the table to see what could be the cause, she spotted Summer's hand—and on it a gigantic diamond ring the size of Texas. "What," she asked, "is that?"

Shaken out of her Drew-gazing state, Summer looked at Lucy confused, asking, "What is *what*, Luce?"

"Is that what I think it is? Because if it is what I think it is, how could I not remember?" Lucy's eyes were wide as she grabbed Summer's hand to study the dazzler.

Snickering, Summer replied, "It is! Oh, and the reason you can't remember is because when Drew popped the question, you were … a little busy." She then glanced Jax's way and smiled.

"What? Busy doing what? I'm confused. This whole morning has been one of confusion, actually," shared Lucy, rubbing her eyes as Drew laughed and patted her shoulder. Then he nodded a hello to Jax as he sat down.

Jax looked at her and explained, "Let's just say you were very persuasive last night. After the third time of asking me to go make out in the back room, how could I say no? I mean, there's only so much a guy can take."

Looking horrified, Lucy exclaimed, "I did *what*? Oh wow. Summer, I blame this on you, no more crazy nights for me!"

Laughing, Summer noted, "Yeah, yeah, but that's beside the point. The point is—I'M GETTING MARRIED!"

Forgetting her embarrassment and confusion, Lucy felt only excitement and joy for her best friend. Getting up and hugging her, she stated, "I can't believe you're GETTING MARRIED! This," looking at Summer and Drew, "calls for a celebration, but I'm a little, well … I think I was over-served last night, so instead of drinks, lunch is on me!"

"Thanks, Lucy. Yeah, I would agree. You were totally over-served last night, but … I might have been too." Laughing at that, Summer grabbed Lucy's hands and added, "Oh, I have something to ask you. I was going to ask last night, but you being over-served and all." Summer cleared her throat, shook back her beautiful blond, shiny locks and continued, "Lucy, I would absolutely love it if you would be my maid of honor. You're my best friend, and I couldn't do this without you by my side. It wouldn't be right without you there."

Looking at Summer's serious expression, Lucy teared up, replying, "Of course, Summer. It would by my honor." Lucy gave her a hug and added, "Did you even have to ask?"

Hugging Lucy back, Summer affirmed, "Well, I knew you'd say yes. But it's a big deal to me, and I just wanted you to know how much I love you and want you to be a part of it."

Wiping their eyes, the girls hugged again and then broke apart when they heard chuckling. Looking at Jax, Lucy questioned, "What? What's so funny?"

Shaking his head, Jax stated, "Women. Only a woman would get choked up about being asked to be a maid of honor." Then he leaned forward and divulged, "I'll let you in on a little secret. Unless it's your own wedding and you actually *want* to marry the girl, guys hate them— weddings that is. They are just waiting for the party after the wedding to start."

Lucy smacked his arm at the same time as Summer who argued, "Hey! Well, I'll let you know, you are going to *love* my wedding. You are going to be so in love with this darn wedding that you yourself are going to want to get married." She looked at him as if daring him to prove her wrong. Then she added, "This wedding is going to be A-MA-ZING."

Drew laughed and commented to Jax, "See that look in her eye? Yeah, it's best not to challenge her when she looks like that. I promise you, you'll never win." He slapped Jax on the shoulder and smiled at Summer.

They spent the rest of their lunch talking about weddings and laughing at the guys' jokes. Summer, winking at Lucy, commented on how well Jax and Drew were getting along, "Seriously, look at those two."

Summer, glancing over at the guys, who were laughing together at something one had said, added in a whisper to Lucy, "You'd think they've known each other forever. It's a good sign, Lucy. Maybe we'll be planning your wedding next." Summer beamed, hopeful.

"I don't know, Sum," Lucy confided, watching the guys. They really were getting along great, "I already have one failed marriage under my belt. I don't want to make it two."

"I get it, Lucy," Summer responded quietly, grabbing her hand and squeezing it softly, "I really do, and I'm not saying marry him tomorrow if he asks. All I'm saying is, sometimes you've got to do what you're afraid to do, to get what you really want. Obviously I can't speak for Jax, but I can tell he really cares about you and you care about him."

Lucy smiled at Summer, she missed this, their time together, agreeing, "You're right, I do care about him. A lot, and I think he feels the same way about me."

Smiling back, Summer said, "Then right now, that's all that matters."

Then it was time to say their good-byes for the afternoon. Summer and Drew were off to check out the Walker Art Center, and Jax had to run in to work for a few hours. Lucy was looking forward to spending some quality time with Opal. They all hugged and promised to meet up later that night.

Jax was quieter than usual as they walked to his car, so Lucy wondered if something was wrong. She hoped if there were something bothering him, it had to do with work and not her.

When he slid into the car beside her, he buckled his seatbelt but didn't start the car right away. Instead he just sat in his seat, staring out of the window in front of him.

When a couple minuets had gone by, and the silence was starting to get to Lucy, she finally inquired quietly, "Jax? Is something bothering you?"

At first she didn't think he had heard her, but right when she was about to ask him again, he turned and looked at her, "I love you, Lucy, I really do. I've spent the last couple days thinking about telling you, wondering if it would be the right move. I don't want to come on too strong, and I know things have been moving fast, but I just have to tell you—I love you."

Speechless, Lucy blushed. He was looking at her so seriously, his eyes big and hopeful, his forehead creased just a little bit. He was biting his lip, something she'd come to realized he did when he was nervous. It was more than she could ask for, and because she could tell he was absolutely terrified, she knew he was being real, honest.

It felt good to know that someone could love her for her, the sometimes messy, often clumsy, usually unlucky her—not the her that someone else wanted her to be, but the real her. Being able to be herself in front of the person she loved, and not being afraid of his reaction if she made a mistake, was refreshing. Jax made her feel that it was okay to mess up, as long as she did her best. He made her feel good just being her, even though she often times felt not good enough, he turned her around and showed her that she was. She was better than good—actually she was great.

Thinking about spending the rest of her life with someone that would build her up and love her and cherish her, it made her heart happy. And that was a feeling that she hadn't felt in a long, long time.

Lucy looked at Jax, smiling at her so warmly—with so much love—and she knew without a doubt he would never hurt her, that he was absolutely serious. He really did love her. She could see it in his eyes, in the way he looked at her.

She knew Opal was right—that she should hold on to him and never let him go. So with that thought, she let all worries and insecurities fly out the window. She didn't need any of those, all she needed was love and an open heart. These feeling and thoughts made her smile, and she knew, right then, with Jax, that she really was lucky Lucy.

"I love you too," she told him, simply, as he leaned over and kissed her. She smiled up at him, pulling back to look into his eyes.

"True love," she thought, "sealed with a kiss."

* * * * *

The rest of the time Summer and Drew were in town flew by way too fast, as time usually does when you are having too much fun and not wanting it to end. Before she knew it, Lucy found herself standing outside her apartment building on a beautiful sunny day, giving Summer a tearful hug good-bye, wishing she didn't have to leave, and feeling like a part of her was going to be missing when Summer was gone.

Turning to give Drew a quick hug, Lucy told him, "Take care of Summer, and if you hurt her ... " she gave him a half-joking half-serious glare, "I will hunt you down, and it won't be pretty."

Laughing, Drew bent down, hugged Lucy tight, and promised, "Don't worry, you have my word, Lucy—I'll never hurt her." He smiled at her as he stood up, and Lucy could see that he meant it.

"Thanks," she said quietly and then looked at Summer, who was tearing up as well, "Now get out of here before I change my mind and not let you out of my sight."

Taking a deep breath and shaking back her locks, Summer laughed, saying, "I'll miss you too, Luce, love you."

"Love you too, Sum," Lucy said as she gave her another quick hug and pushed her towards Drew's car. "Call me when you get home."

Standing in the morning sunlight, Lucy watched her best friend and her best friend's fiancée get into the car and drive away. Waving until they disappeared, she turned and forced herself to hold it together as she walked through the lobby and into the elevator. She didn't want whoever was working at the desk up front to see her bawling her eyes out, especially if it was Oliver. He always gave her the hardest time, even if it was all in good fun. She just wasn't up for it today.

Lucy was still feeling sorry for herself as she stepped out of the elevator and into Opal's beautiful entry. Her newly engaged best friend had just left town, making her feel lonely and a little wistful. Her hunky boyfriend was at work, making her wonder what in the world she was going to do with herself on her last day off. She had been so busy these past few days with Summer. It felt weird to have no plans, and plans were something she was in desperate need of to keep her distracted from this glum feeling she'd probably have all day, missing Summer.

Walking into the sun-filled living room, she saw Opal lying on the couch with a pained look on her face. Her eyes were closed, and from the kitchen Lila glanced over at her frequently, looking a little too worried.

Quietly walking into the kitchen, Lucy asked, "Is everything okay?"

Lila bit her lip, sighed, and then shared, "I really don't know, Lucy. She's been up all night, been in a lot of pain. Now she's finally trying to get some rest, but I'm not sure that it's working. She keeps tossing and turning. I told her she might be more comfortable in her bed, but she insisted on lying on the couch. Says she's sick of her bed, sick of being cooped up in her room." Lila shook her head as she looked at Opal.

"What about the pain? Isn't she on medication to help with that? Is it possible to up her dose or go back to the doctor for something else?" Lucy asked, hating to see Opal in any kind of pain. If there were anything that could help her feel better and get some rest, Lucy wanted to do it.

"Bowden is speaking to her doctor now. He actually went in this morning for her because she was refusing to go herself. She has really grown … well, she really doesn't like the place much anymore, with all that she has been through there. Even if she knows she's going there just to talk with her doctor, she doesn't like it. She tries to stay away as much as possible."

Lila and Lucy jumped in synchrony as Opal shifted positions and moaned.

Lucy looked over at Lila with a pleading look on her face, repeating, "We have to do something, isn't there *anything* we can do?"

Looking at Lucy, Lila shook her head, explaining, "No, she is refusing to go on hospice, which would be the most logical thing for her. So the only thing we can do right now is wait. When Bowden comes back, we'll know more, but until then, we'll just keep her as comfortable and happy as we can, which is no easy task."

Smiling softy, Lila took Lucy's hand and squeezed it.

Lucy squeezed back and asked, "What does this mean, for her ... for her condition?" She swallowed the lump in her throat as she saw sadness cross Lila's face.

"I'm not sure, Lucy. The doctors said that they really have no idea how long she'll ... last, with her treatments not working the way they'd like them to. As of now, anything's possible. It could be days or it could be years. But ... being prepared for the worst is something we all need to do. Talk of hospice only comes up when people are nearing the end. We need to accept that these could be her last days, but then again they might not be, you just never know."

Looking at Lucy's crestfallen face, Lila pulled her in for a hug, offering, "Come here, sweet girl. I know it's hard. I know it's not fair, but it's life. These things happen, and we can't do anything to stop it. The only thing we can do is enjoy our moments together and appreciate every second."

A million feelings and emotions drenched Lucy. They were coming at her from all directions, and she didn't know what to do. Why today of all days, when she was already feeling low because Summer had to get back home, did this have to happen? Lucy knew she should be comforting Lila, who had known Opal for years and years, but she felt so devastated at the thought of losing Opal that she was paralyzed.

She felt regret for not getting to know Opal sooner. She felt anger at her mother for keeping them apart. But she felt pity for her mother as well, for not getting the chance to see this beautiful side of Opal. She felt scared for Opal—and for herself. What would she do when Opal was gone? Whom would she talk to, tell all her fears to and know she wouldn't be judged?

Faced with the overly evident reality that Opal was dying, Lucy could barely breathe. She could barely think. All she could do was feel, and feeling right now was too much. She felt too much and it hurt, and the hurt consumed her until she couldn't even hold herself up. She collapsed onto the floor into a crying heap.

She felt Lila come and sit beside her on the floor, rubbing her back and quietly whispering, "Sh-h, sh-h, there, there, it's okay now, sh-h, sh-h." Lila stayed like that for a long time, quietly whispering and rubbing her back until a door opened and Bowden walked in.

Holding her finger to her lips, Lila slowly stood up and pointed to Lucy who was now sleeping, her breath hitched every now and again, and her eyes were still wet with tears. "She took it hard, poor thing."

"I'd be surprised if she didn't," Bowden quietly commented, bending down and scooping Lucy up. "I'll just bring her to her room. She'll sleep better there."

He carried her away down the hall and into her daydream of a room.

* * * * *

Waking up, Lucy felt confused and surprisingly drained for what appeared to be the middle of the day. Why was she in her room? She hadn't remember walking in here and deciding to take a nice, little nap—something weird was definitely going on.

Sitting up, Lucy stretched her neck and wondered why her eyes felt so raw. Then the memory hit her like a ton of bricks, so hard that she lost her breath and fell back down into bed, her soft pillow breaking her fall.

Taking a few big breaths in and out, in and out, Lucy knew she needed to go and see how Opal was doing and find out if Bowden was back from the doctor's yet. She was assuming he was and that he was the person who had brought her to her room. She really couldn't imagine Lila lugging her down the long hall and putting her to bed. Lucy was as tall as she was, and she was pretty sure Lila couldn't handle carrying her all the way. She was pretty sure someone had carried her because from what she could remember, there was no way she had willingly walked anywhere—but who knew, maybe Lila had some weird super power Lucy had yet to find out about?

Forcing herself out of bed, she walked into her bathroom to wash her face. Looking at herself in the mirror made her cringe. Her blood shot eyes and smeared mascara said it all. After she had cleared that all up, well the mascara at least, there was really nothing she could do about the bloodshot eyes right now, she went into the closet and pulled on some black leggings and a neon yellow tunic with a black tank underneath. If she didn't feel cheerful, she could at least *look* the part. Plus, it was comfy, and comfy was what she needed right now.

Lucy gathered up courage as she walked down the long hallway toward the kitchen and living room. She knew that spending time with Opal and figuring out what, if anything, could help with the pain was more important than her fear of the future. She knew she needed to be brave and strong for Opal, be in the moment. There would be a time for sadness and hurt and sorrow, but this wasn't the time. This was the time for happiness and fun, for love and joy. This was the time for making

Opal's last days or years the best that she could.

Laughing to herself, Lucy thought of the comments Opal would surely make when she took in Lucy's blinding shirt. Opal had the best sense of humor. It was one of the things Lucy loved most about her. Feeling her spirits lift a little, Lucy smiled as she walked into the living room.

Rounding the corner, Lucy stopped abruptly and took in the scene in front of her. There were about fifteen people milling around the spacious living room. Some of them Lucy had seen before, but most she had no clue as to who they were and why there were there. Then she spotted Lila and Bowden sitting on the couch. Lila was silently wiping her eyes, and Bowden's head was bowed low, resting against Lila's, as he softly whispered something in her ear.

It was at that moment, as Lila looked up to see Lucy and immediately started sobbing, that Lucy knew something was terribly, horribly wrong. As Bowden slowly stood up and started making his way toward Lucy, she knew. She knew what he was about to say to her, and she wasn't ready to hear it. Looking at his grief-stricken face made Lucy want to turn and run—run and hide somewhere until all of this was over.

Knowing she needed to be brave for herself, for Lila and Bowden, and for everyone else who was grieving Opal's passing, she braced herself for the news that she was about to hear.

Pulling Lucy into a tight hug, Bowden began quietly, "I think you know what I'm about to say to you, don't you, Lucy?" When she only nodded and put her head down against his shoulder, he continued, "She loved you. She loved you so much, Lucy. Just you being here made a huge difference in her life. It was the only thing that she wanted, for you to be here with her. She wanted to make sure you were okay, that you were happy, and that things were good between the two of you. And you made that happen, Lucy. Thank you, thank you so much for that."

Choking up, Bowden pulled away from Lucy and held her an arm's length away. Then he continued, "Please know that your being here changed her, made her into someone that even Lila and I hadn't seen before. You just brought out her true happiness and joy. Focus on that, Lucy, that you were able to bring her peace and happiness when she needed it the most. Focus on that when things get hard, promise me?" He looked at her, tears running down his face, waiting for an answer.

Unsure of her where her voice had gone at the moment, it had left her somewhere along the way, leaving her with a huge lump in her throat and a stinging in her eyes that she was trying with all her might to ignore, Lucy nodded and choked out a barely perceivable, "I promise."

Nodding, Bowden said, "I'm going to hold you to that promise."

Then he took her arm and led her over to where Lila was sitting, head in her hands, adding, "Oh, and you're not going anywhere my dear, you are going to sit here with Lila and me, and we are going to get through this together. There is no way I'm letting you get away with hiding in your room when there are all these ... people to deal with."

He gave her a stern look, which in turn made her smile a little. He was better at reading her than she'd realized. Even though the room was full of people whom she really didn't feel like being around, she knew she would feel a whole lot worse sitting in her room by herself. So she put on a brave face and tried with all her might to hold it together for the three of them.

CHAPTER THIRTEEN

Stepping into the limo and out of the cold wind and rain, Lucy ran her fingers under her eyes, wiping away all the smeared mascara and tears that she could. Then she put her big, black sunglasses back on and hoped nobody could see what a mess she was. She heard the door shut and looked away, putting her head into her hands. She didn't want anyone to see her, and she definitely didn't want to see anyone else.

Quietly sighing, Lila rubbed Lucy's back as the limo started to drive slowly away. She gave Bowden a look as she nodded at Lucy. She wasn't sure what to do with her. She knew Lucy would come out of this funk eventually, but she was hoping it would be sooner rather than later.

Bowden shrugged and shook his head. He had no idea what to do with Lucy. Women and their emotions constantly confused him, and that was saying something since he had worked for Opal, one of the most emotional and confusing people there was, and he could usually read her pretty well.

Leaning over to Lila, he whispered, "It's okay, she'll come around, we just need to give her time ... and I need to remind her of a promise she made me a few days back."

"Good. Remind her of that today, please. She needs to snap out of this. Her not talking to anyone, even Summer and Jax, has me really worried. It's just not like her," Lila whispered, stealing a quick glance at Lucy.

Smiling softly at Lila, Bowden rubbed her back as she continued to rub Lucy's. He closed his eyes and sent up a silent prayer that they would all be able to get through this together. It was hard enough on Lila that Opal was gone. Having to deal with getting Lucy back into shape was not going to be an easy task. But he had time on his hands now, so he guessed she could be his next project. Now that Opal was gone ... He shook his head and quietly cleared his throat, thinking these next few weeks were going to be harder than he had thought.

Feeling the limo start to move, Lucy opened her eyes and peaked out the window. She knew she shouldn't have looked, she knew seeing their faces, tear-streaked and confused, would just make things worse, but she couldn't help it. She figured it was her payment for not doing what she could have done to keep Opal alive.

As the limo pulled away, Teddy, Jax, Cash, Carson, Benno, Summer, and Drew stood together, huddled in a small group under a few umbrellas. There was a collective feeling of sadness and confusion in the group. No one knew what to say or where to even begin to express how they felt.

Taking a deep breath, Teddy assured everyone, "She'll come around. You know, it's *Lucy* we're talking about here. She's just like, in epic shock, or something."

Clearing his throat, Benno commented, "I don't know, man. The only thing I *do* know is that I'm missing that pizza girl. I mean she just *brings* something to the place. I can't describe it, and then add to that—she is amazing at making those pies and, dang! We've definitely been hurting over at Saucy Baby."

"She'll be fine, she'll come through. She always does ..." Teddy repeated and then trailed off, watching the limo. "It's weird though, yo, to not have heard from her in five days. It's not a lot of time in the grand scheme, but still, not like her," he added.

"I don't know, guys, she's never, *never* been like this before. I've seen her at some bad times, and it's never been this bad. I'm worried—she won't even talk to me. She's completely cut me off, cut all of us off. I just don't know ..." Summer lamented, trying to hold back her tears, "I mean, we are best friends, besties, and she has completely shut me out. This is new, this is new—and it scares me. Before, I knew how to push her to get her to snap back, but now ... I'm not so sure anymore, and I feel horrible. She's my best friend, and I have no idea how to help her."

Pulling Summer closer to his side, Drew shared, "I don't know Lucy, not all that well, just really what you've told me, Summer, but ... I do know that sometimes these kind of things can really change a person. Losing someone you love, no matter how long they've loved them, can almost paralyze you if you let it. Like I said, I really don't know her like the rest of you, but I'd say just be the best friends you can be. Don't give up on her. Don't stop reaching out because one day there might be something that one of you does that pulls her out of whatever's going on inside of her." He glanced at Jax.

Shaking his head, Jax divulged, "I just can't do this anymore, this is killing me." Obviously trying to keep his emotions at bay, Jax stalked off in the direction of his car.

Feeling horrible and wanting to help, Summer started after him, calling out, "Jax!" but Drew caught her hand before she could take two steps.

"Just let him go, Summer. He just needs some time."

"Yeah," Carson agreed, "There are only two people who can heal that broken heart, and it's Lucy and Jax, himself … and right now Lucy's not talking. He needs some breathing room, I'd say."

"Amen to that, brother," Teddy seconded, as he slowly walked toward the parking lot with the rest of them.

* * * * *

Waking to a pounding on her bedroom door, Lucy put a pillow over her head and tried to go back to sleep. No luck there, the pounding simply got louder and a voice started yelling, "Lucy, you open this door right now! I don't care how long and loud I have to stand here pounding and yelling, I will do it until you get your little butt out of bed and open this door, young lady!"

Confused, Lucy sat up slowly and questioned, "Mom?"

The voice continued even louder this time, "You bet your hiney, it's me! Now open up before I have to wake this entire la-di-da apartment building!"

Smiling despite herself, Lucy slowly got up, unlocked the door, opened it a crack, and then slowly walked back to her bed. Before she got there, though, she felt herself being whipped around until she was face to face with Stella, who commanded, "Don't you dare get back into that bed, young lady! You march yourself right into that over-the-top shower you have in there, and you don't come out until you're as clean as a whistle. Understood?"

Lucy blinked a few times. Stella's face was in such close proximity to hers that Lucy had to back up a few steps to see her clearly.

"O-o-o-kay, so what happened to that whole bonding moment we had before I left? Remember that? And the times we've talked on the phone, remember how nice those were? What happened to the new you?" Lucy demanded stubbornly. She didn't want to get into the shower, she wanted to mope.

"We'll talk all about that when you're out of the shower. All I can say now is that desperate times call for desperate measures. And right now I'll do whatever it takes to get your mopey little self out of bed and on with your life. Now get!" she issued while pushing Lucy into the bathroom and then closing the door swiftly behind her.

* * * * *

Stepping out of the shower and wrapping a fuzzy towel around herself, Lucy had to admit she did feel better. She couldn't actually remember the last time she had taken a shower. Probably over a week ago, the morning of Opal's funeral. The thought brought her back to all of those horrible feelings she had been wallowing in since then. She was about to step back into the shower—who cared if she'd showered already?—when her mother cracked open the door.

"Well, I tried to find something for you to wear in that massive closet of yours. I'm not sure what you're in the mood for, so I pulled out a few things." Stella set a pile of clothes on the long bathroom counter and then closed the door.

"Thanks, Mom," Lucy managed as she walked over and looked at what Stella had picked out for her. Surprisingly, her mom had put together some cute outfits, for which Lucy was extremely grateful. She didn't even have enough energy to walk through that closet trying to decide what to wear; just getting out of bed had taken enough out of her.

Lucy ended up choosing a black and white striped t-shirt and white shorts—which she had never seen before. They must have been another of Opal's recent additions and another reminder of Opal that stung more than Lucy could have imagined.

Not able to control her emotions, Lucy sunk to the floor and started crying silently, her grief consuming her again, just as it had ever since Opal's death.

She stayed that way, crumpled up on the floor, until Stella knocked softly. When Lucy didn't answer, Stella came in and sat down beside Lucy, rubbing her back and tucking her long, damp hair behind her ears, just as she had done many times when Lucy was a little girl.

Lucy didn't move, she just continued crying into her towel. Stella took Lucy's chin and lifted her head until they were eye to eye. Then she firmly but quietly advised, "Lucy, you need to snap out of this. You need to continue on with your life."

When Lucy just closed her eyes to try to shut her mother out, Stella commanded softly, "Lucy, look at me. Open your eyes and *look* at me."

Stella then waited patiently, which was never her strong suit, for Lucy to do just that. When she finally did, Stella cleared her throat, continuing, "I know this is hard for you. I know you loved her, and you think it's your fault that she is gone, but it's not. It isn't. You need to get out of this funk and live your life. Think about Opal. You know she wouldn't want you moping around here, not speaking to anyone, not going into work—a job which I hear you love and are amazing at, by the way. She wouldn't want you rotting in this bed, day after day. She loved you, Lucy, and you know she brought you here and gave you all that she gave you, so you would be happy. Bowden told me you made him a promise, and I have to say, you haven't been keeping your word."

Lucy just shrugged her shoulders and looked away.

"Lucy! You need to keep that promise. Bowden knew things were going to be difficult for you. That's why he wanted you to think about what you did for Opal, how you made her happier than she had been in a long time. You really did make these last months of her life better than she could have hoped for. Remember that. This, what you are doing now, isn't a life, Lucy. This isn't what Opal wanted for you. She didn't bring you here for you to sit around and wallow in your misery. She brought you here so you two could get to know each other, spend time together, and you did. She also brought you here, so you could grow, so you could find yourself and know that you are an amazing person, and guess what? She accomplished that, as far as I can tell. So, why are you throwing away what she gave you? Don't let this one set back, this one trial in your life, paralyze you.

"Opal led an amazing life, Lucy. She did more, loved more, saw more than most of us could do in two lifetimes if we had them. If she were here, you know she would tell you to get off your butt, get over it, and go have some fun! No more regrets, Lucy! It's okay to have fun. It's okay to move on. You don't need to punish yourself for her being gone, that's not what life is about. Life is about learning to love and letting yourself heal when you're hurt, being able to move on and know things will be okay. It's about having fun and helping others. It's about joy, Lucy.

"Of course there are going to be hard times. I know that, but how would you know how good the good times were if you never experienced the bad? Opal loved you, and she wanted the best for you. Of course, it takes time to get over a loss like this, but you need to try, you need to give it all you've got. Can you do that for me, Lucy? Can you do that for Opal, please?"

Letting Stella's words sink in, Lucy sat quietly for what seemed like forever, trying to decide if her mom was right. Closing her eyes, she tried to picture Opal—her big smile, her loud laugh, her enormous amount of energy. Lucy wondered what she was doing now. As she thought about it, an image started to form in her mind, a picture of Opal in all of her glory. She was surrounded by friends, people who had been there for her and whom she had let lean on her as well. Her husband was there right by her side, and seeing Opal so happy gave Lucy the most peaceful feeling she had felt in a long time.

Then, as if Opal could sense Lucy's presence, it was as if all of the other people faded away and it was just Opal looking at Lucy, looking at her with love and concern, but also with hope. Lucy felt light and tingly as this image filled her mind, and she could swear that she heard Opal say to her, "What are you doing, Lucy? Why are you in such a funk over me? Look at me, do you see me? I'm fine. Go, go live your life. Go find love and enjoy every single moment of it, good and bad. Please, learn from me, don't waste any more precious time feeling bad for yourself. You have so much to look forward to, I can see it all from here, and I'm telling you, you're going to love it. Oh, and remember one thing Lucy, I love you."

Opal slowly faded away, and Lucy took a few breaths in and out, in and out, trying to dissect what had just happened. Her mother's voice brought her back to reality, "Lucy? Lucy? Lucy, please look at me." Stella's voice was filled with concern, and it crushed Lucy to know she had hurt another person in the process of whatever had been going on with her.

Opening her eyes, Lucy looked at her mom. She saw the love and pain in Stella's eyes, and she was reminded of all the other times she had seen the same emotions there. All of the times Lucy had been hurt, whether by a mean girl at school or a boy who had left her down in the dumps, or even before those things had mattered, and she had been crushed by something that seemed meaningless later.

Her mom had been there for her, in her own way. She had always made things better, even if it was in a way that Lucy didn't understand at the time. Stella had tried, and Lucy wondered why she hadn't realized this before.

"Mom," Lucy said, finally finding her voice, "Mom, I'm okay. I'm going to be fine. I just needed a little extra time, and a little push, I guess." Lucy smiled, thinking of Opal's last words to her.

Stella gathered her up in a hug and then sat back and looked at her, eyes searching Lucy's, saying, "Are you sure? Because, although I love seeing you, I really don't want to be called back here to get your boney butt out of bed again. I know you can do this, Lucy. You're a strong person. You just need to believe it yourself."

Smiling at her mom, Lucy replied, "I'm sure, Mom, and thanks for coming here, getting me out of bed. I don't know what I would have done if you hadn't come."

Feeling on the brink of tears again, Stella waved her hand like it was no big deal. She went on to share, "Okay, now come on and get dressed. We've got a lot to get done before I head back home. Oh, and there are a few people who have been waiting to see you—I just wanted you to know. We've all been worried."

Feeling guilt rear its ugly head, Lucy took a breath and pushed the guilt away. It wasn't a feeling that she needed right now. It wouldn't help her, it would only hurt her, and she'd been through enough hurt to last a lifetime. "Good to know, I'll be out in a few."

Pulling on her t-shirt and shorts, Lucy threw her now dried hair up into a sock bun and braved a look in the full-length mirror. Giving herself a small smile, she decided she didn't look half bad for having been, as her mom had said, rotting away in her bed for over a week. Besides her slightly swollen eyes, she looked okay. She was pretty sure that if she was desperate enough, she could call on Tia to fix her eyes. Being the miracle worker that she was, Tia had to have some sort of cure for red, swollen eyes.

Stepping out of the bathroom, Lucy saw her mom pulling off her bedsheets and tossing them into a heaping basket of laundry.

"Oh yeah, thanks for that, Mom. Me being holed up and all, I haven't really had a chance to do any laundry," Lucy admitted, embarrassed.

"That's what I'm here for, right?" Stella smiled brightly at her, and Lucy again felt a wave of thankfulness that her mom had come to save her. Taking Lucy's hand, Stella asked, "Ready?"

Lucy squeezed her mom's hand and replied, "Ready as I'll ever be." Hand in hand, they walked down the hall together.

* * * * *

When Lucy heard the murmur of voices, she stole a quick glance at the group of people sitting around the kitchen table eating lunch. She stood frozen in place, her heart beating at top speed.

When Stella gave her a questioning look, Lucy explained, "There are so many people out there that I have hurt. I don't know if I can stand to go out there and face all of them, especially at once. I'm just not sure what to do or say."

Stella gave her hand another squeeze and reassured her, "They are all here because they love you and want to make sure you're okay. There is nothing you could do or say to change that. Trust me, it's going to be okay. There isn't one person out there who is going to make you feel uncomfortable or out of place, I promise."

So trust her was what Lucy did, and it went great. Walking out to face all of her closest friends had Lucy's nerves buzzing and her heart racing. But when she approached the table around which they sat, she received only smiles from everyone, and Teddy said simply, "You're back."

Smiling at everyone who had gathered around, Lucy quietly sat down beside Summer, and she accepted the plate of heaping food Lila handed her. Everyone was there—Summer and Drew, Teddy, Cash, Carson, Benno, Lila and Bowden. Everyone, that is, except Jax.

Confused and hurt by the fact that he was the one person who didn't seem to care, Lucy tried to eat her food. She tried to choke down the deliciousness of Lila's cooking, but she couldn't quite muster it. Knowing that if she brought it up, it would cause her to cave back into herself, she decided to ignore the elephant in the room. She decided to work on making sure the friends that did care knew how grateful she really was.

CHAPTER FOURTEEN

Sitting in the cold, dark room of the lawyer's office and looking at the grumpy, old, seemingly irritated man in front of her, Lucy was surprised this was the person and the firm that Opal had chosen to represent her and to read her last will and testament. Maybe it was the name that had done it for her, Lucy thought. If there weren't many lawyers to choose from, and she had to pick, that one with the name of Tinkles might be worth a laugh.

Rubbing her hands up and down her arms, Lucy sat back in the uncomfortable chair and looked over at Bowden and Lila, and then at her mom sitting beside her. "Yes," she decided, "I'm ready."

"Well, then," Mr. Tinkles said, clearing his throat, "let's get started. As there is ... " He then paused.

He was one of those people who dragged out the last word of his sentence, in a way, reminding her of Professor Snape from the *Harry Potter* movies. Lucy laughed, thinking of Professor Snape and Mr. Tinkles in the same room. She quickly shut up when she looked up to find his glare boring into her skull.

Mr. Tinkles cleared his throat again and began reading, "To Bowden and Lila, Opal has left you both a tremendous retirement fund as well as your salaries payable for up to another ten years if you choose to stay employed. If you two were to decide to retire early, these allocated funds are set to roll into your retirement account. So it's up to you both what you decide to do."

He took a deep breath, shuffling papers around. Then he continued, "You both also are permitted to keep your lodging at the penthouse. If you so choose to reside elsewhere, she has provided instruction for you that will help in purchasing a place of your own. She has also gifted each of you a car. Hmmm ... "

He paused, flipping through papers again, all the while dragging out the "m-m-m-m-m." Then he continued, reading, "For Stella, Opal has left you a generous sum of money to do with as you will, with the stipulation that it's for, and I'm quoting this, '*your passion.*' That money is being wired to your account as we speak." He looked up and smiled at Stella.

"Lastly, Lucy, well it looks as if you get everything else." He quickly pushed some papers their way.

"Each of you sign here, please," he stated in conclusion.

Confused, Lucy inquired, "Wait, what do you mean 'everything else'? Can you be more clear for me, please?"

Letting out an exasperated sigh, Mr. Tinkles grabbed the folder full of papers for Lucy, and as he began flipping through them, he stated, "Okay, here we go. Lucy is endowed Opal's entire remaining estate, save the rooms that Bowden and Lila may reside in. She receives Opal's cars, save the ones she left for Bowden and Lila. She receives her beach house, the house in Mexico, the house in Malibu, the house in the Hamptons, and the house in Vail. And, let's see here, the few restaurants she owns are yours now, too, Lucy. You are beneficiary of her investments, all of her savings—basically any money she had is now yours. You get it all, and there is a lot of it. Do you need me to keep reading, or do you want to look over it yourself?" Mr. Tinkles looked at her, eyebrows raised.

Shocked and overwhelmed, Lucy responded, "Wow, I had no idea. I have no clue about investments and how to run a restaurant or how to take care of multiple homes. I'm not so sure about this." She swallowed loudly.

Smiling the first real, well as close to real as it could get with him, smile he had since she had entered his office, Mr. Tinkles explained, "There is nothing you need to worry about. Opal has everything taken care of. You don't need to do anything but enjoy life. Your ownership of the restaurants is really just a majority share or almost like a silent partner with other owners. If you want to be more involved you can, or you can decide to sell or just do what Opal did and just kind of go with the flow. She invested in these places because she was excited about what they could bring to the cities they were in. She wanted to help out friends and provided funds to help them start out. It's really not that time-consuming.

"Stocks and investments, she has, well—you have people managing on your behalf. You'll, of course, have meetings to discuss positions, investments, and earnings, but there is a team of individuals responsible for helping you. The houses are managed by rental companies; they do all the heavy lifting for you. All you need to do is let them know when you are going to come stay, and they'll take care of the rest. When you are not staying at any of the homes, you have the option to rent them out. That is why the rental company is in the picture. They handle everything for you in that department. It's a win-win for you, Lucy."

Still feeling overwhelmed with all of the information coming her way, Lucy looked to Bowden. He had been her rock since she had first walked into this crazy life.

Nodding at Lucy, he assured her, "You're going to do great, Lucy. I can walk you through this later, but it's really not as complicated as it seems. I've helped Opal with all of this for years. I will continue to help you work through the details."

Back to business, Mr. Tinkles pushed the papers toward them again, stating, "Your signature indicates that the will and testament was delivered."

After everything had been signed, Mr. Tinkles thanked them all and let them know that everything would be transferred over to their names as soon as possible. He then led them out the door and slammed it almost before they were out.

"Well, he was something else, wasn't he?" Stella asked, laughing.

"That's Opal for you, throwing in a surprise now and then. She probably picked him as her lawyer because of his poor people skills, thinking how she'd be up there laughing, watching us have to sit there with him," Bowden commented with a shake of his head and a smile at the thought.

"Oh," Lucy remarked, "I never thought of it that way, I just assumed that she thought his name was funny."

Looking at Lucy, Lila inquired, "What was his name? I never did catch it."

Bowden, Lucy, and Stella looked at each other and all burst out laughing.

"What! What's so funny?" Lila demanded.

"Mr. Tinkles!" Lucy managed to get out, before she started laughing again. "The lawyer's name was Mr. Tinkles!"

* * * * *

Watching her mom pack up her clothes, sticking them this way and that into her bag caused Lucy's mood to sink back down although hovering slightly above where it used to be after Opal had died.

Her mom had been staying with her, helping her along for the past week, giving her little pushes now and then when she felt like Lucy needed it. But now that she was leaving, Lucy wasn't sure what she would do without her.

She hadn't really been talking much to anyone else. It was as if she couldn't quite come out of her shell all the way, but she wasn't sure why. The first day when she had emerged from her room and tried to eat lunch with everyone had been great, but for some reason Lucy still felt like retreating back into herself when anyone besides her mom was around.

She felt horrible about it too, especially with Summer, who had taken off unknown amounts of time from work to make sure Lucy was okay. She had been staying there, at Lucy's, driving back home a few times to open the boutique and do her news spots. Summer had pulled Lucy aside yesterday, saying she needed to get back to a normal routine soon and that she was hoping they'd have some time to talk before she left. She was leaving tomorrow.

Lucy wanted to make things right with Summer, but she wasn't sure how. She was so confused about why the person she was seemed to have been taken over by someone else entirely. Normally she would have no problem or hesitation at all going to Summer and telling her what she was feeling. Now, she just wasn't sure what to say; she wasn't sure if Summer would understand.

Sensing her hesitancy, Stella stopped stuffing her suitcase (she had brought all her clothes into Lucy's room, so they could chat while she packed) and asked, "What's going on in that mind of yours, Lucy?"

Shrugging, Lucy lifted her hands and let them fall to her sides, admitting, "I'm just scared. I'm scared that when you leave, I'll actually have to do something by myself, and I'm not sure I'll do the right thing. I'm scared I'll end up back in bed again."

"No you won't, Lucy. That won't happen," Stella insisted, shaking her head.

"I know, but … I just don't know what to do or where to start. I feel like I've hurt all of my friends and how do I even fix it, you know? Then there is Jax, who no one has even remotely tried to talk to me about. No one has explained to me at all why he hasn't bothered to show up. I just feel like I totally screwed up everything that was great, and now it sucks and it's bad and I'm hopeless to make it right."

"Oh, Lucy," Stella said. She sat down on Lucy's bed and patted a spot next to her.

When Lucy sat down, she continued, "Every one of your friends understands what you are going through and why you've been having a hard time. You haven't screwed anything up—yet. If you continue to not speak to them, they will eventually move on, but I know you won't let that happen. And Jax … well, this has been hard on him too. Not that he is devastated by Opal's death. Of course, he was saddened about it because it hurt you. But your not returning his calls, not communicating with him at all, seems to have thrown him for a loop. I don't think he is sure what's going on with you or with the two of you as a couple. I imagine the reason that he hasn't been around is because he's confused and worried you're going to take one look at him and turn the other way."

"But I would never do that!" Lucy exclaimed, upset by the thought.

"I know, but he doesn't know that. All he knows is that from the moment you found out about Opal, all communication between the two of you ceased to exist. Even when he tried talking to you at the funeral and burial site, there was nothing from you. Lucy, it was like you didn't even hear him." She looked at Lucy, waiting for her reply.

"Honestly, Mom, I *didn't* hear anyone then. It was like I was just going through the motions, floating from here to there. I barely remember anything from a few weeks ago."

"*I* know sweetie, but like I said, *he* doesn't, and that is something you are going to have to talk to him about. You might want to talk to those other people who have been hanging around here day and night as well, even though you've still been ignoring them most of the time. You need to change that, and I think that with me out of the way, those things will start to come together. You won't be able to hide behind me anymore," Stella gently explained to Lucy and stood up, walking around the room to double-check that she hadn't forgotten anything.

"But, Mom, I *want* to hide behind you! I don't want you to leave me," Lucy insisted sadly, tearing up.

"Lucy," Stella stated, walking over to her and taking her hands, "you're not a little girl anymore. You don't need me like you used to, you haven't for a long time now. You're an amazing woman, and I know you can do this. You just needed a little push, like you said, and that is what I came here to do. But now it's time for you to finish it, on your own. Now come and see me off. I need to get back home. There are a lot of people waiting for me to finish my column this week, it's about—"

"Mom!" Lucy cut her off, "Okay, I don't need to know what it's about. If I'm curious, I'll read it in the paper." She grabbed her mom's suitcase and started toward the door.

Laughing, Stella confessed, "I knew that would get you moving."

Walking down the hallway toward the elevators, Lucy again heard the murmuring of voices, and when she walked through the kitchen and living room, she saw that everyone was still there. They were hanging out on the big couches, watching something or other on TV. A few heads turned their way as they walked by, and Lucy lifted her hand in a wave as she passed.

"You're one lucky girl, you know," her mom stated as they approached the elevators.

"What do you mean?" Lucy asked, scrunching her eyebrows together.

"You did just see all those people out there, didn't you? Sitting around, just hanging out together, and waiting for you to get better, to come out and join the living. They've been coming, every day," Stella explained, taking her suitcase from Lucy and then giving her a look.

"Ha-ha, Mom," Lucy replied, rolling her eyes.

"No really, Lucy, that's something special in there. I'm not sure how many people could say they had a group of friends camped out in their living room for weeks, waiting for them to appear. You've got something there, something some people spend their whole lives looking for. Don't take it for granted and don't mess it up. When I leave, I want the first thing you do to be walking into that group like you belong there because, believe it or not, you do."

The elevator sounded its arrival, and Lucy gave Stella a tight hug and said, "Thank you so much, Mom, for doing this. I'll miss you."

Kissing Lucy on the head, Stella responded, "You're welcome. Oh, and by the way, in case you missed it—there's someone in there," she pointed to the living room, "who's looking pretty down. Don't miss your chance to change things. Love you!"

Then she picked up her bag and stepped onto the elevator. "Don't be a stranger!" she added, waving good-bye.

CHAPTER FIFTEEN

Unsure of whom her mother had been talking about, Lucy turned and slowly walked back into the living room, quietly approaching her friends, trying to scope out who looked the saddest.

She was about to hightail it back to her room to grab her phone and ask her mom just who the heck she was talking about, when she saw him sitting on the floor, leaning up against the back of a chair where Teddy sat. Jax.

All at once her heart sped up and her breathing started to do that weird thing it always did when she was with him. She was just about to walk away, catch her breath, when he looked up and saw her.

He looked at her with the most heartbreaking look she had ever seen. And in that look she could see all of his pain, all of his hurt and confusion, all of it because of her, and it almost broke her again. To know that she could do that to a person, that she could affect someone in that way was almost too hard to bear. But this time, instead of breaking down, instead of caving in on herself, she stood up tall and faced what she needed to face.

It started with a smile. She wasn't sure how she could make right all that she needed to, especially with all of these people in the room. But smiling made her feel better, and feeling better gave her courage. So she smiled at Jax as he stood up and made his way over to her.

"Hi," she murmured when he was close enough that she could smell him. She loved the way he smelled, how could she have forgotten that?

"Hi," he replied, looking at her with uncertain eyes.

Lucy realized that it was the first time she had seen him without a smile on his face. He always smiled when he saw her, when they were together, and the realization hit her hard in her gut. She wasn't sure what to do or say, so she said the first thing that came to mind, "I miss your smile."

Taken off guard, her saying that definitely wasn't what he expected, he told her, "Thanks Lucy, I—"

Before he could continue, Lucy cut him off, saying, "Jax, please don't say anything right now. I know I have a lot of explaining to do, especially to you. But before I do that, there is just one more thing I need to do, there is one more thing I need to fix. Will you wait for me, please? I won't be long." She looked at him a little sadly, but with hope.

Still unsure, he nodded slowly, replying, "I'll be right here."

"Thanks," Lucy said, turning and walking into the kitchen where she saw Summer talking animatedly on her cell phone.

When Summer saw Lucy walking towards her, she quickly said, "Hey, can I call you back? Great, talk to you soon!" Then she put her phone down and rushed over to Lucy to give her a hug, announcing, "There's my girl! I've missed you, ya know."

Lucy squeezed Summer in a tight hug, then stepped back to state, "We need to talk."

Eyes widening, Summer joked, "Uh-oh, are you breaking up with me?"

Shooting Summer a look, Lucy told her, "Seriously, I'm sorry. I'm sorry that I've been avoiding you, avoiding everyone really, especially at a time like this when I need you more than ever. I'm not sure what my problem was, but I really want to make things right. You've been the best friend anyone could ask for, and I feel like right now, I really don't deserve it." She met Summer's gaze, hoping she would understand.

"Oh, Luce, it's okay! I get it, I really do! I'm just glad you're back. You *are* back, aren't you?" Summer eyed her up and down.

"Yeah, I'm back. I'm trying my best to be back, and you know what? It feels good. I don't know what I was so afraid of." She smiled and looked around, feeling herself relax a little.

"Afraid of change, afraid to move on, afraid to be happy? All those things are okay, Lucy. You just can't let them rule your life. Never let fear rule you, girl." Summer said, shaking her head.

"I just feel like I wasted so much of your time, and now you're leaving tomorrow, and I totally missed out on spending time with you. Instead, I was feeling sorry for myself, rotting away in there," Lucy lamented, pointing towards her bedroom.

"You didn't waste my time, Lucy, I'd do anything for you, you know that. The only way this would have been a waste of my time would have been if you'd have never come out of that room, but I knew you would. I know you, when it comes down to it, you'll make it happen, baby! So …" Summer's face turned serious, "Have you talked to Jax? He's here now, you know." Her face turned towards the place where he had been sitting.

"I know. I talked to him for a second before I talked to you. But to be honest, before I could fix things with him, I had to fix things with you. If we're not good, then nothing else is good, you know? I had to make sure, that, well, you knew I still have your back, and I was hoping you still have mine," Lucy explained, smiling at Summer.

"Of course, I got your back, girl! Now go talk to your man. Then tonight we're going to have an all night girls' gab fest. I need to start planning this wedding, Lucy!" Summer announced, smiling, taking Lucy by the shoulders, and then turning her around to push her towards Jax. Summer whispered, "Make it work, girl."

Smiling, Lucy stumbled towards Jax.

"Whoa, you okay there?" he asked, with a small smile playing on his lips.

"Yeah," Lucy replied, smiling back, "I think I'll be okay."

"So," he began, leaning in closer to her, "What was it you wanted to say to me?"

Feeling her heart start racing again, she replied, "You've *got* to stop doing that."

Smile getting a little bigger, he inquired, "Doing what?"

"You know what you're doing, making me all nervous." Taking a deep breath, Lucy continued, "I wanted to tell you I'm sorry, for ignoring you, not talking to you, not communicating. It wasn't just you, you know, it was everybody, and thinking about it makes me feel so horrible. I don't know why, when I needed you the most, I let you go, and I'm so sorry." Feeling frustrated with herself, she shook her head and slowly looked up at Jax.

"Thank you, Lucy, for saying that," he said, "I'm not going to say it was easy for me. It wasn't. The past few weeks were probably the hardest weeks of my life if I'm honest. I can understand not being able to deal with her death and shutting people out—I guess I can understand that. I thought I was different, that I was someone you'd need by your side, no matter what. I guess I was wrong though, and I'm really trying to accept that, but you're making it hard at the moment." He smiled at her, but his smile didn't reach his eyes.

"No," she asserted, feeling crushed for the millionth time today by something that she had done, "You weren't wrong, Jax—*I* was. I'm not sure if it matters to you anymore, but you are someone I want by my side, no matter what. I did want that then and I do want that now, I just didn't know how to deal with all the emotions that were running through me. I felt like it was my fault that she died, and, I don't know, I should have been able to help her more."

Lucy looked up at him and pushed her hair out of her eyes, continuing, "I know I shouldn't have done what I did, ignore the people that mattered to me the most, and I am incredibly sorry for that. I can't promise that it won't happen again because I can't predict the future, but I hope it doesn't happen again. I'm pretty sure it won't."

She looked at him, trying to read what he was thinking, but she couldn't, so she just kept going, "I guess what I am trying to say, or trying to ask, is for another chance. Please don't give up on me now. Please let me try again."

She cleared her throat, not knowing what she would do if he walked away from her—if his answer was no.

"Lucy," he responded, grabbing her face and tilting it up, so he could look into her eyes without her moving away, "you don't need another chance, I've never given up on you. I love you, that's why it hurt so much. To think about losing you, almost right after I found you, that just wasn't fair. I understand that what you went through was hard, I get that. I'm just glad you're back."

Letting out a quiet laugh, she remarked, "You don't know how many times I've heard that today."

"Well, get used to it because it's true, and I have a feeling you're going to be hearing a lot more of it," he said with a smile, nodding towards the room full of people, full of friends—friends that were now taking an extreme interest in what was going on with Jax and Lucy.

"Okay, people, show's over!" Jax shouted, and then he added, "And in case you are wondering—yes, Lucy's back!"

This statement was followed by cheers and shouts and hugs, as Lucy was pulled into the living room and surrounded by the people who loved her and whom she loved the most.

CHAPTER SIXTEEN

Wiping more tears away with her mascara-stained Kleenex, Lucy turned to Summer, remarking, "This really was the most beautiful wedding ever, and you are the most beautiful bride."

Grinning at Lucy, Summer replied, "I know! And I know you aren't just saying that because you are my best friend and my maid of honor, either."

They were standing in the stunning reception hall, the first dances were out of the way, as were the toasts and dinner. The DJ was turning up the tunes, and there was a group of people jamming on the dance floor.

Watching an old couple "gettin' jiggy with it," Lucy turned to Summer, answering, "You know I'm not. You were right all along, Sum. Your wedding was perfect, you definitely were shining bright, baby!"

Laughing, Summer added, "Like a diamond! Oh, just you wait, Luce, there's more to come. I have one more trick up my sleeve. Before the night is over, you are going to be blown away!"

Shaking her head, Lucy agreed, "I'm sure I will be, but I'm not sure if I'll be blown away by the awesomeness of it or the crazy Summer-ness!"

"What's the difference? No, actually this is going to be something you'd never expect, trust me. Now where'd my *husband* run off to? I can't believe I am actually *married* and have a *husband*!" she squealed and ran off toward where the man in white was standing.

Lucy looked at her best friend as she ran up and gave her new husband a big, sloppy kiss. She was so happy for her. It was amazing that everything had come together at the last minute. Summer really had looked stunning in her strapless, white wedding gown. But of course she did, she *was* Summer, no surprise there.

As Lucy was beginning to reflect on the past nine months and how far she had come since Opal's death, Stella came up to her and pulled her towards a chair that was set off to the side of the dance floor, in a quiet corner of the room.

"Mom, what are you doing?" Lucy asked, bewildered.

"Don't talk, just sit," her mom ordered, pushing her down in the chair and keeping her hands on Lucy's shoulders, so she couldn't stand.

"Mom!" Lucy hollered, trying to get up, but was held down by her mother's stubborn hands.

"Sh-h! I said, don't talk, just sit." Her mom gave her one of her "just try me" looks, so Lucy stayed put.

Just as Lucy was about to ask her mom to *please let her go*, her mom pulled something out of her little black clutch, saying, "This," then handing an envelope to Lucy, "is for you."

"What is it?" Lucy asked, confused. She took the envelope from her mom and turned it over, gasping when she recognized Opal's handwriting on the front.

"Something special," Stella promised, smiling down at Lucy. "Open it. I'll be back in a minute," Stella said quietly, then slowly walked away, wanting to give Lucy some time alone.

Lucy took a big breath to steady herself and then carefully opened the envelope and pulled out the thick stationary Opal always used. She didn't unfold the stationary right away, but took a moment to remember Opal. She wondered why her mom had given her the envelope now, instead of tomorrow or after Summer's wedding celebration was over. Whatever the reason, Lucy knew her mom wouldn't have given it to her if it weren't important. So she opened the letter and began to read.

> *Lucy, if you're reading this, then as you know I'm gone. Wow, that feels weird to think about. Oh Lucy, I'm sorry I left you. I know that must have been a rough time for you. But if I know anything about myself, I know that I'll have made sure you move on and live your life. Have I done that yet? Given you the push you needed?*

Lucy laughed to herself, remembering her vision of Opal all those months ago. Opal had given her just the push she needed. Wiping away a stray tear, she continued reading.

> *I'm going to hope that I have. If not yet, I will soon, I promise you that! Whenever you need me, you know I'll be there in some way or another. But this letter isn't about me being there or not being there. It's about you. It's about you and Jax, actually. Yes, you and Jax. I'll give you a second to let that sink in.*
>
> *You probably don't know this, Lucy, but Jax came to me a while ago, after we all met for dinner together. You know the night where I pointedly asked him what his intentions were with you. He came to me, and he told me that what*

he had said in the car was true, that he loved you. He loved you more than anything, and he wanted to make sure that the day he proposed to you was the most special day you could ever imagine. That it would be something you would remember forever. Now, of course, if there is a special day, I have to be there. At first, I wasn't sure what he wanted. I said I would help in any way I could, but I wasn't sure how much longer I would be around.

Then we came up with this, well it was Jax's idea, really. I'll give him the credit just this once. He came up with the idea for me to write this letter. I think he knew it would be something you would like, a way for me to be there with you. Jax asked me to remind you what a beautiful girl you are, Lucy. You really are special to so many people, I bet more people than you are aware of. Maybe now you are beginning to see that. Always remember what a difference you made in my life. No matter what happens, never forget that. You changed this old lady's life when there wasn't much time left. So thank you, Lucy.

As for love ... well you know what I think of that— never hold back, always go for it. Don't be afraid. Sometimes you need to just jump and fall, and guess what? When you do that, it can end up being the best thing you ever did. Don't think so much, just follow your heart, it'll never steer you wrong. Well, that's about all I have for now, sweet girl.

Remember—I'm always with you, believing in you, cheering you on. Always.

Love,
Opal

Lucy swallowed, trying to hold back her tears. She still missed Opal so much. Even after nine months, the pain could still take her breath away.

She quickly dried her eyes as she heard someone approaching. She didn't want to damper the festive mood of the evening by sobbing in the corner. When she looked up, she saw Jax.

He was walking towards her with hands in his pockets, smiling nervously. Seeing him made her heart skip a beat, as usual. She was assuming this was something that was never going to go away, and she hoped it never would.

"Hi," he said. Then he kneeled down in front of her, took her hand in his, "I hope reading the letter from Opal made your day a little more special, Lucy. I know how much you miss her, and I wanted to do something for you that would remind you how much she loved you, too. And how much I love you. Ever since that day outside Grinder when you bumped into me, I knew you were the one I wanted to be with for the rest of my life."

He paused, caught his breath, and then continued, "There was just something about you that caught my attention, and there still is something about you. I think there always will be for me."

Jax smiled his million-dollar smile, the smile that could melt her heart in a second. He let go of her hand, reached into his pocket, and began to speak again, "Lucy, you have my heart, you have had it from the moment I saw you. I can't breathe without you; it hurts too much when you're away from me. Please say yes. Say that you'll marry me."

Lucy looked into his eyes, his beautiful, dark, loving, accepting, honest eyes and could only think of one thing to say, and that was—"Yes."

With that one word, Jax slid the most beautiful vintage ring onto her finger and then swept her up into a hug. "Thank you, Lucy," he whispered into her ear.

Wiping away tears, she told him, "Jax, I love you so much. Thank you for doing this for me, for thinking of me and knowing that having Opal a part of this day would mean so much to me."

She gave him a kiss and then brought her hand up to get a better look at the ring. "Wow," she declared, her eyes a little blinded by the massive sparkling, "Wow, you did good!"

"I'm glad you like it," his voice serious, "because it was Opal's."

Lucy's jaw dropped. "What?" she asked, shocked, holding her left hand up and examining the ring on her finger. It was almost too much to take in—having Jax ask her to marry him and giving her the most gorgeous ring, which used to be Opal's. She really would have a piece of Opal everywhere she went. His thoughtfulness overwhelmed her, and she started to cry.

"Lucy?" Jax asked, brushing her tears away with the pads of his thumbs, "What's wrong?"

She could hear in his voice, how he thought he might have messed up, so she assured him through her tears, "No, nothing's wrong."

"What is it then?" he asked, tilting her head back and looking into her eyes.

"It's just that everything … is absolutely perfect. Thank you, Jax, for being so thoughtful. For knowing how special it would be for me to have her ring. It's a beautiful way to remember her." She leaned forward and kissed him, hugged him close to her.

All around her people were getting on with the party. The DJ was playing ear-popping music again, and most of the guests were on the dance floor dancing. Summer and Drew were mingling, wanting to make sure they said hello to everyone. Teddy was there with his friends, talking to the DJ upfront about who knows what. Lucy spied Bowden and Lila sitting close to one another at a table not far away, sharing a piece of cake, looking at each other lovingly.

The sight made her smile. Things were going good with Bowden and Lila. They decided to stay in the penthouse and help out with the day-to-day activities as they had been doing for years before Lucy had ever known they existed.

Lucy was fine with that; she was more than fine with that. Actually, she was overjoyed. She had hoped they would stay and do what they had done, but she hadn't wanted to pressure them, so she hadn't said anything to them about it. Then one night they approached her and asked if she would mind if things continued as they had been. She had been so happy about them wanting to stay and help her and just be there that she had let out a shriek Summer-style, which had almost sent Bowden flying into the other room, ears ringing in pain.

Lucy brought herself back, looking around for her mother. When she saw Stella, she smiled. She was dancing with a good-looking older gentleman, laughing all the while. After Stella had returned home, she had put away the money that Opal had left for her, "saving it for a rainy day," as she had told Lucy.

Though Stella and Opal were never able to have the kind of relationship that Opal and Lucy had, they did seem to come to terms with each other before Opal had passed, and that made Lucy happy. She had asked her mom a few months ago if they, Opal and Stella, had ever made up. Lucy had been brought to tears over the story her mom had shared with her of their reconciliation. Lucy was thankful it hadn't been too late, though she could tell her mom wished they would have had more time together.

She knew that the money Opal had left Stella took away the stress of not being sure what she'd do if she didn't have her column to write anymore. Removing the stress about money was the gift that Opal had given Stella, and Lucy knew that her mom was extremely grateful for Opal's generosity. Her mom seemed to be more carefree these days, which seemed to be leading to her having more dates. Lucy wasn't sure what she thought about her mom dating, but she was happy to see her having fun, so she took a page from Opal's book and let it be what it was.

As for herself, well, Bowden was teaching her as best as he could about what Opal had done with everything she had made for herself. And Mr. Tinkles had been right, it was less complicated than it had seemed. If she wanted to be more involved, she could be, but she didn't need to consume her every waking moment with it. She would have a say in major decisions, of course, and with Bowden's help, she was starting to understand the key to how Opal had been so successful. She was even hoping to add to Opal's success one day, but for now, she was content to just live life and have fun doing it, enjoying time with friends and family.

Benno had surprised her with a promotion, not long after she had finally returned to work. She was now one of the managers as well as the one and only pizza babe. Being able to work with people she loved, feeling like she was part of a big family, was something that inspired her, something that made her want to do more, be more. It was something that made coming into work more fun for her and everyone around her. Not long after she was promoted, Saucy Baby was written up in a national magazine for being one of the tastiest and best restaurants, earning it a four-star restaurant status.

Of course, this made Cash and Carson rethink their firing of Lucy, making them wonder aloud to their employees and friends if they should ask her to come back to Grinder/Zippy Computer. This question earned them both a resounding, "NO!" from all of their employees, Teddy specifically saying to Cash, "I will walk, dude. I will walk if I have to do that again."

The comment had earned Teddy a frightening glare from Lucy, to which Teddy responded, "What? Do you *remember* how much you sucked at that job??"

Lucy smiled, thinking about her first days at Grinder, her first days here in this new, foreign place, a place that now felt like home to her. She wondered what she would be doing if she hadn't taken that leap of faith and decided to move here. Come live with and get to know an old, long-lost grandmother that had sometimes scared her to death but had promised to be different this time. She remembered how scared she had been, how worried she was that things wouldn't work out, that it would be horrible, that she would make the wrong choice.

Shaking her head, she smiled again. She guessed Opal really was right. Sometimes you just had to jump, then fall, and see where it took you because it might just be the best thing you've ever done.

"It wasn't all my idea," Jax explained, cutting into her thoughts.

"What do you mean?" she asked, still checking out her ring, watching the light dance off the diamonds.

"The ring," he explained, taking Lucy's hand and turning it this way and that. "It was Opal's idea mostly. I had told her I wanted some help picking out a ring. She invited me over," he smiled at her surprised look, "when you were at work. She had her jeweler there, with rings lined up for me to look at. I had no idea which one to choose, until she brought out this," he said, touching the ring on her finger. "Then I knew. It was perfect."

Surprised, she looked at Jax, declaring, "I can't believe it! I'm so happy you chose what you did. I had no idea!" She laughed.

Smiling big—she loved that smile—he said, "Me too. It was one of the most interesting shopping experiences I've ever had."

When she just continued to stare at him, he went on to explain, "In a good way, though. It was good. I got to know her a lot better that day, and I'm thankful for that." He grabbed her hand.

Looking at Jax, taking the time to really look at him, she saw how much he really did love her. She saw beauty in his eyes and face, not just good-looks beauty, but real, honest, good-person beauty, the kind that just flows out of some people who are truly and honestly good, who are real. She remembered seeing that kind of beauty in Opal, and she realized how lucky she was to have Jax. How lucky she was that on that fateful day, she had decided to go check out the local coffee shop and had bumped into her future.

"You never know," Lucy thought, "what the future might bring. No matter how much you try to figure it out and plan for it, it can't prepare you for what's waiting for you. It can't prepare you for the beauty and pain and joy and sorrow and love that is life."

EPILOGUE

Lucy—

First off, please let me say—I am very sorry for the way I treated you while we were married. I have begun to realize, with some help, that I was 100% in the wrong. Let me explain ... I've met someone!!! I was trying out surfing (yes, surfing!), and I was about to catch a big wave, when I somehow flipped myself over and knocked my head hard on a rock along the way. I woke up sometime later to a surfer girl giving me mouth to mouth! Needless to say, she saved my life, in more ways than one. After spending time with her, and after a few of what she calls "come to Jesus" talks, I started to see how horrible I was to you. I should have never treated you the way I did, and I hope that this apology will help you heal. I know I could have been better to you, Lucy, but I hope someday you will forgive me. I also hope that one day you will meet someone who will treat you the way you deserve to be treated and make you smile that beautiful smile of yours. We have been through a lot together, Lucy, and I hope, that although most of it wasn't great, that we can remain, or at least part, as friends.

Drew

Drew—

Surfing, huh? Actually sounds pretty fun, well minus the almost dying part. Thank you for the apology, it really does mean a lot to me, and even though I could never imagine saying this to you six months ago, I do forgive you. I'm happy that you met someone that can help you become a better you. Guess what? I've met someone, too! He is amazing and definitely makes me smile. As for us being and parting as friends, I'd like that. Have fun in Cali and good luck trying to catch your next big wave.

    Lucy

ACKNOWLEDGEMENTS

First, I would like to thank my parents, for always reading my stories. From the very first story I've ever written (who could forget The Three Twin Sisters, or my own version of *Goosebumps*?) to now, you have always encouraged me to follow my dreams. Thank you for your love, support and belief in me. I wouldn't be here without you.

My husband, for your patience, editing skills, and all the times you took the kids so I could have a few hours to work on my book.

My kids, your excitement about this book makes me smile. A bonus thanks for your input on the book cover, I'm glad you like it.

My brothers, Jon and Chris, thank you for your ideas and advice. Watching both of you live your dreams is so inspiring, I'm proud of you.

Scott and Chris, for your help and enthusiasm, as well as reading and editing my book, thank you. I hope it made the long travel hours go by a little bit faster.

My BFF, Jaimie, thank you for being the best friend a girl could ask for. Through you I have learned what it means to be a true friend. Thank you for always being there for me, listening and not judging, and accepting me for me. From breaking hearts to broken hearts, from learning how to skateboard to learning how to drive, there is no one else I would have wanted by my side. Thank you, you are my very own Summer.

Nicole Garber, for your support, advice, and expertise in all things books, thank you. I am so glad we met at your book signing and have enjoyed our coffee dates.

To everyone that has encouraged me along the way- Jenny H (thank you for taking my picture as well as giving me decorating tips, you are amazing!), Amanda (for your support and interest, as well as your own silly minions), Chrissy (for your help and advice), my book club crew – Allyson, Angela, Angie, Colleen, Dana, Jennifer, Jenny G, Jenny P, Julie and Torrey (for your encouragement and all those fun nights talking about a little more than just books), and everyone else who has helped me – thank you, thank you, thank you!

Also to Book Chix for all the work you've done to make this book a success.